# THE VERNHAM CHRONICLES

John Saunders

en Press

First published in Great Britain by Pen Press
All paper used in the printing of this book has been made from
wood grown in managed, sustainable forests.

ISBN13: 978-1-907499-59-3

Pen Press is an imprint of Indepenpress Publishers Ltd
25 Eastern Place
Brighton
BN2 1GJ

Printed and bound in the UK

A catalogue record of this book is available from
the British Library

Cover design by Jacqueline Abromeit

This book is dedicated to my wife Carole,

Mum and my late Dad
(who wouldn't have approved of parts of this book),

Jennie, Roger, Russell and Andrew

John Ellis
(who unwittingly encouraged me to become an author),

David Shaw-Parker (for helpful advice),

Jo McCafferty
(who puts up with a lot of my waffling missives),

Doris Brendel
(who actually took time to read one of
*The Vernham Chronicles* chapters),

anyone who has enthused in my pursuit of finishing this book,

and anyone who hasn't had the slightest interest in my pursuit
of finishing this book (RASPBERRIES TO YOU!).

# Foreword

The point behind *The Vernham Chronicles* is that there is no point. One reader who assessed this book commented that the narration wasn't conventional, but somehow I managed to bring events and characters to some sort of cohesion. This of course is art imitating life – basically most of us get up some sort of time every day, do things and go to bed later on that day to sleep and repeat the cycle in a sort of fashion the following day. Most stories reach conclusions that make sense, and that is a general requirement of most story threads to make the reader stop and think about the conclusion.

With this book I've written ten of twelve chapters that are chronicles of a day or event in this little village called Vernham. Each chapter is a story that doesn't necessarily end with a neat conclusion. But then that is indeed like life; we very rarely tie up loose ends before we close our eyes at bedtime, and most of us leave a lot of loose ends behind after we close our eyes for the very last time. The other two of the twelve chapters in *The Vernham Chronicles*, 'Of Idiosyncrasies, Ideas and Idiots' and 'Vernham Gossip Update' are details of the ridiculous goings on of the characters of the village of Vernham. There are many normal people in this village; they don't get a mention as there wouldn't be very much of interest in "Old Sid Cotton bicycles to work every day, and after work he returns home for dinner and spends the rest of the evening practising normality."

Many of the characters in *The Vernham Chronicles* are based on people that I have known or had the uncertain pleasure to have met; I have of course completely exaggerated or distorted these characters so that they nearly all seem to have some sort of obsessive behaviour patterns.

This book is intended to make people laugh, if you don't find yourself laughing then this is possibly not the book for you. I very rarely laugh at my jokes, but I have found myself chortling like an hysterical child at times when reading the chapters; this could mean that it is funny, or I need some kind of counselling, reclining on a shiny brown leather couch in a darkened room, being taken back to my childhood… I prefer the former!

# Chapter 1

## A DAY IN THE LIFE OF COMFYTUMS

In the Vernbury Vale is a little village called Vernham, in which most of the buildings appear to be from the 16th century or at least Mock Tudor. There is a little confectioner tobacconist newsagent shop with small square panelled windows which alternate from clear glass to bottle bottom convex panels; they still sell sweets by the quarter and halves from traditional glass jars. There is an open-fronted greengrocer's that has a very fat greengrocer who proudly shouts that his apples are lovely and green and his bananas are ripe, but not too ripe, and his farm fresh eggs are fifteen pence cheaper than the local supermarket. There is a butcher's that always has rabbits and pheasants hanging upside down with flies buzzing around them most times of year, and the most prime and bloodiest beef steaks on display, very proud of his pies, a board outside heralds "THE BEST PIES IN VERNHAM, WITH GOLDEN SHORTCRUST PASTRY!" – mind you, no one else makes pies in the village, even the local pub pies are his. And, oh yes, his local farm fresh eggs are fifteen pence cheaper than the local supermarket's as well!

Now the pub, 'The Grummet and Nut', which is open all day, serves nothing but the finest ales, none of that lager rubbish. The same people stand at the bar in the same place seemingly all day, only returning home at teatime for the evening meal and then back to The Grummet and Nut for another three or four local brews. The barber always stops for lunch at the pub for an hour before reopening for business in the afternoon; it is said that it is always better to have your hair cut in the morning rather than the afternoon, unless you want a crew cut, but even then it is advisable to mask you ears with sticky plasters just in case (prevention being better than cure). The Gent's toilets in The Grummet and Nut are worth avoiding too, neither of the sit-downs flush properly and the urinals are blocked with cigarette ends, even a year after the smoking ban!

There is a toy shop that sells toys that can only be described as collectors' items or antiques. There are only two children in the village as most young couples moved out into neighbouring villages when they became parents due to the lack of cottages. The two children don't seem to be too interested in toys anyway, preferring to make their own catapults and crossbows to kill animals and break old people's windows.

There is a haberdashery that provides all needs for the skilful knitters and sewers of the village with an ambitious name, 'Haberdasher's World', a small world but a world nonetheless.

But the jewel in Vernham's cobblestoned crown has to be the local tea room 'Comfytums'; not just tea and cake here, they also serve All Day Breakfasts, but only until midday when they change the name to Mixed Grill. This badly lit, even in broad daylight tea room, is owned by twin spinsters Milly and Molly Goldsworth – everyone has asked them why they never married, I don't know why as they're quite unattractive. Even in the black-and-white framed photographs dotted around the walls of Comfytums showing them in their 'Land Girl' day (yes they are quite old) with pitchforks at the ready, prove them to be not very good catches; but there does also seem to be great big Friesian cattle in every photo (the ones without udders, so maybe…?). Every day Friesian cattle roam through the village and peer into Comfytums' windows as if searching for somebody; nobody knows where these cattle come from, there's no dairy nearby, they just appear every day.

The food is always good at Comfytums, they even give you little indigestion tablets with your bill instead of after-dinner mints. The omelettes are to die for; in particular the Cajun Four Cheese omelette is popular, a touch on the expensive side perhaps, but they buy their eggs from the supermarket believing the local farm fresh ones to be inferior. The farm fresh eggs are treated with suspicion by both Milly and Molly ever since they saw the local chickens, some of them appeared to be double headed; soon after they bought a batch of farm fresh eggs and they were all double yolkers. Putting two and two together, the spinsters believed this to be a bad omen and could encourage a spate of mutant offspring being born after their women customers ate them. After all anything could happen, when all is said and done – Tommy Perkins the village odd boy is rumoured to have been conceived after his mother was supposed to have had an illegitimate affair with old Mr Williams' St Bernard, and Tommy does bark rather loudly. In reality, Tommy's mother used to take Mr Williams' dog out for regular walks as the old fellow couldn't manage it (not with his hip!), and Tommy had whooping cough when he was eighteen months old and is always 'a bit chesty'. And the supermarket's eggs come from exactly the same farm-fresh farm – they are just fifteen pence dearer, overheads you see!

At 10:00am Milly and Molly open for business; a turn of two keys in two locks, click, click, turn the CLOSED sign to OPEN, open the shop door, tinkle, tinkle, clang goes the bell on a spring. This charming bell adds a touch of homely village business to the atmosphere, at the same time alerting Milly and Molly to customers entering the premises, but after five or six punters come in, it can prove quite damned irritating. "Ooh, mustn't forget to put the specials board outside, doesn't look like rain, the chalk won't run!" thinks Molly.

At 10:02am precisely, tinkle, tinkle, clang! Mrs Bunkerton walks in as she always does every day, looks at the menu and says, "I think I'll try the Welsh Rarebit and a pot of tea please?" as she always does every day. Mrs Bunkerton, kind-hearted, nice to talk to and a nosey moo, recently widowed, as she tells everybody every day – well seven years ago actually but who's counting – makes her way to the ladies room while the Rarebit is being prepared to 'powder her nose' and bumps into the giant brass bedpan 'BONG!' that could do with a bit of

‘Brasso’ hanging on a bitumen-soaked oak beam, as she does every day.

Meanwhile tinkle, tinkle, clang, Mr Selsman walks in, only after changing his Wellingtons for the clean pair always kept by the door that Milly and Molly bought for him to commemorate twenty years of loyal custom. This is a ‘No Muddy Wellingtons Please?’ establishment and as Mr Selsman insists that Wellingtons are the only footwear he can comfortably wear due to his complaint(?), Milly and Molly thought it only kind to present him with ‘indoor Wellies’ and not penalise him as he was such a good customer. A long time ago Mr Selsman walked some sheep doodles onto the terracotta tiled floor in Comfytums and a poor old lady visitor slipped upon the offending excreta, gashing her forehead badly on the corner of a table. Naturally, an all out Wellie ban had to be engaged. The indoor Wellies have a dual purpose – one, that Mr Selsman can enjoy his tea in comfort; and two, people had complained for a long time about the Eau de Pied fromage pong emanating from Mr Selsman’s stockinged feet, so something had to be done! And yet, the postman told me that he had seen Mr S wearing carpet slippers the other day when he had to open the door to sign for the new pair of Wellington boots that he had ordered from last month’s *Country Gent* magazine. Mr Selsman walks over to his favourite table in the far corner of the tea room, squeezes in between the table and chair and sits down, ordering a pot of tea and a muffin with a rude click of his fingers. Molly obliges and shoots off to brew a fresh pot for him. He takes out his newspaper from his dogtooth chequered jacket with traditional teddy bear elbow patches, unfolds the broadsheet, shakes it and knocks the white sugar bowl flying, spilling out grains of white across the ebony-black stained table. If you concentrate, the little sugar granules look like tiny stars in a new galaxy that only Patrick Moore could dream of.

Mrs Bunkerton returns back to the tea room refreshed, God only knows what she's been doing in there, and says, "Oh hello, Mr Selsman!"

"MORNING," he growls without looking up from his daily read.

"Nice day out there I think, Mr Selsman," says Mrs Bunkerton.

"IS IT?" he bellows. There the conversation ends as it always does every day.

Molly brings out Mr Selsman's pot of tea and muffin, and Milly brings out Mrs Bunkerton's Rarebit and pot of tea. Tinkle, tinkle, clang! In walks Miss Somerton-Jove, flustered as usual after the everyday occurrence of heavy-breathing phone calls at breakfast time, or so she says.

"Good morning, Miss Somerton-Jove, how are you today?" asks Mrs Bunkerton, gesturing to a vacant seat for Miss Somerton-Jove to sit, as she does every day.

"Oh, not too good, dear! I had another one of my turns this morning after those blessed phone calls, I feel the end is not too far for me now!" says Miss Somerton-Jove dumping her more than generous rump on the offered seat, letting out a whiff of mothballs from each pocket of her burgundy bouclé jacket. She always smells of mothballs, she feels the fragrance is more unique than any toilet water that you can get from the chemist. Apart from the obvious benefits of keeping those hungry little moths and woolly bear larvae at bay, they also make a very good breath freshener. After too many cups of tea and Milly and Molly's cheese and garlic quiche, should she meet a dapper gentleman that may wish to take her out to the evening play at the Vernham parish village hall, 'Pop a mothball in your mouth, quiche pong gone!' as the song from a fantasy television advert goes inside her head.

Somerton-Jove? Now that's an interesting arrangement of a double-barrelled name. Miss Somerton-Jove's mother was a Somerton by birth, and Miss Somerton-Jove was born a… how can I say it politely? …well, a bastardess! The Jove bit came about after her mother was interrogated by the village in The Grummet and Nut as to who the father was; the young Miss Somerton didn't know exactly. So her father shouted, "WHO DID THIS TO YOU?" The possible guilty party who was present looked at his watch and exclaimed, "BY JOVE!" and dashed out pretending to be late for something or other. Miss Somerton's father looked around the pub and said, "Who is this damned Jove anyway? I've never heard of him!" And so the village conceded that Jove, however a mysterious stranger he was, must have been the sire, and so the tailpiece of Miss Somerton-Jove's name came about to give the new baby a noble start and remove any suspicion that she may be illegitimate, although that is rather like plopping a liberally thick layer of whipped cream on a horrid trifle, underneath that layer is uncertainty. The baby, a beautiful little girl, was eventually fortunate enough to be fostered by a normal family and not have to grow up in a village of weirdos; but later in life, as she grew older, she became curious about her true mother and returned to Vernham.

Molly asks Miss Somerton-Jove what she would like to eat and drink and points to the specials board in case she wants something different from the usual cheese and garlic quiche. This would be preferable because the quiche was off; or rather she had forgotten to make it and is thinking that to distract Miss Somerton-Jove to eat something else would be an advantage. Miss Somerton-Jove has this awful quiche every day and is known to be quite unreasonable if she doesn't get her way. "Mmmm!" ponders Miss Somerton-Jove, and notices a very huge stuffed and mounted brown trout in a glass case, the inscription declaring that the Reverend Thomas Stilton caught it from the River Poddum on April 1st 1926 weighing 11lb 3oz.

"I'll have the trout please?" says Miss Somerton-Jove.

"I beg your pardon?" Molly queries.

“The trout, that great ugly thing swimming around in that tank!” Miss Somerton-Jove points at it with her obese forefinger.

“Oh but you can’t eat that,” chortles Molly, “it’s a taxidermist’s work and quite inedible!”

“Don’t you mock me, Madam, I know a trout when I see one and I’m looking at one now! You can’t deprive me of something that I desire when you yourself have just offered it to me, I know about the trades description act and I demand my rights!” shrieks Miss Somerton-Jove.

It is only 10:42am and already the unpleasantness has begun. Sensing trouble, Molly nods to Milly and mouths the word ‘PHONE’ to her. This is a common occurrence with Miss Somerton-Jove and it isn’t the first time that they have had to telephone ‘Merry Meadow’, Vernham’s local home for the infirm, old and very disturbed.

Before the auxiliaries from Merry Meadow arrive, Miss Somerton-Jove is rolling around the terracotta tiles, foaming at the mouth and shouting, “I WANT THE TROUT, I WANT THE TROUT!” Auxiliaries arrive, despatching Miss Somerton-Jove quicker than a trout angler’s priest, into the van, and off they go back to Merry Meadow to be merry again.

All the while this commotion is going on, Mr Selsman carries on reading his paper and Mrs Bunkerton enjoys her delicious Welsh Rarebit and tea, pretending not to notice. Mrs Bunkerton and Mr Selsman leave before the usual run of normal-ish and noisy customers come in for their cappuccino and Jaffa cake treats.

Another everyday regular customer Mr Wilson arrives – tinkle, tinkle, clang, crash, smash, clump! through the door. Mr Wilson is blind, and Milly and Molly haven’t quite got the concept of blind location and negotiation yet; each time Mr Wilson visits he walks into a table. The reason for this is that both Milly and Molly think that as the table proves to be a hindrance to Mr Wilson, they have to move it to another area so he won’t bump into it next time. Of course poor Mr Wilson never does accustom himself to the tea room as nothing is ever in the same place. Mr Wilson lost his sight during the Second World War – not as a soldier, he wasn't old enough. The story goes that he and some chums as school children used to go up to the top of 'Silver Hill' which is the highest point of the Vernbury Vale and play 'Sungazing'. Sungazing was a character-building exercise and a competitive one at that too. The boys used to lie on their backs and see who could stare at the sun the longest without blinking. Counting more than two skylarks achieved bonus points. What the young Wilson boy didn't realise was that although his pals didn't blink, they cheated and had their eyes closed all of the time. One day, 'Wilson Champion Sungazer' pushed the bar too far and lost his sight.

At one time even though Comfytums had a 'No Dogs' policy, Milly and Molly did allow Mr Wilson to bring his beautiful old Golden Labrador guide dog with him. The only trouble was that the old dog suffered from terrible flatulence and used to clear the tea room in a trice. Molly once suggested to him that "Charcoal biscuits are very good!" but Mr Wilson said that he'd prefer the buttered scones that he normally had and didn't quite take the hint. Nowadays he prefers a white stick because, as all dog owners know, it's hard to come to terms with an old friend being put down – just as well because all of the spinster twins' profits were going on potpourri and incense sticks! Other than that, dear Mr Wilson is no trouble at all, although he insists on a pot of tea to pour out for himself and either Milly or Molly rush around making sure that the tea ends up in his cup; unfortunately the same principle as the doorway table is applied here. One thing I have noticed though is that Mr Wilson is always aware when a pretty young woman comes into the tea room, he seems almost as though he's following the girl around the room with his eyes – surely not?

Tinkle, tinkle, clang… Tommy Perkins the odd boy walks into Comfytums, coughs loudly and walks out again.

It's lunch time. Mr Wilson has long departed, having gone in the opposite direction to home – don't worry though, he's sure to get home eventually, and after all Milly and Molly can't be held responsible for moving his home.

A new visitor arrives with a tinkle, tinkle, clang and looks around the tea room – it's a young lady newspaper reporter from the *Vernbury Trumpet*, a weekly local rag that tells you that nothing very much happened last week and well worth the twenty-five pence cover price. Her name is Monica Millstone and she's here to report on a sighting of the 'Vernham Bog Stomper' – a local, possibly mythical beast that is said to stomp around Sweetwater Marsh on the outside of the village. She sits down at a table near the counter and orders an expensive cheese and ham omelette. She explains to both Milly and Molly what she is about and the twin spinsters enthuse. The legend of the Vernham Bog Stomper goes back no further in time than twenty-three years; Milly and Molly confess that although they have never seen the beast, they have heard it regularly, particularly on very still nights and always after 11:00pm.

"Ooh terrible stomping noise it makes!" grimaces Molly, shaking her head and screwing her face up as though she has just sucked on the sourest lemon in the world.

"Ooh yes, STOMP, STOMP, STOMP," concurs Milly portraying the sound visually with an 'I thought I was going to break wind but was horribly wrong' kind of walk.

Now I'll let you into a secret that I wouldn't want to tell anyone else as it would spoil the myth, and the fun… Not so long ago I saw Tommy Perkins trying out some new shoes – they aren't everyday shoes, they're very special. The shoes are made from the round discs that form the lid and bottom of a beer barrel; these discs, strapped to Tommy's feet with old pieces of leather trouser belt nailed to them, act as a sort of snow shoe, but are BOG SHOES!

Unbeknown to the village, Tommy works the night shift at the Velstrum baker's across Sweetwater Marsh as he has done for nearly twenty-three years. Velstrum, a neighbouring village, is a twenty-minute bus ride away which takes you all around the village and around the marsh before finally reaching Velstrum where it terminates and returns half an hour later to journey back to Vernham. After 10:32.5pm the buses stop running and if you don't have a car or tricycle you have to walk for forty-two minutes, or roller skate which can knock off three or five minutes depending on wind direction.

With Tommy's Bog Shoes, walking across the Sweetwater Marsh is a fifteen-minute doddle and gets him to the baker's in time for a quick cup of tea and a smoke outside before his shift 11:30pm to 8:30am starts. Tommy may be odd, but not daft. Tommy has also heard of the Vernham Stomper but doesn't realise that it is he who started the myth. On some nights when it is very still, dark and paranoia rising high, Tommy can hear the beast chasing him; that can knock off another five minutes and give him a bit more smoking time.

All of the Vernham populace unfairly think that Tommy is a 'benefit sponge', I don't think they realise just how hard he works! Tommy never seems to sleep, which is a worry to his mother; she's told him that he eats too many of those special under-the-counter sweets from the chemist called 'Whizz Balls' – just as well that they are expensive and he spreads them out over a week, or he'd be gnashing his teeth like a pneumatic road drill.

Monica Millstone, the *Vernbury Trumpet* reporter (just in case you'd forgotten her after all of that waffle) notices some attractive butterfly paintings on the shop window and compliments on how lovely they are. Milly says, "Oh yes, we call that accidental art!" 'Accidental art', because they are modified graffiti made by the two children of the village. Outside Comfytums in the summer are alfresco tables, and the two children thought it would be great fun to paint each other's buttocks with bright yellow vinyl gloss paint that they'd stolen from Chris the painter, stand on the alfresco tables and press their little botties against the window. These 'bum prints' looked too much like bum prints to both Milly and Molly and so they decided to modify them by turning them into butterflies, ingenious!

Monica Millstone shovels down her cheese and ham omelette and says that she'd better get her skates on, as she has eight interviews with locals who say they have seen the Stomper, before camping out on the edge of Sweetwater Marsh in hopes of catching some footage of the beast on her infrared camcorder. From there, if she succeeds, the footage will be posted on the *Vernbury Trumpet's* website. I hope she fails, it'll ruin the fun!

No sooner after Monica leaves, the Reverend Parsworthy enters tinkle, tinkle, clang into Comfytums – he's here to scrounge a scone and cup of coffee under false pretences. He comes in every day to collect for the church door fund; the church needs a new door after it was stolen three years ago. The church door had silver and gold embellishments and was worth a great deal of money. The only way to keep the weather out of the church is to stick polythene bin liners to the door frame with cellulose tape, cheap but effective. There's no need to fear a break-in as everything inside has been stolen as well. So 'Old Rev' visits Comfytums every day in the hope of raising a little more badly-needed funds.

Sadly, after the tea room the next visit is The Grummet and Nut where he stays until kick-out time. Somehow the church door fund always seems to get stolen every night when poor 'Old Rev' gets mugged, looking like he's been dragged through a hedge backwards, or fallen into one perhaps? Hopefully the collection at the Sunday morning meeting will help. Reverend Parsworthy walks around the twenty-strong congregation with a wooden tray collecting the freewill offerings; anything less than fifty pence gets a 'God bless you!' with clenched teeth. I heard some cynical swine suggest the other day that 'Old Rev' may have sold the church door and the church's silver communion cup to finance his craving for liquor, how very unchristian! Reverend Parsworthy distracts the Goldsworth twins most of the afternoon with tales of his missionary work in the Sudan, most of his tales untrue, but he did serve the missionary position once or twice.

Tinkle, tinkle, clang! It's Nelly Birdham – she's come here to play the piano for afternoon tea entertainment. With a clanking of gin bottles in her tartan shopping basket, she makes her way to the upright piano that has a board nailed to the back with 'NELLY WILL BE ONLY TOO HAPPY TO PLAY ANY OF YOUR REQUESTS' and unlocks the lid revealing ebony and ivory tinklers that look like the dentures of a very happy piano. The locking and unlocking of the piano lid is an important ritual as Nelly fears that some wag might swap the keys around when she's not about. One afternoon the tea room was subjected to a cacophony of melodies and Nelly swears that when she wasn't looking, or swigging a big gulp of gin maybe, somebody swapped the notes around. When the old gin kicks in good and proper, Milly and Molly know of a little button at the side of the piano that can flick it into pianola mode, thus saving a mass walkout and keeping Nelly happy thinking she's doing a grand job. The man in the off-licence once asked Nelly if she drank 'London Dry', and she said, "No, I think there is plenty more to be imbibed yet!"

"Hello, Nelly how are you? Your hair looks nice!" chirps Molly. Nelly nods her head and her very nice hair tilts forward, it's a wig, a grey wig and no one is ever sure whether she has got it on the right way round or not. Underneath this wire wool bird's nest is a beautiful mane of white hair, so why the wig?

Nelly peers into a dark corner and spots Mr Barnford and mentions that he's asleep again as he often is. Mr Barnford, now in his one hundred and second year, regularly nods off and Milly and Molly don't like to wake him as he gets very confused when he is woken abruptly, often running around searching for his ARP helmet. The only trouble is that Mr Barnford has been like that for the last five days without going home, even the flies that keep landing on him can't wake him from his slumber, I think somebody should phone for a doctor!

Across the road from Comfytums, Mrs Bunkerton is trying to make her way through a herd of Friesian cattle, bobbing up and down with arms sticking upwards being carried away as if in a fast river current. She finally makes her way back to Comfytums – tinkle, tinkle, clang, GASP, “The Fire Station has burned down!” she yells.

“Ooh that’s a bit of a silly place to have a fire!” says Milly.

“Yes very silly!” agrees Molly.

“Yes it is!” says Mrs Bunkerton as she leaves to find someone who’s really interested, as she does every day.

Reverend Parsworthy, now convinced that he’s got about all the dosh he’s going to get from the frigid purses of the tea room, gets up and makes his way to The Grummet and Nut.

A coach load of naughty school children arrive outside Comfytums and herd into the tea room like a swarm of locusts. The gaggle of pre-pubescence catches Milly and Molly with their defences down, and the counter and all of its contents are raided. The ruffians are gone as quick as they came without paying for anything, even the poor old tea room door bell can’t cope under the strain of so many openings and closings.

Well, there’s nothing left for the Goldsworth duo to do but close up shop for today, Milly looks around at the aftermath and notices Mr Barnford gone. As she tinkle, tinkle, clangs her way outside to get the specials board in she sees the school coach disappear with old Mr Barnford hanging out of a broken side window, arms flapping about like a rag doll. “Well! The little blighters have even stolen Mr Barnford!” says Milly quietly to herself.

Milly closes the tea room door, click, click both the locks locked, CLOSED sign turned and the twins prepare food in the kitchen for another cheery day at Comfytums.

Walking with a purposeful zigzag from The Grummet and Nut towards Comfytums is hairdresser Harry Helmson. Too late to open up shop for the afternoon, he trips up on a curb stone and falls against the tea room window. Face pressed tight to the window, his face smears downward with a piggy nostril expression, fast asleep – he’ll stay there all night, as he does every night!

# Chapter 2

## YE OLDE SWEETIE SHOPPE OF VERNHAM – ANOTHER DAY

Deep in the heart of the Vernbury Vale, the little village called Vernham is a village almost suspended in time. The buildings are mostly 16th-century with a few Mock Tudor buildings thrown into the gaps made by 'Old Jerry' when he flew over during the Second World War and dropped his bombs. Vernham wasn't a deliberate target for bombing, it was just that the Luftwaffe didn't want to go home after a bombing raid in the cities with any leftovers.

Technology is a new word to the population of Vernham, so don't expect to find any technological wotsits and thingamabobs here.

Lining the cobblestoned 'Low Street' of Vernham are quite a few shops that provide just about anything one could possibly need to buy – NO! not that kind of anything, if you want that kind of smuttery you can jolly well buzz off to the city and take a very opaque shopping bag with you to hide your naughtiness. The butcher's, the greengrocer's, the baker's, the haberdasher's, a tea room and more all provide the village's everyday needs. But the lifeline to the outside world is a confectioner tobacconist newsagent called 'Ye Olde Sweetie Shoppe', a place to get gossip from the outside world and indeed the outside underworld of the seedy city named 'Busted'.

The newspaper van brings all the newspapers and magazines to the sweet shop but never takes any unsold newspapers back. The reason for this is that the owners of Ye Olde Sweetie Shoppe, Ken and Bettie Griggs, sell them as 'Oldspapers' at a reduced rate for anybody needing yesterday's news should they have missed it if they were beamed up by aliens, or when they'd had too many in the local pub 'The Grummet and Nut' and lost a complete day of their lives, comatose.

This 'Day lost' malarkey is a common phenomenon in Vernham, so Ken and Bettie have found the system of Oldspapers to be quite a green attitude to recycling, and also very lucrative! Ken and Bettie open for business at 6:00am every morning, except Christmas day when they open a little later at 8:00am and only for a few hours. The usual customers that have to commute to Busted are the regular early punters to buy newspapers, fags (for those not in the UK, cigarettes, not funny boys!) and sweets; normally Wendy Wilson is the first.

Wendy Wilson, daughter of Blind Mr Wilson made blind by a game of 'Sungazing' in his youth, is a very busy sales rep for a city toothpaste company called 'Peggy White's' and she has to be on the road early to visit numerous independent chemists all over the place. She pops in every morning to buy a copy of *The Stun* which is Busted's answer to *The Sun* and *The Daily Star*; turn to page 9 and you'll see what I mean. She also buys 3lbs of 4X mints, and Ken and Bettie always don wartime respirator masks to complete the ritual. How can I describe Wendy? Beautiful is a word that doesn't meet her ravish worthy appearance. Wendy 35 years old, with a complexion of a 16 year old, gorgeous eyes with lashes so long they need no mascara, naturally blonde and very silky hair, a figure that even gay men would turn their heads to hold against them. It's sad that Mr Wilson has never seen her… Wendy also has extreme halitosis, and that puts the mockers on any dalliances with would-be boyfriends; this problem has limited local Casanovas to wolf-whistling from the other side of the street to her, but hey! still better than nothing.

Around Ye Olde Sweetie Shoppe are old promotional display boards for Fry's Five Boys chocolate bars, Will's Whiffs, and Sun Pat HOT PEANUTS SOLD HERE! Both Ken and Bettie are aware that you can no longer buy these products, but like to keep them up as an antiquarian statement, adding a touch of homely wholesomeness to the shop. Not that the shop is really modernised in any particular way – the windows are small panelled, alternating between plain and bottle bottom panes, and there are faded old window display boxes of Milk Tray with dummy chocolates. The windows are smeared with saliva from the two small children of the village who don't quite understand that the chocolates are fake. There is a local services board up on the wall where local workmen can put their calling cards to promote their businesses – here's an interesting one: RACING SNAILS FOR SALE!

One of village odd boy Tommy Perkins' hobbies, apart from coughing, is coach-painting garden snails with enamel model paint, The Humbrol Flyer is one of his favourites. It's not that easy painting them, the trick is in keeping the little blighters still, but he finds distracting the snails by touching their eyestalks and making them retract is the best way. Grand Prix versions are one pound each, go-faster stripes one pound fifty! The 'V-Twin Supercharger' prototype, which is two snails with their shells superglued together, was shelved because snails, being single-minded and naturally argumentative, try to choose their own course and the weakest one always gets dragged about all over the place. He's currently considering buying some giant African land snails as a sort of big truck version, although his first thoughts were tortoises, but they are too expensive. Sadly, snail racing has yet to catch on in Vernham, but they are rather beautiful if you like that sort of thing. Surprisingly the brighter coloured escapees one would think should be easy prey for thrushes to spot – not so, they probably can't believe anything so daft looking would be edible and ignore them.

There are no customer restrictions in Ken and Bettie's shop, even farm animals are welcome, and it's not unusual to see ducks and geese waddling around when you visit. The goats have proven to be a bit of a problem as they favour crisps, bag and all, so Ken and Bettie keep them behind the counter.

After the usual flurry of early morning workmen buying their bits, it's 8:00am and Fred Flasher bursts in, flings his greatcoat open revealing all and shouts, "A quarter of Strawberry Bonbons and a Walnut Whip please? Way-hay, Woo-Hah, Woo-Hah!" followed by a tongue-wobbling shriek much like a Masai tribesman's war cry warble.

"Good morning, Fred, how are you today?" says Bettie, trying to ignore the tattoo of a pair of glasses just above his curlies with a comic book speech bubble saying 'Can you see what it is yet?'

"Oh not too bad, Bettie, Woo-hoo, Way-Hay, Ooh-Yah, Ooh-Yah!" says Fred, at the same time joggling up and down.

There's a sudden 'THUD' above the shop ceiling and Ken, Bettie and Fred look upwards. "Do you want me to go up and sort 'em out for ya?" says Fred followed by a "Wee-Hee and Woo-Hoo-Hah!"

"NO! No, it's alright, it'll be the new tenants moving things about!" Ken assures Fred. Now let me explain as to why Fred was so keen to 'sort 'em out'. For many years the flat above Ye Olde Sweetie Shoppe has been uninhabited until now. The reason being, that Ken and Bettie couldn't rent the flat out due to a presence of two poltergeists causing mayhem on a regular basis. The flat above was empty of furniture except for a cast iron bed which couldn't be moved due to a force beyond the strength of any man, it just would not budge. There were even attempts to cut the bed up into more manageable pieces, but it blunted the sharpest power tools. The poltergeists were said to be the lost souls of a young courting couple who were caught in bed by the girl's over protective father. The father saw red and reached for the nearest weapon he could find, to kill the boy who had defiled his daughter, which was a blunderbuss. He aimed at the young man, but unfortunately due to the funnel-like barrel, blunderbusses tend to spray the shot in a very wide angle, the result being that he killed his daughter as well. So for many years you could hear a boing, boing, boing, gradually getting faster and climaxing in a great 'THUD!'

Ken and Bettie grew tired of this bedspring bouncing duo and decided to employ the Reverend Parsworthy of Vernham parish church to exorcise the evil spirits above. Old Rev, as his parishioners call him, arrived with his Holy Bible, Holy Water and Crucifix to rid the unrest lovers' souls. He had only been upstairs for five minutes when there was a banshee-like shriek and a terrible scraping and banging noise, followed by Old Rev rushing down the stairs, ashen-faced and holding the tattered remains of his trousers and long johns, all bare-bummed and dangly. Ken and Bettie administered a half bottle of finest cognac to the shell-shocked Parsworthy before he showed any sign of calming down, and then he drank another half bottle just to make sure.

It is said that it was here that Reverend Parsworthy's drink problem began. Kind Bettie knocked up a pair of trousers made out of *The Stun* pages and cellulose tape so that Reverend Parsworthy could go about his daily business. He later retired to The Grummet and Nut for a few swift pints of medicinal ale, but left when too many people were trying to read his trousers, and as if someone doing the crossword wasn't bad enough, spot the ball was the absolute limit – the pencil was a bit sharp!

The poltergeists were eventually exorcised in an unconventional way by Fred Flasher; he told Ken and Bettie he'd "give 'em what for and sort 'em out!" Fred dashed upstairs into the bedroom and flung his greatcoat open with a Woo-Hoo, Wee-Hee and a Way-Hay-Hay, shook everything he had and a huge high-pitched howl and scream erupted with the iron bed crashing through the bedroom window onto the cobblestoned street. Ken and Bettie were indebted to Fred and have since agreed to give him a quarter pound of Strawberry Bonbons and a Walnut Whip for every day of his life, and turn a blind eye to his exhibitionism.

Fred is a common sight in Low Street and people have almost become used to his flashing. To the casual observer Fred appears to be a normal person wearing a greatcoat; he has half trousers which are just the legs held up with elasticised suspenders. He wears that greatcoat all year round and can get a bit stinky during a heatwave. In the winter when there is a cold north easterly or frost about, he tends to curtail the flashing, preferring to approach people and describe himself; personally I don't know which is worse! You might be thinking "How does he get away with it, why hasn't he been arrested?" It's difficult you see because Fred is the local Bobby 'PC Fred Sweetman'. It did get a bit too much for him one day when he exposed himself to a tray of cherry-topped pink iced buns in a baker's shop window – he thought it was symbolic of St Tropez. He was so shocked by his own behaviour that he nearly turned himself in, but he had a bit of trouble with the handcuffs as no one was willing to help him put them on. Fred leaves Ken and Bettie's shop after receiving his free sweets, bidding them adieu with an upward flick of his coat tails revealing a tattooed rump, the left cheek reading 'Way' and the right reading 'Hay'.

Mrs Bunkerton, recently widowed seven years ago, pops in to buy a copy of *Women's Friend with Crochet Monthly supplement* and 2oz of liquorice cream rock and says, "Good morning, Mr and Mrs Griggs, looks like it'll be a lovely day providing it doesn't rain, ho, ho!" as she does every day.

"Yes!" say the Griggs.

"Well mustn't stop!" says Mrs Bunkerton, "I've got to go round telling people that the Fire Station has burned down like I do every day!"

Exit Mrs Bunkerton, enter Mr Selsman complete with filthy Wellingtons; he's come here to buy his huge newspaper *The World Today* and a block of 'Angel Kiss' aromatic pipe shag to stoke his meerschaum pipe with. This tobacco, with a heady aroma of butterscotch and soft notes of banana is his favourite; he doesn't realise that for years he has been smoking strands of brown sugar-coated coconut which are leftover stock from the children's sweet section originally called 'Pirate's Swag' – no wonder it keeps going out and has to be lit several times! Ken and Bettie found it difficult to sell this item as all of the children of the village grew up, so they emptied it out of the original wrappers into a jar and renamed it Angel Kiss. Mr Selsman looks up at the magazines on the top shelf, mutters “Disgusting!” pays for his paper and shag, makes a smell and leaves.

Bettie grabs a bulk box of ‘Bobby the Clown’ white candy sticks, or sweet cigarettes as they used to be called, and proceeds to remove them all from their boxes. She takes one of the little water-colouring brushes from a children’s paint box called ‘Water Colour Fun’ that has been hanging around the shop since 1967, and with dilute cochineal, paints the ends of them with a little red dot, believing that ‘Killjoy’s’ the confectioners established in 1908 have made a mistake. She’d rather not return them and upset that very nice man from Killjoy’s who supplies a whole range of sweets. She leaves all of the little sticks out to dry and will put them back in their boxes later. Oh look! there’s a little picture card of ‘Bobby the Clown’ kicking another clown’s bottom – there’s one in every pack! On the subject of burning things and pretend cigarettes, in walks Mr Jedson, part-time Fire Chief, part-time pyromaniac who’s always busy – he’s here to buy a bumper box of cooking matches, although to call them safety matches is a manner of speaking in Mr Jedson’s hands. I’m wondering how long it will be before the thought dawns on him that ‘The Fire Station Plot’ was a bit of a faux pas!

And now it’s Harry Helmson the hairdresser/barbaric hairstylist’s turn to come in. Still a bit booze-bothered and bedraggled, he’s peeled his face from Comfytums’ tea room window where he’s spent the whole night. He’s just been being woken by one of the two village children firing a pebble from a catapult, making a direct hit on the back of his head. Harry’s here to purchase his usual – a packet of paracetamol, a 2 litre bottle of Irn Bru and three packets of cheese and onion crisps. This for Harry is a far better hangover cure than any ‘Hair of the Dog’ he’s tried – It completely dulls that feeling of somebody trying to push your eyes out from behind with a sharp stick, although the combo of Irn Bru and cheese and onion make him quite unapproachable once he begins to belch.

One might think that I paint an ugly picture of Vernham, alluding that there is an inherent drink problem here, well there is mostly!

"Night on the tiles then Harry?" smirks Ken.

"I've been worse!" sighs Harry. A stray bulldog toddles in and looks around the shop, looks at Ken and Betty and then fixes a stare on Harry, shuffling on his front two paws. The bulldog seems to be mesmerised by Harry, bloodshot eyes unmoving, the bulldog's eyes are also bloodshot. The staring-out competition seems to go on forever until the bulldog 'BLOOP!' vomits on the shop floor and sends Harry shooting out cupping his hand over his mouth and painting last night all over the cobblestones. The bulldog follows. Harry, hangover already forgotten, is feeling much better now and has a number two 'better than a Hair of the Dog' to add to his catalogue. Bettie opens up two bottles of Cherry Buzz Bomb fizzy soda that don't seem to sell too well and uses them to swill the bulldog stomach contents onto the outside pavement with the help of a broom. The pungent aroma of overripe cherry and the caustic burning action seems to do the trick… but is that steam or smoke?

There's a BANG! THUD! RATTLE, RATTLE, DONG! up above from the new tenants. Bettie looks at Ken and knows he's thinking that he wishes he'd sent Fred Flasher up to "sort 'em out". The new tenants, Vic and Maureen Grinham, hate noise of all sorts, but make a lot of their own racket. They've already upset next-door neighbour Mr Swale by shoving a note through his letterbox reading, *Hello, we're your new neighbours, SHUT UP! Yours sincerely, Vic and Maureen Grinham.*

Poor Mr Swale, retired but still active member of 'The Busted Philharmonic Orchestra', practises his bassoon every morning at ten o'clock for one hour only and has done for the thirty years he's dwelled there. No one else minds Mr Swale's music and have become quite attached to the regular parping belting out from his cottage. Now there's a big FOR SALE board mounted on the outside of his home and everyone is disappointed, that is except for the Grinhams who feel that it's mission accomplished for them! One giggle for Mr Swale to be had is that in the Vernbury Vale Estate Agents, you are allowed to add your own selling points to the adverts – for instance, the good points you think may persuade the viewers to buy your home. So Mr Swale has put his little bit in and it reads thus:

*Two bedroom luxury period cottage in a friendly village
*Large kitchen/breakfast room
*Beautiful meadow views from the rear
*Modern bathroom/shower/WC
*Ample sized lounge
*Would suit Punk Rocker with Gibson Les Paul
and 100-watt Marshall valve amp with 4 x 12" cab

The Grinhams are an odd couple; Vic is a window cleaner/peeping Tom and Maureen leaves the flat fairly early loaded up with vacuum cleaner, mop and bucket and dressed up in a floral apron. Both self-employed, Vic and Maureen have their business calling cards on Ken and Bettie's local services board. Vic's is straight forward really:

"SPARKLEGLASS window cleaner, no pane too big or small, competitive mate's rates. sparkleglass.com".

Maureen's is more dynamic:

"SUPERCLEAN MAUREEN, all size houses cleaned top to bottom. Be prepared to be swept off your feet!" Again no telephone number but a rather subliminal website address – naughtynancy.com.

Now I'm not saying anything, but Maureen spends virtually all day working and always comes home with her hair ruffled and apron torn – I'll leave that to your imagination. Vic seems to come home as often as he goes out to do a job, in and out like the proverbial fiddler's elbow – it's easy to look busy when you're rushing about doing everything and nothing. The website addresses are pointless for the people of Vernham as no one else has a computer except the Grinhams, but there is a PC store in neighbouring village Velstrum called 'EEZEE PEECEE' so technology is burgeoning in the Vernbury district.

Outside Ken and Bettie's shop a crowd of screaming teenage girls can be heard, Bettie rushes to the door to see what the commotion is all about and sees a very pink and sexy Cadillac Eldorado with the soft top down. In this huge American automobile sits Rock star Tricky Turnspike coming back from LA to visit his parents after another sell-out tour with his band The Transincidentalvestites. He's looking cool even after the '75 date tour, Braeburn Sunglasses with huge lenses the shape of apples and a gargantuan quiff which can only be described as a beehive the wrong way round. The quiff itself is a work of art; Tricky's fringe now four feet long is combed over a flame-retardant foam prosthesis, hairspray and pins are the finishing touch. This act of coiffeury is a 'soft top down and whizz up the highway baby' only hairstyle, although Tricky has had the soft top of his car customised with a little waterproof sheath to keep his hair dry on rainy days. This bulbous bulk can withstand force 10 storms easily; the video to Tricky Turnspike and the Transincidentalvestites song 'While You Were Snoring' is testament to that – it was filmed in Miami when tropical storm Gertrude was wreaking havoc, and you can see as Tricky reaches the part were he sings "I blew my mind while you were snoring". Both he and The Transincidentalvestites appear to take off in flight and Tricky landing flat on his back with quiff fully intact, finishing the song with "While you were snoring, you blew my mind!"

Tricky's real name is Richard Turnpike (or Quiff Richard as his chums nickname him); his manager thought the addition of an 'S' in his surname added a violent edge to a typically twee English name, and the Tricky bit came about after he had difficulty thinking of a raunchy Christian name, "Um, I'm having a bit of a job thinking of a Christian name, it's quite tricky!" BINGO! and the name was born! And as for the screaming girls, Vernham is totally unaware of Tricky and his Trannies, so he plays a tape loop recording on his car stereo of teenyboppers screaming from 'The Beatles Live at the Hollywood Bowl' album just to make himself feel at home. As he progresses down Low Street the stray bulldog pukes up again and PC Fred 'Flasher' Sweetman flings his greatcoat open and gives old Tricky what for!

Back at Ye Olde Sweetie Shoppe, Mrs Bunkerton rushes in and bumps into a rotary display stand of Music For Pleasure LPs sending it into a spin like she does every day. One of the LPs has fallen out, it's one of Lulu's and apparently… She's a tiger… GROWL! Not bad value though, still only 59 pence and there's a T.REX one too! Mrs Bunkerton is full of fluster, rush, blush, and flush – she wants another 2oz of liquorice cream rock as she's stumbled on a very proud cobblestone, dropped the bag of sweets and a stray bulldog has eaten them. There'll be a complaint registered to Vernbury district council for that, rest assured – she does it every day about something.

"Quick, quick, 2oz of express liquorice cream rock – Oh hurry please?" Mrs B is in a panic it's nearly ten o'clock and she's going to miss her 10:02am entrance to Comfytums – she's not missed a single one since 1973, even when she was recently widowed seven years ago! Bettie scoops out 4oz from the liquorice cream rock jar just in case, although given the effect these little demons have on Mrs Bunkerton's IBS she could well miss tomorrow's 10:02am entrance due to a different type of flushing – that'll be a complaint registered to The Department of Environmental Health then! Off Mrs Bunkerton flies just in time; she's just heard the tinkle, tinkle, clang of Comfytums' doorbell as Milly Goldsworth opens up for another day's business and unpleasantness.

Blind Mr Wilson walks into Ken and Bettie's, walks around the shop tapping his white stick carefully, decides that he's in the wrong place and clears off. It's to be hoped that he'll eventually end up for his pot of tea and a buttered scone at

Comfytums – I do hope Milly and Molly haven't moved that wretched doorway table again!

Fred Flasher bursts in, "A quarter pound of Strawberry Bon… oh, I've already been here haven't I? Alright, see you tomorrow then!" Completely out of people to shock, Fred goes back to the police station to do a bit of serious Bobbying and hopefully catch a bit of The Archers on Radio 4 – I wonder what Shula's up to? Fred still likes listening to The Archers but feels it lacks something that used to be there when Walter Gabriel was in evidence, and indeed Genesis haven't been the same since he left either!

Ah! Chris the painter has just walked in to the sweet shop to buy this month's edition of *Decorating Universe*, the be all and end all to décor. This month there's a twelve-page pull-out entitled 'POLLACKIZE YOUR WALLS!' (I'm assuming they're referring to Jackson here) ***THIS WEEK A FREE TURKEY BASTER INSIDE***. Chris, as everyone calls him (no one knows his surname because they haven't asked), is a quiet man who's very good at his job and starts the morning on a natural high every day. Everyone likes him and he always has time to say 'good morning' – come the afternoon things are quite different due to his manic depression, so don't expect a 'good afternoon' from Chris!

Chris's problems began when his beloved wife left him for a bricklayer called Bernard Bunsen (his real name despite his party trick of passed wind and disposable lighter routine) who cajoled her into eloping with him to Worthing for plenty of S, S and S, which in old money is Sand, Seaweed and Stink in translation. Worthing is an elephant's graveyard for retired and successful business people to rot, and some of the young people speak with a West Indies dialect even though they've never been to Brixton. I hope Chris's wife Lucy sees the light and acknowledges her mistake. Bernard is probably cajoling somebody else now, telling her that she'd be better off running away with him to Vernham, rather than staying with that hard working loser that truly loves her. Poor old Lucy… Silly moo!

Apparently Wendy Wilson has been a distant admirer of Chris for some time now; sadly Chris has a heightened olfactory system even after twenty years of snorting the old gloss vinyl, so maybe Wendy should try gargling paint!

*Decorating Universe* is currently at a cover price of £2.99 and Chris hands over three £1 coins. Uh, Oh! Big mistake, because Chris does a fair bit of work outside Vernham he gets a lot of these coins as tips. Now, and this is the peculiar bit, the village of Vernham has yet to recognise the £1 coin as acceptable currency; shops will only except £1 notes, so don't start me on the £2 coin. What one has to do is either buy something small with a £5 note and take the change in acceptable currency, or alternatively go to the Bureau de Change in Busted and exchange your coins for notes. The former alternative is more economical because the exchange rate at the Bureau de Change is £1.20 for a £1 note; on the way back changing your notes for coins, you only get £0.80p. There is always a busy lithographic printer beavering away at the back of the Bureau de Change, churning out these little green slips of paper in sheet form, later to be guillotined into usable bills. Realising his mistake, Chris draws the coins back and pulls out a £20 note and gets, "Have you got anything smaller?" from Bettie. Chris hasn't and looks around the shop for something else to buy. He looks up at the magazine rack and spots one called *COSH!* The magazine for lonely men with a front page flash ***How to win your wife back and fix the swine who took her for good!*** at another £2.99. Bettie accepts the £20 note and gives Chris fourteen £1 notes and four halfpennies which are also acceptable currency in Vernham. It looks as though Chris has the choice of being ripped off or spending the change only in Vernham.

The local rag delivery of *The Vernbury Trumpet* is just about to be unceremoniously dumped on Ken and Bettie's shop floor – FLUMP! It goes sliding across the floor. The headline 'THE VERNHAM BOG STOMPER CAUGHT ON VIDEO TAPE!' Oh No! It won't be long before scores of reporters and thrill seekers will be lining the perimeter of Sweetwater Marsh trying to catch the beast, and before long there will be commercialisation as has happened to Loch Ness. Good old Nessie keeps her head down though and there is yet to be a definite sighting of her. Puzzlingly enough, Tommy Perkins has taken a great deal of interest in this local folklore and may well take a night off of work to see if he can spot old Boggy too! Ken picks the newspaper bundle up, cuts the string and places them on the shop counter. A herd of Friesian cattle walk through Low Street and two of them poke their heads in through the shop door opening; they look around cud-chewing, one sticks a hoof onto the step as though to come in, Bettie shouts "SHOO!" and they do with the clumsy panic that only cattle can.

Another regular customer, Mr Robson, glides in elegantly as though he is wearing invisible roller skates. "Helloo one and all, and hoo are ye todee!" says Mr Robson in a terribly false Scottish brogue. Mr Robson thinks he has Scottish ancestry after having a dream about Rabbie Burns – he considers the dream to be about his past life, or a 'postmonition' as he wrongly calls it. He is quite English but likes to wear kilts and sporrans.

"We're very well, Mr Robson, thank you," says Bettie.

"Can I bother ye for a quarter poond of thae Winter Mixtures, so help ma boab, crivvens and jings!" says Mr Robson, giving a 1971 Christmas annual of *Oor Wullie* on the magazine rack a knowing wink. Mr Robson is looking forward to going to the Vernham Parish Pensioners Picture Show this afternoon – they're showing *Whisky Galore* and *Greyfriars Bobby*, these films are right up Mr Robson's street. He plans to see both films and crunch his bag of Winter Mixtures all the way through; for the people sitting anywhere near him it can be most distracting and soon Mr Robson has the picture show to himself.

"Will ye not be going to the picturehoose this afternoon Ken?" asks Mr Robson with a faint whiff of Haggis wafting out when he pronounced the H in picture house, or hoose as he says.

"No, I shan't be, Mr Robson, pensioners only you see!" replies Ken, hoping that the subject will end there.

"Oh, ye'd be surprised, there's many an ol' goat that looks younger than ye, I might just be able to smuggle ye in, d'ye ken what I'm aboot, Ken?" says Mr Robson cheekily and winking an eye that becomes adhered in the shut position after a night of conjunctivitis.

"Eh, no thank you, Mr Robson, if it's all the same to you I'll leave it for now," Ken responds in a squirming fashion, thinking 'and forever amen too!'

"Och aye, Ken, and remember ye can call me Rabbie from noo on!" quips Rabbie Robson and invisible roller skates out, one-eyed and very disappointed. Mr Robson is off to queue up outside the parish hall as he likes to get a good seat, it's now only a midget gem past midday and the picture show isn't until 3:00pm. Now, I've seen people queuing up five or more hours before a Marillion concert but this is just silly. Ridiculously, the projector screen used is so small that most of the old folks prefer to sit near the front, and the sound system is so quiet that it makes sense to be as close as possible, and yet ol' Rabbie prefers to sit at the back, which he could obtain by just being last in the queue… silly old git!

At the sweetshop the afternoon passes fairly quietly until Mr Jedson, Fire Chief extraordinaire jumps in wearing a disguise; it's a fluorescent orange shell suit and a false Groucho Marx moustache, nose and glasses. "Good afternoon, Mr Jedson," Bettie says with a cheery blush.

Showing slight dismay that his disguise had been sussed, Mr Jedson launches into a shrill tirade of terror, "Some call me Albert the Arsonist, some name me Pyromaniac Pete, but you shall know me as Fire Raiser, your nemesis for all the matches that you've sold to children, and you will know my flames!"

With a proud overlord pose, Fire Raiser fumbles around in his shell suit trouser pocket pulling out a very big box of matches. Now this is where Fire Raiser's plan falls foul – the plan being to strike a match, throw it into the newspapers, smirk, pose with his hands on hips and flee. The next part of the plan is to quickly put on his fireman's suit and helmet, dash into the shop with a bucket of water and appear to be the hero saying, "That's another evil deed of Fire Raiser's extinguished, but I must be off to catch the villain, Pip-Pip Away!" Unfortunately, due to the tight squeeze of ramming a big box of matches into his trouser pocket, a stray match fell out of said box, with the not-so-safety match lying against the striking pad and a sudden fast movement of the matchbox… we have ignition!

With shell suits not being the most flame-retardant garments, Mr Jedson becomes a fireball and frantically rolls around the shop floor trying to put himself out. Bettie reaches for a 2 litre bottle of cheap Cola and dowses Mr Jedson with it; meanwhile Ken beats the flames back with a yard broom and an intense look of enjoyment on his face – he hasn't had so much excitement since Granny's shed was infested with rats! With the flames put out and thankfully only Mr Jedson's pride hurt, Bettie telephones for PC Fred Sweetman to come round and "sort 'im out!" What a tragic waste of a very good Fireman's career and also a very nice shell suit! With Fire Raiser being whisked away to spend a night in the cells where he will subjected to a night of extreme flashing, normal sweet shop business can resume.

Miss Somerton-Jove blusters in, sending the Music For Pleasure stand into another spin. Out pops a copy of 'The Tijuana Brass band plays Lennon and McCartney', probably of limited appeal but, with those lovely photographs of John and Paul there's bound to be someone daft enough to buy it! "I can't remember what it is I've come in for, but I'll have 2oz of it anyway and 4oz of what I usually have please, Bettie?" asks Miss Somerton-Jove with a puff of mothball No. 3 whisping out of her burgundy bouclé jacket pockets.

Now there's a dilemma for Bettie, she knows Miss Somerton-Jove has 4oz of aniseed balls but she now has to remember what she has had 2oz of in the past – "Pineapple Chunks? Cola cubes? Whirly birds? No it can't be Whirly birds, they're so light you'd need a very big bag and I'm certain she's never had them! Dolly Mixtures? Oh dear! What does she have in 2oz?" Bettie thinks to herself with all those sweetie words milling around her noddle. "Ah Liquorice Comfits, that's it, Liquorice Comfits!" Bettie breathes a mental sigh of relief. Ting, ting, tumble, ting! go the Comfits rattling around in the weighing scales bowl.

"What in Jessie's name is that you're putting in there?" shrieks Miss Somerton-Jove.

"Liquorice Comfits!" declares Ken. Miss Somerton-Jove chooses to ignore Ken as she feels he may be one of the fiends that has been giving her morning grief with those heavy breathing phone calls.

"Liquorice Comfits!" Bettie concurs.

"I didn't come here for 2oz of Liquorice… whatever they're called. I've never eaten them before in my life, and even though I can't remember what it is I came here for, I think I'd remember those silly little psychedelic things if I wanted them, you stupid woman!" bellows Miss Somerton-Jove.

Oh no, she's going into one of her tantrums, Ken thinks. "I'll shove a psychedelic gobstopper in your cakehole if your not careful!"

Within moments Miss Somerton-Jove is rolling around the shop floor screaming "I DON'T LIKE THEM. I WON'T HAVE THEM!" It's funny how the telephone number of Merry Meadow is indelibly marked in everyone's memory, Ken performs the ritual. She's an absolute menace that woman and I feel it's time to lock her up for good!

Now that Somerton-Jove woman has been taken back to Merry Meadow for tranquillisation, Bettie can get on with putting those little sweet cigarettes back in their boxes, which is something she finds quite therapeutic and she puts them back ten by ten, not really sure if they're going back into their correct homes but that doesn't matter.

A couple of Vernham Bog Stomper hunters walk into the sweet shop to buy a few supplies to make the dark damp night by Sweetwater Marsh more comfortable – comfort foods like chocolate bars, crisps and cans of fizz. I hope they dispose of their litter properly! PC Sweetman is intending to keep an eye on the watchers and is going to paint himself with phosphorescent green paint so that he shows up properly, though I think that one flash of all that lot in the dark will be enough to freak the most intrepid hunter out for good!

A dear little robin flutters into the shop and lands on an Aztec bar; these bars haven't been around for a while and this is an original copy with the Cadbury's purple wrapper. There's no sell-by date on this bar so it must safe to eat. They don't make chocolate like they used to; things were made to last and this one is from 1973. The robin jumps from the Aztec bar onto a display stand of Beechnut chewing gum and leaves one of its little droppings behind as it flutters off bumping into one of the small window panes before finding the doorway.

Ken looks up at the shop clock, it's 5:05pm; thank goodness, only twenty-five minutes to go before closing time. The trouble is that this can be the busiest part of the day as people rush in to get stuff after they've finished work. The two small children of the village come into the shop hoping that the 5:05 – 5:30pm rush might cause enough distraction for them to steal things unnoticed. They wait patiently pretending to be interested in women's magazines, at the same time keeping an eye on the batch of goodies they intend to pinch. Something's wrong, it's now 5:09pm and nobody's come into the shop yet! It's normally teaming with punters dashing in and dashing out, now it's time for plan B. One of the boys asks for something that he can't see in the shop, a sherbet fountain, and Ken goes to the store room to see if can find some. Bettie, wise beyond their few years, who's been out of view filling the last few boxes of sweet cigarettes, moves towards the doorway and blocks it with her plump figure. One boy keeps watch while the other fills his shorts with just about everything he can cram in; some of it is falling out from the legs of his shorts. “Quick let’s scarper, he’s coming back!” whispers the watchman boy, and they make a beeline for the doorway. Bettie, arms folded, all she needs is a tattoo of an anchor on one of her forearms and she’d be truly frightening, screams “PUT THEM BACK!” with a vocal technique that even Peter Hammill would be scared to use. The boys burst into tears as they know their fate is to be whisked off to their parents by the ears with PC Sweetman, and their parents have told them, “If you don’t learn to behave you’ll grow up bad, and PC Sweetman will give you what for!” Think on, you little miscreants!

It’s nearly 5:30pm and time to shut up shop. Ken does a bit of sweeping up before he counts the float from the till, Bettie leaves by the back door and cycles home to prepare dinner. With a final sweep of dirt out on to the street, a rain beetle struggles upside down to right itself and scurry off out of the dust, Ken turns his OPEN sign to CLOSED, remembers it is Wednesday and thinks, “How lovely for the other shops in Vernham, that they can close half-day on Wednesdays and go without all of this lunacy!” and locks the door.

# Chapter 3

## HEAVEN OPENS ABOVE VERNHAM

It's 5:55am, and it's sunrise over Silver Hill, the sun momentarily sitting like an orange septic head on top of a great green boil. It is said that it never rains in Vernham and a cloud never floats by, but today is different. Already the fauna of Vernham is scurrying away, large and tiny creatures preparing for something horrid. Worms are fleeing their subterranean ghettos to higher ground only to be decimated by the safe beings, predatory crows and other winged offenders. The water table in Vernham is excellent, even during drought Vernham remains moist, being so low lying and with underground springs that steal water away from other villages, everything in the garden is green and rosy. During the dry summer of 1976, the surrounding villages came to Vernham every day to fill up containers with water from the Vernham village pump and the supply was never depleted. Indeed Sweetwater Marsh is always wet, sphagnum moss and peat being its main solidity. Low Street was the original course of the River Poddum before the ancient settlers of Vernham thought it a good idea to divert it around the outside of the settlement – why they didn't consider building a village to the side of the river which would have been fairly straight, one can only wonder. Whatever the reason, they did it and we're stuck with it.

A huge black cloud emerges from behind Silver Hill wrapping around the sun like the disappointment of a TV commercial with a beautiful women retiring from a bath and folding a bathrobe around herself before you get to see anything. This is the blackest cloud that Vernham has seen for a very long time.

Ken from Ye Olde Sweetie Shoppe unlocks the shop door and looks out to see the fluffy carbon spectacle and calls Bettie to have a look. "It looks like rain," they say to each other. Bettie excitedly runs to the stock room to find the barely-sold plastic Rain Macs and see-through plastic Rain Hats, from a dusty corner. There they are, still on their rigid cardboard display boards with an inviting slogan ***JOLLYMACS & JOLLYBONNETS MAKE RAIN FUN! Pack one in your bag TODAY!*** She has also found some clear polythene umbrellas that are shaped like jellyfish domes; they cover your top half completely and they never blow inside out, they just steam up and cause other accidents instead! Well, no prizes for guessing what the big sale for Ken and Bettie will be today, Wendy Wilson has just bought a Jollymac and Jollybonnet to keep her 3lbs of 4X mints and copy of *The Stun* dry.

It's beginning to rain quite hard now and PC Fred Sweetman has just bought a quarter of Strawberry Bonbons, a Walnut Whip, a Jollymac and two Jollybonnets, one bonnet to keep his helmet dry and the other... well I shan't be too explicit, but he's just excitedly run out of the shop singing his own adaptation of a Neil Diamond song "Thong, thung blue, PC Sweetman wears one!" As I said, today is different, PC Sweetman has even forgotten to give Ken and Bettie 'what for' in his haste. The rain is really lashing down now and word has got about that Ken and Bettie are selling protective rainwear – the price seems to inflate with each item sold!

For the last two years, Reverend Parsworthy has been collecting planks of unwanted wood and there's been a certain amount of banging and sawing recently – he thinks he has had a divine message about a flood happening in Vernham, it's odd what dreams one can have after a skinful! Nevertheless, this one-man ark could be quite useful, though I think that Reverend Parsworthy could have taken the odd note about Noah's story and made one a little bigger, the selfish git!

The rain is making Low Street look like a fast and shallow river, all the litter left by careless people is being swept along by the current to end up looking untidy somewhere else.

A very proud Mr Selsman parades Low Street shouting "Who's the fool now, who's the fool now eh?" Well done Mr Selsman, who would have thought it, all these years you've worn those Wellingtons preparing for this day and now it's here!

If it carries on raining this hard, the River Poddum will burst its banks and then there will be trouble. Goofy Gordon the beaver freak has been practising dam building using his bare teeth to trim branches and twigs, his front teeth are all his mouth owns. In his beaver studies he has learned the techniques that these little mammals use to build the perfect dam to hold back the flow of water, but will it be of any use? Gordon's dentist has warned him that if he persists with his habit of wood chewing he may well lose his two big front teeth – they do look rather odd though, it seems almost as if the tooth fairy stole them and replaced them with somebody's big toenails. Well, if he loses them he'll be known as Gummy Gordon that's for sure, perhaps he'll take up studying ram's horn water snails instead.

The water level is getting much higher now, nearly all of the buildings have very high steps fortunately, but there may still be a need for emergency sandbags yet.

Mr Selsman is making his way to Ye Olde Sweetie Shoppe to buy his broadsheet and baccy; the sweetshop's step is a little lower than most in the village and already one inch of flood water has made its way onto Ken and Bettie's shop floor. With careful footsteps, Mr Selsman just about manages to avoid getting a boot full, and as he steps into the shop he frightens a small shoal of sticklebacks, sheltering after they've lost their home in a little nearby pond, darting for cover in different directions, each tiddler halting with the bent tails like sticklebacks do. The display stands are quite high in the shop though, so hopefully Ken and Bettie won't suffer a stock loss;

insurance cover is something that most proprietors in Vernham don't bother to take out as they consider it to be dead money and rather spend any extra in The Grummet and Nut or Comfytums. Mr Selsman takes his leave and carefully steps out of the sweetshop and the water is over Wellington boot level – have you ever considered chest waders, Mr Selsman?

Mrs Bunkerton, determined as ever not to miss her 10:02am entrance to Comfytums, arrives by inflatable life raft – now there's something she doesn't do every day! "I shan't be needing anymore liquorice cream rock today, Bettie, I've still got plenty left from yesterday," says Mrs Bunkerton with joyous shrill, and paddles her way down to Comfytums to lash and moor her vessel to the D-Ring that Milly and Molly Goldsworth had specially installed into the shop front wall outside the tea room for dog owners to tether their dog's leads to.

The specials board normally boasting Comfytums' goodies is not there, but there is a makeshift handwritten sign taped to the door… ***CLOSED DUE TO ADVERSE WEATHER CONDITIONS*** BE BACK SOON! Oh, Mrs Bunkerton, what are you to do now? Distressed beyond her wits, Mrs Bunkerton unties the life raft from the D-Ring and throws her arms up in horror, drifting downstream towards despair. One of the two small children of the village, always at the ready for fun, fires a very sharp pointed stick from his home-made crossbow right into the side of Mrs Bunketon's life raft, DOP! WHEEEEEEEESH! The air rapidly hisses out leaving Mrs Bunkerton floundering in eighteen generous inches of floodwater.

A loud cry comes from further down the street, "FEAR NOT, FINE LADY, I SHALL SAVE YOU!" It's Tricky Turnspike, and he's running through the water in Baywatch-style. Unfortunately pretending to be in a slow-motion movie shot doesn't quite work as the water doesn't behave in the same way – something to do with gravity and stupidity I think! The water isn't that deep but when it comes to heroics, who cares! As he approaches Mrs Bunkerton, Tricky removes the pins that tack his hair to the flame-retardant foam quiff prosthesis he styles his hair on, and passes the spongy beehive to Mrs Bunkerton as a buoyancy aid. She embraces the bulk of polycarbonate foam like a grateful child with a teddy bear and Tricky drags her ashore to shallower water on the other side of the street.

As she lays exhausted on the raised pavement, Mrs Bunkerton looks up at her aquatic saviour with his fine figure and very long wet hair and says, "I take back everything I've ever said about long-haired men that make loud noises!" She looks at Tricky in wonderment and feels something inside her she's not felt for a long time… EXCITEMENT! Mrs Bunkerton hasn't experienced true kindness for a very long time and has always believed that people only tolerate her. She can't take her eyes off Tricky and she sees him in the same way as a romantic movie with petroleum jelly on the lens of a camera – that'll be your glasses steaming up, Mrs B, and behave yourself, Tricky's twenty-five years your junior! Tricky picks Mrs Bunkerton up in his muscle-bound arms and carries her to the only establishment nearby that hasn't taken any water in yet, The Grummet and Nut. Tricky sits her down on a wooden chair and orders a very large and medicinal brandy. Normally Mrs Bunkerton doesn't partake of alcohol, only breaking her temperance at Christmas with a 'Snowball', but as I say, today is different. She sips the warming nectar rapidly and appreciates the glow that she feels before it rapidly goes to her bonce and she passes out. Mrs B will be alright and I'm certain someone will make sure she gets home safely when she comes to!

The banks of the River Poddum have burst and the water retains its memory of where it used to flow, increasing the turmoil as ducks and swans get swept down into Low Street. The mystery herds of Friesian cattle make their daily visit and wade up Low Street like water buffalo; the cobblestones are very slippery and most of the cattle have panic attacks as their hooves lose purchase on the road. Even today some cattle stop to peer into Comfytums where Milly and Molly are completely flooded out, the twins' tears only adding to the problem. The cattle move on and out of the village to wherever they go.

PC Sweetman, who is on his best behaviour and trying his best to help people who are in distress, suddenly remembers that he has left Mr Jedson the disgraced Fire Chief in the cells and he may be in trouble. PC Sweetman thrashes through the water but his greatcoat now completely waterlogged is slowing him down. No choice but to take the greatcoat off, and he does so in a flash, excuse the pun. Everyone around expecting to be subjected to more unnecessary nudity are shocked to find him completely dressed in his police uniform – what on earth is going on? PC Sweetman reaches the police station to find Mr Jedson waist deep in water; he unlocks the jail door and lets Jedson the Fire Raiser out. PC Sweetman warns him that although he is free to go home, he mustn't leave the village as there will be further questioning about other arson incidents of recent, in particular the burning down of the fire station.

Oranges, melons and other floating fruit and vegetables are bobbing downstream now as Jim Phillips the greengrocer loses most of his stock. Punnets of cress are white-water rafting down Low Street like thousands of little green refugees looking for a new home. Jim Phillips is trying to retrieve his melons using a large landing net, placing the melons in a tethered keep net that he normally uses for his coarse fishing matches at weekends.

Despite the heavy rain, over the other side of the street is a group of good-sized chub and they're waiting in the slacker water for odd bits of food matter to drift towards them. Jim Phillips can't believe his eyes as he spots these piscatorial barrels, estimating them all to be between six to seven pounds. Acknowledging that he'll never get another chance like this, Jim rushes to the back of his greengrocer's shop and rigs up a fishing rod to float bread crust past them and catch at least one of them before they get spooked. He needn't have bothered; by the time he gets back a miserable old cob swan has a peck at the back of one of the fish and they bolt away, "Bastard!" Jim curses. The cob swan spots Jim with the huge chunk of bread in his hand and with a bullish stiffening of the wings, swims with the ramming speed of a Viking longboat, or at least a very white short boat. The cob propels itself by both webbed feet with boastingly proud upward chest movements towards his prize. Jim grabs some melons out of the keep net and throws them in the direction of the cob; one melon makes a direct hit on the cob's back, accelerating its anger and speed.

Jim is actually quite afraid of swans, a phobia he has had since a short-trousered knee-pecking incident when he was a schoolboy. Jim moves to the back of his greengrocer shop and the cob swan follows; all the cob wants is the chunk of bread that Jim is gripping in his frightened hand. With a milk-curdling shriek Jim cries, "NO, NO! NOT THE KNEES, NOT THE KNEES!" The cob stops and looks at Jim with a 'What are you on about?' sideways tilt of its head, and then proceeds to peck at his bum instead.

The two small children of the village watch this rump-pecking happening with glee, it's better than anything on telly. The water is now almost chest-deep for the children and they're having difficulty in staying still, such is the force of the flood water. Seeing the trouble that the children are having, Jim forgets his swan phobia and lets go of the bread to help them. The cob swan's interests are diverted to the bread crust and slap, slap, slaps at the mushy disintegrating loaf portion with its bill. Bum-pecking now a recent memory, Jim pushes through the water to save the children. Picking both brats up with each strong arm, Jim pops them onto his American footballer width shoulders and double St Christophers them across Low Street and off to the downstream home of their worried parents.

Ooh! Now there's a spectacle, Tommy Perkins is somehow surfing down Low Street on his Bog Shoes! I'm not sure if it's with intent or accidental, but Tommy seems to be in complete control of the elements – he's laughing or is that crying, it's hard to differentiate rain and tears, unless of course it isn't raining!

Not to be beaten, Tricky Turnspike swims to his parents' home to get his surf board from the garden shed. Now you see… normal people in normal villages and hamlets would be in absolute terror if their homes and businesses were under threat from catastrophe, but not this lot!

At the north end of Low Street, the road dips down to a 1-in-8 slope; this acts like a weir and at the bottom of the long slope is 'The Vicarage' and 'Vernham All Faiths Church', the church so named because it accepts people of all faiths, basically, be you Buddhist, Moslem or Mormon – if you've got more than 50p for the freewill offerings plate on Sunday morning, you're welcome. Reverend Parsworthy, now deep into his fourth bottle of Côtes du Belch communion wine, only £3.99p in Breecher's the supermarket, is swaying from side to side like a terrace chanting football hooligan, shouting "You've all been warned, none of you believed me that there would be a second flood and now it's here, there's no room in the Ark for you!" I think you've got your Bible stories a bit on the mixed-up side Rev!

Close to the original principle of Noah, Reverend Parsworthy has taken two of everything into his Ark – two bottles of Chablis, two bottles of Bordeaux, two bottles of 12-year-old single malt and so on, and two squirrels who are stowaways and currently enjoying one of the two boxes of his cashew nuts on board. This flood is, in Reverend Parsworthy's reasoning, an Armageddon for the human race and sees no point in taking heathens onboard as they are only bound for their judgement day. With blurred vision and fumbling thumbs, often turning over more than five pages of the Holy Bible at a time, he has managed to muddle up a very abstract story based on the finer points he can remember, to join together the pieces and come up with a surreal notion. With the flood water now rushing underneath the Ark, Reverend Parsworthy launches into a lunatic laugh shouting, "YES, YES, YE-HE-HE-YES!

HA-HA-HA-HA-HAHA!" Parsworthy's Ark is washed off of its mounting and Rev, the booze and the squirrels are drifting off into the main course of the River Poddum where they will pass through many villages of the Vernbury Vale and most probably end up in the Busted canal basin to be pointed at and ridiculed for looking so silly. Not that the squirrels will give a tinker's cuss, as all they need to know is what is in the cashew nut boxes and how much is left.

Back in the flow of things, Tricky Turnspike has found his surf board and waxed it. Tricky, with waterproof MP3 player, is listening to 'The Beach Boys Live In London' – handy things those earphones; it's a bone of contention for recording engineers and producers – Tricky and headphones don't mix. Due to his insistence on going into the studio fully quiffed, recording studios have to be equipped with custom-built headphones made with an extra long bracket to accommodate his huge foam bump. What a spectacle it is to see a renowned Rocker toeing from the back of his board to the front, well in his mind anyway!

One thing to be said about today is the noticeable absence of two of the regular characters of Low Street. Blind Mr Wilson had a brief tap around with his stick outside his front door, found it a bit splashy and decided to stay in. Miss Somerton-Jove hasn't been allowed to walk about today as she may get herself into trouble and it might prove to be difficult getting Merry Meadow's ambulance to her should she have one of her tantrums.

At last the rain seems to be easing up, but the floodwater will take a long time to diminish. At the deep north end of Low Street, Tommy Perkins' Bog Shoes can be seen floating upside down, side by side – oh no, not Tommy? It would be very difficult to turn yourself up the right way if you lost control in deep water, but… wait a minute… either Tommy is very deft at doing the splits or he isn't wearing his Bog Shoes – they are now about twelve feet apart from each other! Suddenly with a huge vortex and bubble Tommy rises from the depths and splutters, "I've found the plug," cough, cough, wheeze, "I've found the plug!" Tommy is holding what seems to be a regular manhole cover, so it could be that his joy is about to turn into heartbreak. But there does seem to be another vortex in the water, and the water level does seem to be dropping – could it be that the manhole cover has been a plug in a very big plughole? Be careful now, Tommy, that whirlpool could drag you down! Tommy swims to an oak tree trunk and hugs it for safety. Meanwhile Tricky is finding inspiration from this scenario and makes up a lyric for a new song, "Whirlpool, I'll draw you into my whirlpool, you can call me Eddy!" Wow that should be a smash, Tricky!

The floodwater in Low Street is draining off down to the plughole – well done, Tommy! Before long, all owners of the shops and buildings are sweeping out the remains of the flood; hopefully the same will happen to the gents in The Grummet and Nut, they haven't seen a broom or mop in years! The sun pokes its cheeky face out through the clouds bearing a huge marmalade grin and the warmth of its smile evaporates the damp from the cobblestones leaving will-o'-the-wisp steamy ghosts rising to heaven.

Parsworthy's Ark hasn't reached Busted canal basin; instead, it is stranded on a hillock just on the edge of Sweetwater Marsh. Here the Wrong Reverend Parsworthy sends out a squirrel to collect nuts to bring back so he can be sure the flood has subsided. There he will wait patiently for the squirrel's return; after the bellyful of cashew nuts that those little fellows had it could be a long night!

# Chapter 4

## AN EVENING AT THE GRUMMET AND NUT

In the village of Vernham, set deep in the heart of the Vernbury Vale is a hive of adult activity enjoying the spoils of life. Like every good or bad soap opera, the local population meets up in a Rover's Return or Woolpack Inn to fight or fall in love; Vernham has its own version called The Grummet and Nut. This original 16th-century inn is currently run in a sort of fashion by Landlord and Landlady Roger and Susan Spur, proudly celebrating their 40th year as publicans in this very alehouse. This is a Free House selling the finest ales from around the Vernbury locality, and French wines both red and white made in small wineries from regions of the north to far south. Any visitor, or 'Spruggles' as the Vernham natives call them, requesting a pint of Fartmeister Lager or a large glass Kangaroo's Pouch Merlot is after a punch on the nose, or at least friendly advice as to which drink they should choose.

Alcohol is a big pastime in Vernham, and there's no bigger participator than the Reverend Parsworthy, although he does stress to all of the younger influenced regulars that he serves as a sermon to the easily led, 'Don't do as I do, there won't be any left for me!' kind of ethic. Harry Helmson the hairdresser isn't far behind; he does like to down the odd pint or so during his lunch break and, as I've said before, afternoons are a write-off for decent haircuts.

There is one intrepid customer of 'Helmson's Hairdressing Salon' – Tortoise Terry is a regular punter for the 'short back and all gone' afternoon haircut. He has no fear of drunken Harry's mutilation, he doesn't have any ears. Terry lost his ears in an industrial accident at 'Woodmill's Joinery'; he was getting the teas in from the tea machine when he slipped on a couple of doweling rods and fell onto a circular saw which sliced off one of his ears. Why he went back for second helpings with the other ear is anyone's guess. Terry spent a considerable time out of work relying on SSP, and when he was about to return to work, the works foreman warned all of Terry's colleagues not to mention anything about his ears as it was a sensitive subject for him. Terry was one of the best workers at Woodmill's and any upset would make him leave for good.

All was fine for a few days and Terry was on top form, getting on like a house on fire with his old chums, everything was back to normal and Terry was enjoying job satisfaction again… Until one day in the canteen when workmate Billy Buxton, not the brightest spark off of the firework chirped, "Terry, I see your eyesight has improved!"

"What do you mean, my eyesight's improved?" questioned Terry.

"I've noticed you haven't been wearing your glasses recently!" replied Billy with sincerity. That was it; Terry burst out of Woodmill's in tears and never returned. It's a long time ago now and Terry seems to be over the worst of it, although he is still self-conscious about his lack of lugs and has been known to stick a couple of large potato crisps to the side of his head with chewing gum when a pretty girl enters the bar at The Grummet and Nut. In the low light of 'The Snug', a place for courting couples, he can almost get away with it, that is of course until one of the girls tries to get off with him and whispers sweet somethings or starts to nibble at his earlobes! He does however, get the cheapest haircuts.

It's early evening at The Grummet and Nut and most of the daytime drunkards have gone home to lie to their wives, each armed with a bunch of flowers stolen from Mrs Bunkerton's beautiful garden. What are they to say to their very disappointed spouses to change things? "Sweetheart, I've been abducted by some strange purple beings from the planet Sphincton, where they force-fed me with alcohol by some way of experiment!" To get the line properly rehearsed let alone perform it when you're that pickled would be difficult enough, and to convince the old bag would be harder! Dynamite Dan the pyrotechnic fanatic is on to a loser, he grabbed hold of a bunch of stinging nettles by mistake for some pretty flowers and thrust them into his common-law wife's face saying "Shmell theesh, they're beautiful!"

At a table near The Snug, there are three young girl Spruggles who are excitedly hoping to catch a glimpse of their pop hero Tricky Turnspike; they've heard tell of him being back in the country and back home with his parents for a while. With a bit of luck they may be able to get their Transincidentalvestite fanzines autographed. Through the frosted glass in the pub door the girls spot the silhouetted form of a giant quiff, "Here he is!" squeals one of the girls. All of the Vernham populace missed out on Bay City Rollermania so I'm not sure what they'll make of this! The door opens and the shrill squeaks of idol worship are extinguished with the same annoyance of a gramophone winding down while you're listening to a tasty 78.

It isn't Tricky at all, it's Eddie Jedson, Mr Jedson the ex Fire Chief's brother. Eddie was born with the affliction of having an extra long head, even when he was a 10 year old he was 6 feet tall. His mother had a difficult pregnancy and in those days there wasn't ultrasound, it was also a very long labour for Mrs Jedson too! The midwife decided it better to plump for Caesarean section as his mum was so tired, there was shock when this otherwise perfectly formed baby's head came to light! Having such a long head caused problems for little Eddie – one-piece romper suits weren't available with hoods to fit, perambulators never had canopies big enough and despite that, the cruel jokes and Mickey-taking were all too much when he went to school. He wasn't allowed on the school bus because he was continually pressing the bell strip in the roof by accident every time he moved his head. The school bus driver grew tired of stopping at the next stop when it was a false alarm, and with his already bad nerves in tatters the driver asked Eddie's mum if she could make other arrangements for his transit to school.

As he grew older, Eddie's heart was set on being a fireman just like his brother but to no avail; in the name of safety, helmets are required to be worn at all times and they don't make them that big. The 'can't let you in because of safety helmet regulations' excuse is a bit farcical really, despite rumours that his brain is also the same shape or that his brain is normal size and all above is hollow – the last part is almost true but above his normal-sized brain is a honeycomb of very strong bone. So really Eddie is better protected than most people and the safety helmet regulation is just a kind way of saying 'No thanks!' However the 'brain the same shape as his head' rumour has worked to an advantage for Eddie as a lot of people believe that he must be more intelligent than most having a brain that big, and so he is always requested to be in the local pub quiz team – fortunately for Eddie he is very intelligent!

Things are a lot better for Eddie now and he is a very successful chef in a busy Busted restaurant named Raresteak's renowned for its famous cream of tomato soup, and they do have hats that fit him! All of his friends call him Big Ed (yawn!), how original! Eddie has a bit of a problem with the low beams in this 16th-century pub and it's common to hear, "Dock! Ooh! Dock Ow!" as his nut collides with the old oak beams. If Eddie drops money and bends down to pick it up, run for cover or you WILL get head-butted!

Until Eddie has a few pints in him, he has a problem with words – it's probably down to confidence, but a few swift pints normally does the trick. It's always fun listening to Eddie ordering his first drink at the bar, and he's just about to…

"Hello, Eddie, what do you want today, the unusual he, he, ha ha!" chortles Roger the landlord.

"Er… Ye, er… Yes! A bint of pist better and a spracket of cork patchings please?"

"So that's a half of mild and a bag of dry roasted peanuts then, Eddie, a he he a haw haw?" guffaws Roger.

"Er, Ye, er… Yes please R-Roger?" concedes Eddie. Don't worry, after three more halves of mild, Eddie will be able to order what he really wants!

There's a thunderous crash at the pub door, it's 19-year-old Barry the butcher's delivery boy on his bike! Ever since Barry's last delivery bike was stolen outside of The Grummet and Nut, he prefers not to take any chances and insists on bringing it into the pub. It's no ordinary bike; it's a converted full suspension mountain bike with a delivery rack conversion kit installed at the front. With this bike, Barry has no problem in getting into establishments with the typically high doorsteps of Vernham. All of the locals are intrigued to see such a machine. To see Barry bunny-hopping up and down the curbs of Low Street is a delight, although Dick Sperling the master butcher has told Barry to make sure the rain canopy is secured on the delivery rack as he's lost too many pies that way, also it encourages a certain stray bulldog to get very fat! That is though, that nobody has seen the bulldog since the great Vernham flood a few weeks ago and it could be that he disappeared down the Vernham plughole when Tommy Perkins removed the plug. Still, nevertheless there are always hundreds of ravenous ravens and crows in waiting for a free nose bag, and the rain canopy must stay on!

Roger has asked Barry if he could walk his bike in rather than ride it around the pub – there isn't really the room and it's dangerous, it's just that Barry keeps on forgetting. The pies are handed over to Landlady Susan to put in a heated glass incubator to keep them hot, a sight not seen very often in pubs nowadays, and I'm not sure that it's legal. I know a health inspector mentioned something about condemning the incubator to Roger and Susan on the grounds that the pies may not be sold that day and if they remained in the incubator or were reheated it could be a health and hygiene matter. Master butcher Dick Sperling was there that day and took great exception that a statement had been made suggesting that his fresh pies may not sell out on their first day. Dick suggested the health inspector should go outside for a quiet chat and the health inspector was never seen again, although oddly enough a pair of his shoes was found on Sweetwater Marsh!

"So how do I know which are steak and kidney and which are chicken and mushroom then Barry?" asks Susan.

"Oh that's easy, Susan, Dick puts a pastry SK on the steak and kidney and a pastry CM on the chicken and mushroom!" swaggers a very smug Barry.

"Ooh quite clever really isn't it, but… what about if any of our customers are dyslectic then?" puzzles Susan.

"Oh just give 'em a bag of crisps!" Barry cockily quips and rides out of the pub and forgets that the door is inwards opening. CRASH! he'll be singing castrato for a few days now after that brief encounter with his crossbar!

Roger ignores the fuss and ogles one of the pies, "So what would you like, Eddie – a Kate and Sidney pie or a Micken and Chusroom pie? Hoo Hoo Ha Ha He He Haw Haw Ha Ha!" Roger splutters with a wheezy laugh, wishing that he'd packed up smoking before it had taken hold.

"Er, er… N-No thank you, er R-Roger!" says Eddie with bags of disinterest.

After her pie duties, Susan attends to the lost property case which is on full display hoping the owners of the junk that they've left behind will recognise and claim them. Amongst the usual umbrellas and cigarette lighters is a pair of spectacles that have been unclaimed for the last seven years. Susan gives them a bit of a dust and polish and puts them back on a piece of paper which has 'WHO'S GLASSES?' written on it with indelible marker pen. Most people who've seen this spectacle of spectacles have often been intrigued with the punctuation, does it mean who IS glasses, who owns them or indeed did Roger Daltrey wear them at any particular time? None of this matters really because seven years ago Mr Bunkerton passed away after a bit of a heavy session at the pub where he left his glasses behind in the Ladies toilet, went home and had a massive heart attack! Luckily Mrs Bunkerton doesn't go in there very often except by mistake or for her Christmas Snowball, a few weeks ago; though she was there after Tricky Turnspike rescued her from her punctured life raft during the flood and she didn't see Mr Bunkerton's glasses on display due to the large medicinal brandy she scooped back before passing out. If she had seen his glasses she would have been extremely upset – to know that Mr Bunkerton had been frequenting a place of such ill repute would be more than her mind could bear.

Over in the far left corner by the Gent's toilets is the gentle donk, donk, donk of The Grummet and Nut's darts team practising for the 'Vernbury Darts League Cup'. Their next match is in Velstrum at 'The Queen's Ankle' which has a marvellous swinging sign depicting Queen Victoria hitching up her gown and baring her ankle – now that in those days would have been porn! However, 'The Grummet Arrows' as they proudly call themselves, have got a lot of practising to put in and it's not looking too good. Having a dartboard next to the entrance of the Gent's isn't a good idea – that isn't woodworm in the door, they're dart holes. It's not uncommon to see men standing at the urinals with a dart or two sticking in the back of their heads; most of them think though that it is the kicking in of the very strong ale that gives this sensation. To judge when and when not to come out of the toilet is easy though, once you hear three donks you can dash out before the next three are thrown. Roger and Susan did move the dartboard away from the toilets at one time but it didn't seem to make any difference, as they're all a bit rubbish at darts and they could fly anywhere!

Eddie Jedson's feeling a bit more relaxed now and he's fumbling around in his trouser pockets for some coins to put in the Duke Box, it's called the Duke Box because at one time all of the records in the Juke Box were Duke Ellington records. Fortunately now things are a bit more varied as the locals can bring there own 45s in to put in the Duke Box. "What are you going to play now, Eddie – a bit of Slack Babbath or Zed Leppelin? Hee, Hee, Haw, Haw, cough, splutter, hack!" jokes Roger.

"Er, N-No, Tuthro Jell a-actually!" retorts Eddie.

"Isn't that the group with Ander Ianson who plays that shiny whistle pipe on one leg?" asks Roger with a cheeky wink at other cruel punters who think it's fun to mock Eddie.

"Er, Y-Yes, and it's a flute actually er, R-Roger!" says Eddie with an 'I know a lot about pop music!' kind of smirk. Now which song to choose? Ah there it is 'Oo Told To R-Rock 'n' R-Roll, Oo Doung To Yie' – a wise choice, what a shame 'Heavy Horses' wasn't a single, it would be much easier to say!

The Reverend Parsworthy walks in later than usual; he's here to collect for the church door fund, and he's also got a William Holman Hunt painting 'The Light of the World' as a raffle ticket prize, only it doesn't look like the real thing to me. In fact I'd go as far as saying that it's a very cleverly painted-over photograph of Parsworthy holding a Tilley Lamp outside the church before the door was stolen, hopefully no one will be daft enough to buy a ticket. "Turn off that filthy vile Juju music, if thine ears offend thee, then cut them off!" yells Reverend Parsworthy getting his Holy Bible facts confused again.

Tortoise Terry pretends not to hear what the miserable so-and-so said, but he is offended. "Steady on, Rev, it's only a bit of pop music!" protests Roger.

"Call that music? It's the devil's work I tell you, the pipes and drums of Beelzebub luring innocent sheep to their doom!" preaches Reverend Parsworthy.

"Ah shee-ut up, you silly old goat," an anonymous voice says in the background. Shortly after, a dart makes a direct hit with the William Holman Hunt bootleg.

"WHAT YE! DESECRATERS OF HOLY WORK, I PRAY FOR YOUR SOULS!" roars Reverend Parsworthy with a big waggy finger.

It's quite obvious that old Rev is already on the way to being drunk and unreasonable and so Roger tries to calm him down, "Rev, Rev, Rev, calm down now and have a drink?"

"Rev, Rev, Rev! That's all I hear from you, what do you think I am a motorbike? Hell's Angels, filthy chapters of decadence, you will perish in eternal flame!" wails Reverend Parsworthy at the same time as Ian Anderson sings 'Death's Head belt buckle...Yesterday's dream'. Naturally this infuriates the Reverend and he throws his tacky old 'Light of the World' fake at the Duke Box causing shards of glass to explode everywhere.

"Alright, alright, that's enough, you silly old religious nut, get out of my pub. You're barred!" screams Susan.

Ooh now that's calmed him down! Reverend Parsworthy hasn't been shouted at by a woman since his beloved mother did when he was a teenager. The Reverend inexplicably becomes quiet and turns to Susan with tears in his eyes and whimpers, "Yes, Mummy!" Reverend Parsworthy's mother Mary, Welsh by birth, had a week-long fling with an Irish merchant sailor called Fergal O'Rear when his ship was docked at Tiger Bay. Reverend Parsworthy was the fruit of a passionate Guinness and Leek fuelled affair which was doomed because Fergal was already married. The lovely baby boy was Christened Dai Parsworthy, but when you think about it, it's fortunate that the Welsh-Irish couple didn't marry as it would have been torture for the poor boy at school registration... 'Daffyd Simpson?' 'Yes Miss!' 'Glynnis Williams?' Yes Miss!' 'Dai O'Rear?' 'HAHAHAHAHAHAHAHAHAHA!' 'Stop it, children, stop this laughing at once or you'll all be staying in at play time!'

Reverend Parsworthy who now prefers to be known as David, is still very attached to the memory of his mother. She passed away after a short illness while young Dai was still in his senior school. He wasn't born into a Christian background but had his calling when he was at his mother's funeral. Reverend Parsworthy heard his mother's voice telling him to be good and serve God. But with teenage rebellion, the drunken Irish sailor half of his genes dominated his every move and although he became a man of the cloth, he has merely used it as a smokescreen to his advantage. Nevertheless, the sound of a raging woman rebuking him is enough to extinguish the fire in his soul and reduce him to a gibbering schoolboy idiot, and Susan's wrath has done the trick! With an uncharacteristically gentle click of the pub door Reverend Parsworthy sobs off home to the vicarage to question 'WHY?' through to the bottom of a bottle of Glenfunnel 12-year-old single malt, and a bag of cashew nuts. When Reverend Parsworthy heard many years ago that even as far back as the Tudors, people used cachous to freshen the breath, he mistook the name and has put great faith in the deodorizing properties of cashew nuts – well these cashews don't help and he does reek of booze!

All's peaceful in The Grummet and Nut now and Eddie Jedson's words are assembling in the correct order, but only for a few more pints! At one of the centre tables of the bar, Mickey Farshott and his pal Graham Bird have settled down for a game of 'Battling Bellies'. The game of Battling Bellies can only be played by certain people, physique has everything to do with it and this can only be achieved by quaffing copious quantities of real ale for a long time. The object of the game is to whop your beer bellies out on opposite sides of a single pedestal round table and press down very hard (this is obviously a variation on arm wrestling), and the winner is the man who tips the table down on his side. The prize for such efforts is more beer bought for you all evening by the loser and a trip down the Chinky afterwards, at least there would be if there was a Chinese restaurant in Vernham, but one of those ready-made takeaway's from 'BREECHER'S THE SUPERMARKET, NOW OPEN 24 HOURS A DAY!' will suffice. Incidentally, the supermarket's name is simply 'BREECHER'S', but since the store obtained a licence to be open all day and night, the local folk think that the name has changed. And so it's "Ooh, Beryl! This rice pudding is delicious! If I may be so bold, where did you buy it from?" "Yes it is nice isn't it, I picked it up from Breecher's The Supermarket, Now Open 24 Hours a Day!"

Anyway, digression over, Battling Bellies has been going on for seven and a half minutes now, it's stalemate! And then, from absolutely nowhere, a bee lands on Mickey Farshott's stomach – it doesn't matter whether it's a bee, wasp, hornet or horsefly, if it's got a nasty sting or bite it's freakout time for Mickey. Mickey has suffered with apiphobia ever since he was a schoolboy when Sally Smith threw a half-chewed fruit pastille up the leg of his shorts (strange little girl!) in maths, and a wasp followed stinging his under thigh. Mickey panics and his belly loses grip on the table... CRASH, SMASH, TINKLE! It would have been a good idea to put your beer glasses on another table, lads, now there's smashed glass all over the place! If Miss Somerton-Jove comes in and goes into one with her usual rolling about the floor routine, she could hurt herself badly – mind you, if she does you'd better put an Iggy Pop record on the Duke Box to add to its authenticity!

Susan rushes out from behind the bar to sweep up the broken glass and mop up the beer; she then sprinkles some new spit and sawdust out of a bucket to replace that, which has been swept up. All of this unnecessary stupidity is only reinforcing Susan's thoughts on replacing the traditional beer glasses with plastic ones; she's seen some nice ones in a discount shop in Busted Arcade. It's an everything for 99p shop called '99's' and many upset children have come out of there crying because they thought they were going to get an ice cream cornet with a flake in it. Miss Somerton-Jove was thrown out of 99's the other week after one of her tantrums when she couldn't have the CCTV camera and monitor for 99p. Well, in defence of Miss Somerton-Jove, it is a bit silly advertising everything for

99p when it isn't! Anyway, where was I? Ah yes, the plastic beer glasses! They are superb – pink with white polka dots for girls and blue with white polka dots for boys; each one has lenticular eyes that wink when you tip them up. They're called 'Winky Pint Pots'. Susan will probably buy more blue ones as it's mostly men that frequent The Grummet and Nut. I'm not sure what the reaction will be to the plastic mugs though as it's a 'Man's Man' pub!

Mr Robson the counterfeit Scotsman has just popped in for a nip of scotch, "A large whusky and goo steady on the wutter please, Roger?" says Mr Robson with as much authenticity in his Scottish accent as Dick Van Dyke's cockney in *Mary Poppins*.

"Any particular whisky, Rabbie?" asks Roger.

"I'll have a large glass o' that Glenfunnel single malt please, Roger?" says Mr Robson wrongly pointing a dirty fingernail at an upside down bottle of Armagnac du Gascon.

"Any particular water, Rabbie?" enquires Roger.

"Aye, I'll have a wee splash o' that Strathpeffer Spring please, Roger?" says Mr Robson pointing with the selfsame filthy fingernail at a bottle of lemonade. Mr Robson looks around to see if anyone's noticed him being there and noticing that they haven't, or rather are pretending they haven't, says "Aye, if ye gonna have a whusky, it's got tae be the real McCoy!"...Nobody is interested! "Aye it's a braw moon oot there tonicht!"...and still nobody's interested.

Roger puts Mr Robson's Armagnac and lemonade on the bar counter and says, "That'll be £3.20p please, Rabbie?" Mr Robson grunts at the price and dips into his sporran pulling out three Scottish pound notes and a beer bottle top. "Ye can keep the change, Roger!" says Mr Robson generously, then vehemently muttering, "Muserable auld skinflint!"

I think the reason why people aren't too keen on poor old Mr Robson is because they aren't too sure about his sexuality. Take his kilt for instance – at a cursory glance it appears to be an everyday kilt, but the clan from which this tartan is from is uncertain and the inside label reveals the hallmark 'Madame Brigitte – Garments with the larger woman in mind'. The fact that he never passes the four old gentlemen playing dominoes at the same table every night without asking "Good evening, ladies, and hoo are ye toodee?" doesn't help him either! And he has taken a bit of a shine to Ken Griggs the newsagent too, but if you analyse everything he does it becomes clear that Rabbie Robson's eyesight isn't very good. For instance, any self-respecting fake Scotsman wouldn't order a brandy in mistake for a scotch, neither would he confuse lemonade for spring water, and he could have accidentally bought the tartan skirt from a charity shop thinking it was a genuine kilt. But the sporran – that's a different matter altogether; it's an old bus conductor's leather bag with a couple of false joke shop beards glued to the outside. The kilt pin is a lady's brooch he had inherited from an auntie many years ago. I think as an epilogue to these queries, I will settle on my assumption that he is trying to make his life appear more interesting, he's very lonely… and quite mad!

Rupert the burly rugby league prop, who is sitting near Mr Robson, makes a grab for his crutches that he's been hobbling around on for the last two months after he broke his leg during a friendly match. After a bit too much local brew he needs the loo but knocks over his crutches that are propped up against the table. The crutches fall with a clatter and land in a cross. "Hoo kind of ye to offer me to dance De'il Amang the Tailors!" says Mr Robson with joy. And so, getting things wrong again, Mr Robson confuses De'il Amang the Tailors for the Jacobite sword dance and starts hopping around. Meanwhile Eddie Jedson has put Peep Durple's 'Moke on the Swater' on the Duke Box… "We all came out to Montreux, Och aye the noo!" as a very fake Scottish Ian Gillan might have sung.

Rupert swipes his crutches back with anger and sends poor old Rabbie flying; if you've never seen The Flying Counterfeit Scotsman before, now's your chance! Mr Robson plummets to the spit and sawdust carpet with the grace of a sack of spuds, his Glengarry and ‘not so secret now’ ginger toupee scuttling across the floor as though it has a life of its own. Along with the other strange things Mr Robson does, is the habit of sticking toupee tape on the inside of his Glengarry to keep his hair in place. Embarrassed, Mr Robson picks himself up and dusts himself off, bidding goodbye with, “Weel, that’s me done for tonicht, I’m off to practise ma caber tossing noo!” and places his Glengarry the wrong way round on his luncheon meat patterned bald head.

With Mr Robson now leaving, Mr Mussel has just walked in to sell his wares. Mr Mussel is actually William Mustard and Mr Mussel is his business name. William visits all of the pubs in the Vernbury Vale hoping to flog the odd whelk or so. “Cockles and mussels, alive alive-o!” William proudly sings, although they all smell quite dead to the sniffing of the general public. No one buys the seafood salmonella suicide snacks from Mr Mussel. No one that is except for Greedy Griff Johnson, Griff’s cast iron digestive system is immune to all sorts of gastric nasties and Mr Mussel’s seafood is a walk in the park for him. Griff eats anything that doesn’t move, and many a poor soul that has nodded off in The Grummet and Nut has woken within inches of their death as Griff’s tartar encrusted choppers have nearly bitten them. There’s been a mysterious vanishing of barstools recently since Griff’s favourite crisps, Smokey Cedar Wood Barkchip flavour, have been off the menu and Roger is keeping a beady eye on Griff as people have to stand at the bar when they’d rather sit there.

Now completely fluid with mild, Eddie Jedson makes a fluent request to Roger, “I say, Roger, when you have time, dear boy, could I trouble you for a pint of your best bitter and packet of your extremely delicious pork scratchings please?”

“Okay, Eddie, half a pint of mild and a packet of dry roasted peanuts coming up… Hehe haw haw hoo hah!” jokes Roger, the naughty so and so! And much to Eddie’s surprise, a pint of Velstrum brewery’s finest bitter and a humongous bag of pork scratchings ends up on the bar counter in front of him. “Sorry,

Eddie, we're all out of mild and dry roasted, will this lot do instead?" smiles Roger.

"It'll have to do!" grins Eddie.

The Tricky Turnspike girl fans are getting a bit bored now and are thinking of leaving, as the last bus to Velstrum leaves at 10:25pm; they'd better not leave it too late, otherwise they'll miss the connection to Busted where they've booked into a hotel for the night. As the girls make a move, the famous quiff of Tricky Turnspike bursts through the door. Noticing the Transincidentalvestite fanzine in one of the girl's hands, Tricky coolly slips his Braeburn shades down to reveal his heavily made-up eyes and sexily says, "Hi girls, how would you like to spend an evening with a rock star?"

One of the girls replies in a no uncertain manner, "We'd love to, you look good, but you're not a bit like him, he's much taller!" And off they go very disheartened that they never caught a glimpse of their idol.

"Evening, Tricky, what can I get you?" says Susan in her best Bay City Roller fan voice.

"I'll have a tomato juice please, babe!" Tricky says, pointing a pretend pistol-shape hand at Susan and whispering 'POW!' before giving Susan a saucy wink.

"What's that, on the rocks then, Tricky? Heehee haw haw, hack, cough, spit!" sniggers Roger.

"Very funny, Roger, stop it, you're killing me!" Tricky snarls. It's not funny; Tricky is off of the booze for good, due to his doctor's orders. For obvious rock 'n' roll reasons, Tricky has embraced the world of excess too many times and now it's time to stop. Tricky turns to Eddie and says, "Allo, Ed me old mucker, how are ya?"

"Yeah good thanks, Richard!" Eddie says cheerily, and they both chat about the old days ten or so years ago. From behind, Tricky and Eddie look like a couple of Grenadier Guards in civvies that have forgotten to take their bearskins off. Tricky has a soft spot for Eddie, they always used to enjoy going to Busted to buy records from 'Spinster's Record Bar' and it was

Eddie that first got the young Richard Turnpike into rock music when he put Flink Poyd's 'Giper at the Dates of Pawn' on his mum's radiogram. And it was Eddie that inspired that notorious quiff of Tricky's. Tricky reminds Eddie of the time when they both went to see a local band 'The Raspberry's Answer' at a club in Busted called 'Maximum Headroom' and how the ceiling was so low that Eddie kept on bashing his head on it when he tried to pogo. Eddie bursts into raucous laughter and gets so excited he knocks the bar bell making everyone think it's last orders.

A lot of people in Vernham don't bother wearing watches and so they rely on Roger ringing the bell to tell them whether it's last orders or time at the bar. Consequently, all of the drinkers in The Grummet and Nut scoop back their pints and rush up get another drink in before closing time. This mistake of Eddie's is a boon to Roger and Susan as they have often dreamed of having an early night in, and with a bit of luck if Tricky keeps the funnies going, Eddie might even ding the dong again for closing time. Roger and Susan haven't had a single day off in the forty years that they have been publicans in The Grummet and Nut, let alone a night off.

It was forty-two years ago when Roger and Susan met, they were both working in a busy pub-restaurant in the East Midlands called 'The Tamworth Pig Grill', part of the famous Charfood chain. It was there that they fell in love and became married after a whirlwind romance. Shortly after they wed, the landlord of The Tamworth Pig Grill ran away with all of the money and Charfood's, who weren't doing too well since the very popular Chinese and Indian restaurants and takeaways began springing up all over the county, decided to close The Tamworth Pig Grill down.

With both Roger and Susan now out of work, they had to look for new jobs; all they really knew was pub work so they took temporary bar work, often times at different pubs. Then after four months of pittance, Susan's mother's sister, Auntie Shirley was tragically killed in an accident at the archery club she was a member of. The circumstances of her death are unclear, but she was killed when an arrow penetrated her heart; nobody else seemed to know anything about it as it happened very early in the morning. Stranger still, she was killed by one of her own arrows; the coroner's report was vague stating 'Possible suicide with an archer's bow the wrong way round, OR an accident'. Whatever the cause, Shirley was Susan's only blood relative; Susan's parents were killed on safari in Kenya by a raging bull elephant, so Shirley became Susan's mother.

Shirley left everything to Susan in her will, her house and £55,000, which was a huge amount of money in those days, and even today you could buy loads of fruit salad and blackjack chews and still have plenty left for the bus ride home! It was Susan's proposition to Roger, that they buy a free house pub of their own, and after a bit of pondering for two seconds Roger thought it to be a capital idea. And so after a time of browsing in *Which Pub?* the landlord's monthly bible, they found this beautiful inn nestled in the heart of the Vernbury Vale. Alfred and Alice Spillingham, the then landlords of The Grummet and Nut, were retiring and wanted a quick sale.

And so it came to pass that the Spillinghams and the Spurs shook hands on the princely sum of £15,000 pounds for the pub and one and a half acres of meadow land with riparian ownership of a small section of the River Poddum. Since then, Roger and Susan have never looked back – they haven't had time to! So for one more false ding of the pub dong with Eddie's big bonce, an early closing for just once would be a gift for Roger and Susan. Unfortunately, Tricky and Eddie have decided to leave and take a trip down memory lane to listen to some old albums at Eddie's mum's house. Mrs Jedson always had a soft spot for the young Richard Turnpike so he might be in for a bit of luck and get some of Mrs Jedson's lard fried chips… MMMM!

All of this of course is of no help to the Spurs. Roger makes a brave move and decides to ring the bell and shout, "TIME AT THE BAR PLEASE?"

PC Fred Sweetman who's been loitering outside the pub for this moment jumps in and yells, "ALLO, ALLO, WHAT'S ALL THIS THEN, A LOCK IN?" And with a quick flash of 'Way Hay!' and 'Woo Hah, Woo Hah!' everybody runs out of the pub just in case they get any more 'what for'. It's only 10:07pm and Roger and Susan can close up and retire for a cosy evening with a packet of smoky bacon and a bottle of cherry pop each… Ah Bliss!

# Chapter 5

## OF IDIOSYNCRASIES, IDEAS AND IDIOTS

The Vernbury Vale would be poorer without its unique villages, and none of them more unique than Vernham. Outsiders, visitors and accidental tourists all earn the title of 'Spruggle', a term used only by Vernhamites. The origin of the name Spruggle dates back to 1066 when a small number of William the Conqueror's bunch of Charlies took the wrong turning, missed Hastings and wandered on blindly north to stumble upon Vernham, a settlement of very basic and ancient Britons (who somehow managed to miss out on the 5th-century Anglo-Saxon invasion). These Norman soldiers, outnumbered by the Vernhamites, were overpowered and taken hostage.

These Normans were an intelligent and friendly bunch and taught the Vernhamites a lot of useful things. This knowledge was taken on by Vernhamites and the teachings became known as 'Norman Wisdom'. They helped these lesser intelligent villagers with farming methods that revolutionised their ways of thinking as regards cultivation and irrigation. One problem Vernhamites had was the lack of food in springtime; the food, like root vegetables, kept well during the winter months in storage, but as the temperatures rose in spring the food began to decay. This famine period was known as 'The spring struggle', but the Normans showed the Vernhamites how to dig underground cellars to keep the food cooler and prevent frost from biting it. This worked well because by the time they had finished the old stock of food, the newly grown food was just about ready to eat. The spring struggle was an unpleasant memory for the Vernhamites and so anything nasty or unwanted was referred to as 'spring struggles' as a term of dislike, this later became shortened to Spruggles. As all visitors to Vernham were treated with dislike, they became known as Spruggles too, and the term is still used to this day.

Many visitors to the village are affected in one way or another, both good and bad. Martin Paste, poet and winner of 'The Oliver Sprigg poetry trophy 1955' wrote:

> I walk down Low Street
> On lambswool moccasin feet
> Led like a wasp to a jam pot
> To arrive at my favourite spot
> In a village named Vernham
> I read my words and burn them.

He didn't win the Oliver Sprigg trophy with that poem, that was rubbish! But the lambswool moccasin feet part is significant to Vernham, and it was the 'Vernham Village Noise Before 6:00am Abatement Society' that put forward a ban on all noise between 11:00pm and 6:00pm. The milkman, who still delivers milk by horse and cart today, has to put hoof silencers on his horse and the wheels of the cart have inflatable tyres which glide silently on Low Street's cobblestones. The milkman has to wear regulation slippers and the milk is in cartons so to eliminate the traditional clanking of glass bottles. The final part of that short poem portrays Paste's feeling of uselessness, the inability to write about a village that haunts and inspires him so much, and yet his words don't touch the spirit of Vernham. His final act is to set alight the feeble page of words in disgust and watch them burn on the cobblestones. Unbeknownst to Martin Paste, a young Mr Jedson the Fire Chief was watching, and this event made a marked impression on the small boy who would grow up to be a pyromaniac.

The world of American country and western music has also found influence. On a visit to the United Kingdom, country and western artist Wild Wesley West dropped in on his pal Tricky Turnspike and stayed in Vernham for a week. It inspired his song 'Sweetwater Fever' which recounts a tale of a lusty night with a young girl on the edge of Sweetwater Marsh, their passion interrupted by the eerie noise of the Vernham Bog Stomper. They both fled in different directions, trading their passion for fear, the lyric tells us:

It was a hot steamy night by a marsh
I could feel a thumpin' in my sternum
We both got high, stared the devil in his eye
And we lost our souls in Vernham

These words, though apparently nonsensical, have made a huge impression on American country and western fans, and the name of that faraway village called Vernham has acquired a mystique that has earned the same intrigue as English Rock and Roll fans of the 1950s had for places with American names.

It is said that John Constable came to Vernham seeking inspiration for his paintings, but didn't stay for long though because of the lack of gloomy clouds.

To the Spruggle, some the people of Vernham may appear to be eccentric, but Vernhamites believe themselves to be the height of normality and the Spruggles the eccentrics. I suppose when you think about it, if one was to put a bucket on one's head every day from very early on in life and found no unpleasant side effect from such an act, one would assume it to be a normal thing to do. But some people would see that as an act of eccentricity. It would be interesting to hear Ned Kelly's view on that subject if he was still alive!

Vernham has had clever inventors who may be viewed as eccentric to some. Arthur Range for instance developed a street lighting system for Vernham Village. The Vernham Rate Payers Society opted out of having streetlights installed so that their rates weren't increased. They also raised objection to car headlights shining around all over the place during the hours of darkness; now this is obviously flouting a standard safety requirement and law in motoring. So Arthur Range built a street-illuminating compromise – this was a light in a streetlamp-like stand mounted on the roof of the car; he named them 'Mobilights'. These worked well but were not such a good idea as there are a lot of low bridges in the Vernbury Vale and it would be impossible to travel very far. So these were scrapped and Arthur went back to the drawing board and came up with 'Lamplids'. Lamplids are little shields that fit over headlamps with little suction pads. These little accessories make the cars look as though they have very sleepy eyelids, but they are extremely effective and shed controlled illumination only where it's needed. Any driver caught driving in Vernham without these Lamplids is likely to get 'what for' from PC Fred Sweetman and learn a bit about another sort of flashing!

On the subject of cars, another inventor and innovator named Rodney Beauthorpe put Vernham on the motoring innovation map for a short while when he produced the prototype 'Dentmobile'. The Beauthorpe Dentmobile was developed as an answer to the prime, new car owner's fear – getting a dent in your new car! Rodney's reasoning was that people are often afraid of leaving their pristine motor cars unattended in case they get dented by a careless driver when they're parking. Simple, if you make the car pre-dented then you have beaten the careless drivers to it, thus all fear is removed. These went into production and the cars were quite popular around Vernham and its neighbouring villages until 'The Night Of The Panel Beaters' occurred.

One morning, every proud owner of a Beauthorpe Dentmobile woke to find their lovely new cars completely dent less. Much like crop circles that are made overnight, all of this reverse vandalism was executed without a single noise and the miscreants that performed this panel-beating were never caught. All of this did not deter Rodney Beauthorpe in the slightest; it only inspired him to find another method to alleviate dent paranoia... 'The Beauthorpe Latexia' was Rodney's new approach – a car made from solid surgical rubber panels; put simply, you could bash into any old thing and your car would be totally dent free. The windscreens were made from glass clear rubberised PVC, so smashed windows would be a thing of the past. The Latexia's downfall was that it wasn't very good driving round sharp bends – the car would take on a banana shape due to the grip of the tyres on the road, and finally as the tyres lost their hold, the back end of the car would spring out and catapult the car off the road. Also, during safety tests, the flexible windscreen's chemical make-up was faulty; there appeared to be too much stretch, and if a crash test dummy was used to simulate a driver not wearing a seatbelt, the window would wrap around the dummy's head like a melon in cling film. Although facial injuries were minimized, the windscreen's substrate didn't seem to retain its memory and so risks of a driver suffocating were high.

Courting rituals are quite eccentric in Vernham too; if a man finds a woman appealing and wants to take her out on a date, he must first make his intentions clear to her. If the woman says 'maybe', which invariably she will, the man has to place a small pebble on the woman's doorstep, every day for five days. These pebbles are called 'The Five Stones of Maybe', and if the desired woman picks up a pebble off her doorstep and takes it indoors, that is a stone of maybe. Each day that a stone is taken indoors, it becomes more likely that she will go out on a date with him. If the woman goes off the idea she will leave the next stone untouched; this is a rejection and the man is out of luck and must leave her alone. If a woman accepts the man's request, she must let him know by throwing her deciding stone at his bedroom window at 11:15pm. The deciding stone can be any one of the five, and the lucky fellow that gets the first stone of maybe is in for a hot date. The amount of heartbroken men that have had their fifth stone untouched are few, but it does happen – poor old Mr Robson, the counterfeit Scotsman, had the one brick of 'DEFINITELY NO!' crash through his window when he proposed to Miss Somerton-Jove.

One sad tale is of village odd boy Tommy Perkins who fell deeply in love with a pretty girl called Cynthia Bustle. Cynthia said maybe, and so Tommy was very excited. On the first night a stone came smashing through his window, he could hardly sleep that night – fantasy scenarios of eating fish and chips, and walking together in the country lanes rattled around inside his head. All this was before Tommy becamc unwittingly addicted to amphetamines. He very rarely sleeps at all these days; he works a nightshift at the Velstrum Bakery and his free time is spent painting snail shells and coughing. Anyway, the following day, Tommy happily skipped all the way to Cynthia's house only to find his first stone of maybe still on her doorstep. It later transpired that it was one of the small village children that fired a stone at Tommy's window from a catapult. The parents of these infant terrorists are obviously not very concerned that their children are out late at night, it's a sign of the times, and even Vernham isn't immune from this modern culture.

As regards Tommy's amphetamine addiction, the Velstrum chemist 'Booth's' which is owned by Charlton Booth, supplies him with these drugs. Charlton Booth is a chemist who knows just what one needs for their ailments; he also has a wicked sense of humour and will prescribe things for people purely for experiment. So when Tommy turned up at Booth's complaining that he found his night shift at the bakery was tiring him out and he felt very sleepy, Mr Booth said that he had some special sweets called 'Whizz Balls' that can help, and suggested that Tommy give them a go. These sweet cinnamon-flavoured balls are impregnated with an accurate dose of amphetamine sulphate, but they do taste rather good! Tommy loves them and eats a mountain of them, but his mother worries that he sleeps so little.

As mentioned before, Tommy is also unwittingly the fabled Vernham Bog Stomper, and his Whizz Balls enable him to skim across Sweetwater Marsh on his Bog Shoes effortlessly. These little balls are costing Tommy a fortune and he seems to be getting through more and more, and Mr Booth is doing very well thank you very much! Mr Booth once prescribed a laxative for Mrs Bunkerton as a cure for her IBS, his thinking being that if she offloaded everything, her bowels wouldn't have anything to be irritable about. Gladly, Mrs Bunkerton bumped into Bettie Griggs the newsagent lady on the bus home who suggested that Mrs B threw away the laxatives and tried some liquorice cream rock. This was a good idea, it saved Mrs Bunkerton from loo-time disaster, and Ye Olde Sweetie Shoppe was better off from the profit of 2oz of liquorice cream rock every day. Charlton Booth will hopefully meet his nemesis one day, until then people will continue to suffer from his lab rat sense of humour. One thing is for sure, the place most unlikely to have a 'drugs bust' is a chemist!

In a Spruggle's eye view, the people of Vernham would appear to be content with their lot, and in general this is true. Of all the things that are aplenty in Vernham, ambition is in short supply. I mean real ambition, a desire to see what is outside, and some of Vernham's natives have never ventured out as they feel that all they need is in the village. But every now and again a Vernhamite feels the desire to venture out – they are all certain that the far off places that they have seen on the television do exist and aren't just inside the box. Indeed Tommy Perkins was sixteen years of age when he realised that Columbo was a real person and not just a figment of his television, the sad truth dawned on him when he went to a friends for tea in Velstrum and watched the glass-eyed detective on his friend's TV.

But some have aspired to much more world widely things – of course Tricky Turnspike is a good example. In his teenage years, the young Richard Turnpike's father made him his first guitar, fashioned from a plank of wood with a bicycle brake cable stretched between two screws impaled in the wood. Tricky's musical journey began. This plank type of guitar thing was purely acoustic and wasn't very loud, it was also very monotone. The single bicycle cable did make a very good sound though but it needed something else. Then one day, like silly teenagers do, Tommy decided to plug the microphone of his mono compact cassette recorder in and put the machine into record mode whilst plugging in the little earpiece. With this earpiece wedged into his ear hole he discovered that an amplified version of his voice could be heard with a slight distortion. So what if he connected a lead from his cassette recorder into the DIN socket of his stereo record player? He discovered that apart from an unpleasant squealing noise, he heard his voice very loudly. So with a bit of imagination, Richard stuck the microphone to his plank guitar with sticky tape and 'HEY PRESTO!' the electric plank was born.

Some of Tricky's early songs were written on this instrument, and one song in particular was 'While You Were Snoring' which was penned when he was strumming the plank in quiet mode with the earpiece plugged in. The title of this song came about because he composed it late at night when his mother and father were in bed and the original sentiment of the lyric was not as Rock and Roll as it seems in the current version. Tricky also found that if he ran one of his mother's vacuum cleaner nozzles up and down the brake cable while he twanged, the musical pitch of the plank changed. Some of Tricky's early recordings had a definite Hawaiian flavour to the sound, notably the song 'While My Plank Gently Whinges'. All of this cacophony became very popular and has made Tricky the icon that he is today – there's no accounting for taste is there?

Some Vernhamites leave the village unintentionally – 102 years old Mr Barnford, for instance, was kidnapped in the Comfytums tea room raid by pupils of Blagworth Junior School. He now stands sentry in the school corridor, though he doesn't look a very good colour nowadays and smells a bit odd. Mr Barnford, too young to fight in the First World War, too ill to manage the Second World War, became the village ARP man. Most of his time was taken up sorting out the mess left behind by the Luftwaffe bombings. At a Vernham summer picnic, young Mr Jedson sat on Mr Barnford's knee, wide-eyed, for two hours listening to his wondrous stories of burning wood and explosions. Despite his ill health, old Mr Barnford was a wartime hero and he is highly respected. There are newspaper cuttings in Busted's historical museum with an account of how 'Old Barney' (as he liked people to call him, even though no one ever did!) saved the beer cellar of The Grummet and Nut from burning after embers from a nearby incendiary incident ignited some old potato sacks. With a photograph of Mr Barnford, ARP helmet cockily on the tilt, sticking two Churchillian fingers up at the sky and holding a pint of ale in the other hand, the headline reads 'EAT, DRINK AND BE MERRY, YOU CAN'T SPOIL OUR FUN, OLD JERRY!'

Very few Vernhamites did fight in the two wars; there was always a reason not to be able to, be it due to ill health or other excuses. I'm glad that very few did fight, as any loss of its characters would rip the heart out of the village and the surrounding area would become less rural and nodding towards the suburban.

One building that was severely affected by wartime bombing was Grummet Hall, the home of Lord Wenville. Although Lord Wenville wasn't killed that night, the bomb damage was so severe that he didn't feel he could stand the emotional pain of seeing Grummet Hall, the proud home of the Wenville's for over 200 years, being pulled down. Merry Meadow the home for the infirm, old and very disturbed was built on the site using a lot of the bricks left over from Grummet Hall. The original and beautiful landscape gardens designed by Incapability Saunders are still there and the Rhododendrons in May are a treat for the eye to behold.

Although there are parallels with the outside world with Vernham, this little village will always remain odd. The refusal to accept £1 coins as legitimate currency (and heaven knows decimalisation was a nightmare), common notions that completely disregard scientific fact, deviants that would be either chastised or locked up for their misdemeanours are accepted as normal and the implacable belief that Spruggles are the weirdos and 'The Vernhamite is right!' all make up the ingredients of a very strange world that few could survive in.

# Chapter 6

## PC SWEETMAN'S IN LOVE

PC Fred Sweetman, part-time flasher, part-time Bobby is a strange character. He is however a vital ingredient, a cog in the machine of the village of Vernham, and a character that would be sorely missed if he disappeared. What makes Fred Sweetman the exhibitionist that he is? It dates back to his childhood when he was raised by a strict Christian uncle and auntie; this predicament came about because his mother and father were both busy business people who were often away from home. So his parents gave the job of bringing up a sweet little boy to his uncle and auntie, Toby and Winifred Sweetman.

Toby, the elder brother of little Fred's father Terence, was a Methodist minister and ruled with a rod of iron. Toby and Winifred brought little Fred up in a loving caring environment, even if a little bit dull, he was very well protected and cared for. He was taught to say grace before meals, pray before bedtime and read his Bible. He was allowed to play with toys (except for guns and soldiers) during his free time in the week, but taught to observe abstinence of all unholy things on Sundays. Sundays were television and radio free, and the highlights were going to Sunday school and the evening church sermon performed by Toby Sweetman. Fred enjoyed singing hymns and he belted his little voice out. Minister Toby Sweetman was a stern man, with an Abraham Lincoln beard and Ben Turpin eyes; you didn't know if he was talking to you or someone else, but you took heed just in case it was you that he was preaching to!

One thing that was impressed on little Fred was that 'NUDE WAS RUDE!' and blindfolds at bath time were compulsory. At school, Fred had to wear a frog suit under his uniform on swimming lesson days. The sight of neoprene leggings poking out from underneath Fred's little grey shorts were a great guffaw for his classmates, a topic of ridicule with plenty of mileage for years to come. Having a wee wee was a task, as he wasn't allowed to look at what he was doing in case he had ideas about the 'devil's tool'. Sitting down on the WC was the answer for a tinkle as he wouldn't have to worry about direction, and again the trusty blindfold was pressed into use. General toilet duties had to be executed whilst singing or whistling hymns to take his mind off of the job, and only briefly at the end was he allowed to concentrate on the aftermath for cleanliness. I shan't dwell on that subject any longer as it is obvious what problems can occur with a small boy.

He was allowed to watch television but Uncle Toby was the control over what to watch, any hint of the bikini or swimming could only mean flesh, and so Toby would be up and down changing television channels to watch something more suitable. One year during the Olympics, swimming featured heavily and so television was a virtual blackout for part of that summer. Fred was allowed to watch television until 8:00pm and then it was off up the wooden hill for prayers, then sleep. Then one evening when Fred had been asleep for a couple of hours he woke after a bad dream about bare bottoms floating like Nimble balloons over Silver Hill, singing hymns as they soared away to oblivion. As he became more awake he found that he needed a wee wee as he had had a large glass of milk before he went to bed, but he couldn't find his blindfold and so he dared to go downstairs to ask his uncle and auntie if they knew where it was. As he timidly walked down the stairs with his right foot always being the first down, followed by an obedient left foot, he became aware of laughter in the lounge.

Uncle and auntie were obviously enjoying something, and as Fred got closer, the door was ajar – ajar just enough to see both Uncle Toby and Auntie Winifred completely naked enjoying a game of hoopla, Winifred was throwing the hoops at Toby! A sheer electric shock ran through Fred as he felt the feeling of bewilderment and disillusion. Overcome with the urge to urinate, Fred tore upstairs in a 'peeline' for the loo. Down with the pyjama trousers and bugger the blindfold, Fred felt immediate relief, and looking down a feeling of freedom and well being. Shortly after, Fred had the urge to run all the way to the top of Silver Hill and expose himself, singing hymns at the same time, Fred felt like one of the bum balloons in his dream… FREE! That is what it is all about for Fred, freedom, nothing sexual, just freedom. The flashing at the cherry-topped pink-iced buns in the baker's window incident was purely out of respect for topless bathers in the South of France. He only felt guilty because he remembered that food was provided by God and he had a flashback of his Uncle Toby's crossed eyes looking very cross at him, or were they looking at Fred? The rod was definitely not spared with Fred, but the child was spoilt, and ruined!

Of recent, Fred hasn't been seen exposing himself and he's been in full uniform minus his smelly greatcoat. Neither has Fred been collecting his daily freebies of Strawberry Bonbons and Walnut Whips from Ye Olde Sweetie Shoppe. There can only be a few reasons that can make a man change his lifestyle, and one of them is women. And it is a woman that has transformed the life of PC Fred Sweetman, so how has this happened? Well, it all came about one dark evening when Fred was on patrol for naughties, nasties and things that go 'Way Hay!' in the night.

Walking down Low Street at 11:45pm, Fred turned the corner after Haberdasher's World and was confronted by the very beautiful Wendy Wilson. Both of them startled each other and both reacted with an opening of their coats revealing all and shouting 'Way Hay!' at each other. Fred was dumbstruck as he saw the most beautiful sight he had ever seen in his life, and something no man had ever seen, Wendy naked! Although the night was very dark, the rods in Fred's retina were very accustomed to darkness and Wendy was no scotopic illusion. In that brief moment of exhibitionism, Fred and Wendy discovered parity.

Wendy's reason for being an exhibitionist is loneliness, despite being the ravishing beauty she is, her extreme halitosis has always put the mockers on getting to know a man. Fred is also lonely, and this is due to his over-strict upbringing; it has made him shy. This is a strange situation for any couple to meet, but Fred and Wendy hit it off straight away and soon found themselves deep in conversation about the days gone past of Vernham. Yes, I know what you're thinking, 'How can Fred bear the smell of her breath?' Well, if I tell you that Fred has no sense of smell, then you'll understand! When Fred was very small, his Uncle Toby went into one of his Holy rants and accidentally whacked poor little Fred on the nose with his heavy black Holy Bible. This broke Fred's little bugle and he completely lost all sense of smell, which was an advantage for Fred at the time as it meant that he would never have to smell Auntie Winifred's horrible lamb casserole with those horrid pieces of swede ever again. He still had to eat the filthy muck but at least half of the misery had gone! This also explains why he doesn't know that his greatcoat smells so much. So, Wendy had met a man that could appreciate her beauty and Fred had met a woman who understood the freedom of nudity.

It's now three weeks since Fred and Wendy met and they have completely bypassed 'The Five Stones of Maybe' ritual and gone straight into 'The Big Snog of Absolutely!' They both enjoy running up Silver Hill to fling open their coats and feel the air on their bodies, but all public display has been curtailed. They are planning to live together but Wendy would prefer to get married first; this is okay for Fred because he is quite old-fashioned about that kind of thing, and in any case he's had to wait so long for this moment, a little while longer won't hurt. Yes, it's true, PC Fred Sweetman is in love!

We are now in the present, and Fred and Wendy are out on a date, wining and dining in Velstrum at 'The Mozzarella

Wizard's Pizza Den'. Fred has opted for the Margarita because it's cheaper, Wendy has plumped for the Quatro Formaggi, and they are sharing a delicious bottle of Chianti. They both laugh as Wendy has a long string of Red Leicester stretching from her chin to the pizza plate. They also question if Italians would use Red Leicester in their pizzas or whether there is a place in Italy called Leicester. Wendy gazes at Fred and sees the most wonderful man she could ever meet, and it's true – whatever mental picture you have of Fred, he is a very handsome man!

The restaurant is unusually empty, a number of people have walked in and then walked out shortly after. Whether the prospective customers have decided against dining here because they have recognised Fred and are afraid of getting what for, or whether it's because they could smell the foetid whiff of halitosis is unclear. Whatever the reason, who cares, this is romance! All the restaurant staff are drawing straws to take turn in serving the lovebirds, and the pretty little fat Italian girl keeps drawing the short one.

Fred and Wendy talk about their future – do they want children, will they take turns in walking the Labrador, does Wendy like swede and does Fred believe in Father Christmas? Both Fred and Wendy agree that it is going to be an exciting journey, but are trying to be mature about it and not rush into things. Money won't be a problem, even if Wendy falls pregnant and has to leave her job, she has tens of thousands of pounds saved from her well-paid toothpaste representative job for Peggy White's the tooth cleaning specialist.

Fred asks Wendy if she wants to move into his home or buy a new home of their own, which could be a problem as Fred lives in the police house next to the police station. There has been a rumour that the Government may close small police stations and if this happens Fred could lose his house anyway. Fred being 45 years of age has still another 10 years to go before he retires, but he has been thinking of a change of career. Wendy says that there may be a job becoming available at Peggy White's in the city of Busted, but it's a long way for

Fred to cycle. Wendy says that it won't be a problem because she could take him in most mornings, although he would have to make his way home on some nights as she often has to travel to various counties far and wide as the sales pitch is broadening. Fred thinks about it and says that it would be a very long day considering how early she has to start out. Wendy says, "Well, just think about it, if the position comes up, you'd be the first in!" The subject moves back to where they will live together after the're married. Wendy would prefer not to move too far away as she feels she would have to pop in and see her old dad, Blind Mr Wilson, at least once a day. Although Mr Wilson can cope on his own with most things, he does have a problem with the gas cooker. At one time he was able to cook for himself, but ever since Wendy had the fright of her life after finding her father with a sleeve of his Fair Isle sweater alight, she has prepared all of his meals. Fred suggests 'meals on wheels' but Wendy says that her daddy can't abide fast food, Ha, Ha, Ha! Oh how they laugh!

Wendy orders another bottle of Chianti and the dessert menu and tells Fred that this has been the loveliest evening she has ever had. Fred says that it is the only lovely evening he has ever had, apart from last Wednesday when they went for a walk around Sweetwater Marsh, and then of course there was the Friday after that when they had a late night picnic on Silver Hill where he had a mosquito bite on his bottom, and… Oh shut up, Fred?

Fred asks Wendy what her hobbies are; Wendy stops to think, because being a busy career women she has little free time to have hobbies. She says that she used to like jigsaw puzzles but had to stop because her dad kept knocking the little card table over that she used for assembling the jigsaws on. Pieces would scatter far and wide and often the lost pieces were only found when they rattled up the pipe of her cylinder vacuum cleaner.

Fred looks at the dessert menu and says that he thinks he'll have the lemon sorbet, Wendy thinks that's a nice idea and they both order an ice cream sundae instead. Fred asks Wendy what she thinks would be her idea of a romantic afternoon together, "Ooh well, a pot of tea, a packet of chocolate digestives and both snuggling up to watch a video of *Brief Encounter* and later I could be Celia Johnson and you could be Cyril Raymond saying, 'You've been very far away, I'm glad you came back to me!' and after that we'd go for a walk!" swoons Wendy. "What's your ideal romantic situation then, Fred?" asks Wendy warmly.

Fred stops to think and says, "Well the pot of tea and packet of chocolate digestives would be nice, and I think sitting on the sofa listening to 'The Archers' would be great!" Wendy stands up abruptly with a look of abject horror on her beautiful face, her bottom ruby lip quivering. "Whatever is the matter, my sweet?" asks Fred with deep concern.

"Oh no, I couldn't do that, not that, I could never marry a man that listens to 'The Archers', not ever, not ever I tell you, never!" cries Wendy running to the door, "NEVER, NEVE-E-E-E-E-R-R-R-R!"

Fred, acutely embarrassed, is left to pay the bill – only he hasn't got enough money on him as he put the wrong jacket on leaving the one with the big wallet at home! The pretty little fat girl says that the bill comes to £48.90p. What is a man to do in this situation, offer to do the washing-up? No not Fred, with a drop of his trousers and pants he 'WOO HOO, WAY HAY, WEE HEES!' his way to freedom. All the staff of the restaurant flee to the back of the shop in panic, leaving Fred all he could wish for – a free meal!

Fred walks home and contemplates the evening; how words can change a situation from good to bad, and how lucky he is to have been in love and never to have loved at all, also how lucky he found out now instead of after they got married, that Wendy wasn't an Archers' fan. He couldn't marry a woman like that, not ever, never, NEVER!

# Chapter 7

## THE JOLLY VERNHAM COACH EXCURSION

Every year, Roger and Susan Spur, Landlord and Landlady of The Grummet and Nut, arrange a mystery coach tour of the Vernbury Vale. As there are only nine villages to speak of in the Vernbury Vale, the only mystery is when you first get onto the coach, by the time you've turned into one road or another, you sort of know where you're going. Actually, the main mystery is why this event is still so popular after 39 years, but as most of the village of Vernham don't go out that often it's probably a treat for them to look forward to.

It's the usual affair – some blighter can't wait for lunchtime to eat his picnic, cracks open a boiled egg, everyone looks around accusingly to see who it was and a small child is travel sick before the driver turns the key in the coach's ignition. On the subject of small children, the two little horrors of the village go on the mystery tour chaperoned by their mums and dads, but there is no real comfort in that knowledge.

This event is always held on a Wednesday in the second week of July. Wednesday is half day for most proprietors, and so just about anyone who is anyone participates, taking it as a day off. The main two who don't enjoy this escapade every year are Milly and Molly Goldsworth of Comfytums fame, which is a blessing for Mrs Bunkerton because she can do her usual 10:02am visit to the tea room. The coach doesn't leave until after 10:30am, so there is always plenty of time for Mrs Bunkerton to have a daft chat with Milly and Molly, just like she does every day.

Today is Wednesday in the second week of July; it's 10:00am and the coach is arriving outside The Grummet and Nut with a squeaking and wheezing of airbrakes. It's a lovely sunny day, but then it always is in Vernham, no matter what the weather. Roger and Susan have made a change to the tour this year, it is called the ‘Blind Man’s Bluff Mystery Tour’. The reason for this change is due to complaints over the last two tours from people saying that they all knew where they were going. This year everyone will be given blindfolds to wear, only to be taken off at the last moment. PC Fred Sweetman prefers not to wear a blindfold as he says he needs to keep his eyes peeled for naughties and nasties, but as we all know, it’s the sad and dark corridors of his memory that make him wish to abstain, that is of course if you were paying attention in the previous chapter. Mr Wilson doesn’t give a fig about the blindfold, but wouldn’t like to be left out.

The coach driver, Willy Tynebull, a great lumbering oaf of a man with a raspberry-red face and a terrible yellow wig that even Andy Warhol would’ve laughed at, lumbers out of the coach and lands heavily on the pavement. Roger, who has been waiting outside and has had a few cigarettes while he was waiting, greets Willy, “Good mornin’, Willy you silly old fat nit! AH HE HE HA HA HO HO HAH,” (cough, splutter and spit).

“Morning, Roger you ugly old toad, HOO HOO, HOO HOO! can I use your toilet?”

“Of course you can, Willy, use the bucket round the back, HA HA HA HA HA!” chortles Roger.

“Oh, Roger!” complains Susan, “The last time you told him that, he did!”

“Ooh Flippin’ ’eck, I’d better go round and stop him!” panics Roger. Just in the nick of time, Roger manages to stop Willy and directs him to their loo.

Ken and Bettie Griggs who normally take it in turns to go on the mystery tour so that they can keep Ye Olde Sweetie Shoppe running, are both participating this year. They’ve managed to get Vic Grinham, the noisy tenant from the flat above the shop, to mind the business for the day. There’s no need to worry about Vic eating too many of the confectionery profits, he doesn't really have a sweet tooth; come to think of it, he doesn't really eat very much anyway, he is rather skinny! Ken and Bettie have just finished giving Vic instructions for the day and are excitedly walking down to The Grummet and Nut to board the coach. Bettie's tartan shopping bag is full of crisps and nuts to share out with their friends, and a Walnut Whip and a quarter pound of Strawberry Bonbons for PC Sweetman.

Mr Jedson the ex Fire Chief isn't going, he hasn't been seen since he set himself alight in Ye Olde Sweetie Shoppe and was arrested under suspicion of arson. The last person to see Mr Jedson was PC Sweetman after he released him early due to the great Vernham flood filling the police station with water. Rumour has it that he has left the country to travel the world and find himself – silly sod; he's been here all the time! I do know that CCTV footage of a man who looks just like Mr Jedson has been seen at 'BREECHER'S THE SUPERMARKET, NOW OPEN 24 HOURS A DAY!' buying a box of matches; although the picture isn't that clear, behind that false nose could lurk the soul of a pyromaniac!

Hopefully Miss Somerton-Jove won't be coming, she's never invited and yet somehow she always turns up at the final mystery destination. It is said that she, as her mother was before her, is psychic! There are accounts of Miss Somerton-Jove and her forecasts of the foreboding; one in particular was The Great Vernham Flood. Although 'it looks like it could rain!' could be said by anyone if they saw a black cloud, the Vernham natives would take it as a prediction! Seven years ago when Miss Somerton-Jove was sharing a table with Mrs Bunkerton at Comfytums, she made an outstanding prediction. Mrs Bunkerton had just got to the bottom of her cup of tea and she found there to be tea leaves. As she made a friendly comment of, "Oh, Milly dear, I think you forgot to use the strainer!" Miss Somerton-Jove grabbed the cup from her hand with a "Let me see?" Miss Somerton-Jove stared at the bottom of the teacup and made a groaning noise, and then she fumbled around in the pocket of her burgundy bouclé jacket and pulled out three mothballs. She shook the mothballs in between cupped hands and rolled them on the table like gambling dice.

From the pattern formed, which would have been triangular, she read a forecast out to Mrs Bunkerton. Normally this act would only be of worry to moths, but what she said to Mrs Bunkerton will be remembered by all that were there in the tea room that morning. She moaned and wailed with eyes closed, her hands hovering over the mothballs, "My forecast to you is troublesome, today will be dry and sunny with light south-westerly winds, becoming cold and damp overnight with clear skies, and your husband will DIE!" Poor Mrs Bunkerton nearly fell off her chair with that final unexpected outburst, and in the evening of that day, Mr Bunkerton died after a massive heart attack! In reality of course, Milly always uses tea bags in the pot, so a tea bag must have burst, after all no one strains tea before they put it in the pot – how could they unless they had already brewed another pot prior to that? Also, Mr Bunkerton would die eventually as everyone does and Miss Somerton-Jove didn't exactly say that he would die that night, she just added it on to a very good weather forecast. As regards the mothballs, they were just a load of old balls!

More and more people are turning up for the coach, PC Sweetman is already onboard to hand out the blindfolds, and Blind Mr Wilson is the first on. PC Sweetman hands Mr Wilson a blindfold, and being independent he prefers to take the blindfold by touch location rather than have it put in his hand. Mr Wilson feels around for the blindfold and grabs hold of the coach driver Willy Tynebull's tie, walking away and nearly strangling him. Oh dear, Wendy Wilson is here too! (Fortunately, being a nice day, everyone can have their windows open!) PC Sweetman tries to hide his hurt and hands a blindfold to Wendy, "Do have a good day, Madam?" he says in an indifferent manner as though they'd never met before. This could be an awkward day; the ex-couple haven't spoken since their disagreement at the pizza restaurant in Velstrum.

But time heals, and anyway PC Sweetman has got his pocket transistor radio and earpiece so that he doesn't miss The Archers – it's an act of defiance of sorts!

Ah! Here's Greedy Griff Johnson, he is only allowed to sit at the front of the coach because one year, impatient for his picnic, he started to eat the padded headrest on the seat in front of him. Fortunately the coach arrived at its destination before he started to tuck into Nelly Birdham the Comfytums pianist's wig. Greedy Griff will eat anything that doesn't move – as a child he was malnourished due to his parents being poor, food was hard to come by, and so the furniture became more and more appealing. Griff truly did eat his parents out of house and home!

Now here's Mr Robson, I hope he hasn't brought his Winter Mixtures to crunch on! Oh No! It's Reverend Parsworthy, and he's bound to spoil things, he'll probably try and get everyone singing Robert Lowry's 'Shall We Gather At The River' and various other hymns of joy before the musical menu morphs into bawdy Welsh Rugby League songs. Thankfully, most of these songs of rugby rudeness are sung in Welsh, but there are a few arm and hand gestures that can be offensive to those that already have filthy minds! Eddie Jedson has just come aboard; he'll have to lie down for the journey's duration due to the height of his huge head. The coach driver Willy looks at Eddie and has a horrid flashback to his school bus driving days when an unruly child with a long head used to plague him with false bell rings as his noddle kept accidentally hitting the bell strip, "Surely it can't be him?" thinks Willy.

Right, I think that's just about everybody on board; Willy takes a head count, not including Eddie Jedson's. Willy looks at his list, no, there's one missing – it's Mrs Bunkerton still chinwagging with Molly and Milly. Willy beeps his horn; Mrs Bunkerton looks up and runs to the coach waving with a 'WAIT FOR ME?' kind of desperation. "Come on, get in, love?" says Willy with a friendly wink. Roger and Susan will be driving on to the secret final destination in their van to set up the outside bar.

Everybody in, blindfolds on, Willy turns the key in the ignition and speaks over the public address:

"GOOD MORNING, LADIES AND GENTLEMEN, I TRUST YOU'RE ALL SETTLED IN YOUR SEATS AND YOUR BLINDFOLDS ADJUSTED PROPERLY. TODAY I'LL BE TAKING YOU ON A MYSTERY TOUR OF THE VERNBURY VALE, AND JUST TO MAKE IT INTERESTING, I'LL BE DRIVING WITH A BLINDFOLD ON TOO! NO, NO, IT'S ALRIGHT, LADIES AND GENTLEMEN, IT'S JUST SILLY OLD WILLY HAVING A BIT OF FUN WITH YOU!" The passengers breathe a sigh of relief. "WE'LL BE DRIVING OFF TO OUR FIRST MYSTERY DESTINATION, WHICH WILL TAKE ABOUT A HALF OF AN HOUR ROUGHLY, WHERE WE SHALL STOP AND ENJOY A CUP OF COFFEE OR TEA IN A LOVELY SETTING. THERE WILL BE TOILETS AT EVERY STOP SO THAT YOU CAN MAKE YOURSELVES COMFORTABLE IF NEEDS BE. THAT'S ALL, LADIES AND GENTLEMEN, I'LL SHUT UP AND LET YOU ENJOY THE JOURNEY!" (Thank goodness!)

It's a bumpy old ride, so I hope that the sight deprivation won't encourage travel sickness for the queasier sort. Reverend Parsworthy takes a swig of Glenfunnel from his hip flask – well, when I say hip flask I mean an army canteen bottle, but he has got very big hips! When Reverend Parsworthy goes on these coach excursions he gets quite philosophical after a couple of swigs, "You know when I was a small child in Wales, I used to walk around the dock of Tiger Bay and wonder at the ships. One day a sailor, a huge black man came up to me and spoke, he said, 'something, something, something', and to be truthful, I can't fully remember what he said to me, but he was right and it has affected me for the rest of my life!" Of course, old Parsworthy isn't actually talking to anyone, but it just makes him feel comfortable to hear his own voice, and so it doesn't have to make sense, just as well really because no one was listening anyway, except for Mr Robson.

Mr Robson who always sits next to Reverend Parsworthy likes to talk about odd things too, "When I was a wee bairn in one o' my Scottish past lives, I made a scientific discovery when I was sitting in a cave and a large spider walked oot in front o' me, and I said, 'Helloo, Mr Spider, hoo are ye todee?' and the spider stopped in its tracks and turned to me and I said, 'It's alright, Mr Spider, I mean ye no harm!' and he went on his way. Then I said, 'Stop, Mr Spider' and the spider stopped! So, I carried oot an experiment on the wee beastie, an admittedly cruel experiment, but all in the name o' science. I picked up the spider and pulled one o' its legs off. I put the spider doon and telt it tae shoo, and it shooed! Then I telt it tae stop, and it stopped again, so I pulled another one o' its legs off and shooed it again, and it shooed away. This carried on until the last leg was left, and I noticed that the wee beastie was more reluctant to shoo. And so when I removed the last leg and put it doon and shooed it away, it just stayed put. I came to the conclusion that when a spider loses its legs, it becomes completely deaf!"

Everybody that hears this nonsense bursts into hysterical laughter with comments such as 'Nice one Rabbie!' and 'I've heard that one before!' This provokes an untypical outburst of anger from Mr Robson, "This is no joke, it's true I tell ye, ye Sassenach heathen!"

Graham Bird the Battling Belly champion, who is sitting at the back of the coach next to his pal and belly opponent Mickey Farshott shouts out, "Ya shut up, you silly old Spruggle!" Whoops! That's done it! In a second Mr Robson is hurled into a quandary, how can he argue with the Spruggle accusation? If he retaliates with 'I'm not a Spruggle!' he will renounce his claim that he is of Scottish bloodline! Mr Robson wisely opts for the asylum of feigned deafness and keeps his mouth shut; after all, these belly battling ruffians aren't averse to handing out the odd punch on the nose when they get riled, and they will probably punch each other on the nose eventually, once Roger and Susan's outside bar gets inside of them! This year we have also been saved from Mr Robson's bagpipe concertos due to Greedy Griff Johnson taking a bite out of the bag. Mr Robson can't really play them properly anyway and his music is more like a Middle Eastern dirge played over an asthmatic drone, the tune is never the same twice!

Mrs Bunkerton, who is sitting next to Nelly Birdham, opens her heart about the woes of being a widow as she has done to someone every day for the last seven years, "Of course the worst part for me is waking up and not seeing his lovely old face on the pillow next to mine. Just briefly while I'm waking up, I'm thinking 'It's alright he's just gone to the toilet, he'll be back in a minute!' but he never comes back and then my day is full of sorrow. It's a wonder to me how Queen Victoria kept up her mourning for so long, I've just about had enough of it, it tears me apart every day, I long for this pain to ease! I used to love hearing him snoring next to me, a lovely deep nasally noise that I used to imagine was a tuba in a Salvation Army band. I'd sing hymns over the rhythm of his snoring – gently mind, so as not to wake him, he used to get very tetchy if I woke him during the night. Of course that's the problem with the youngsters nowadays, if you can't love your spouses snoring then you can't be in love, they put it down to the pressures of finance or even the S word, but it's the snoring that makes or breaks it! Mind you, I almost see the point in the young ones living together before they get married – don't get me wrong, I'm not in approval of it, but it would probably stop a lot of messy divorces. Funnily enough, there was a couple over Velstrum way, they lived in a flat opposite 'BREECHER'S THE SUPERMARKET, NOW OPEN 24 HOURS A DAY!' lived together for twenty-five years seemingly happy; they decided to tie the knot and were divorced within a year. Snoring, it's snoring that does it, once you've signed that licence you're committed to the snoring, it'll make or break you!" Nelly Birdham is quite asleep and has been for the last ten minutes.

Willy the coach driver switches on the PA to make an announcement, "RIGHT, LADIES AND GENTLEMEN, WE HAVE JUST ARRIVED AT OUR FIRST PORT OF CALL, YOU MAY NOW TAKE OFF YOUR BLINDFOLDS. WE ARE NOW AT MILSTON GARDENS. WE SHALL STOP FOR AN HOUR WHERE YOU CAN TAKE A STROLL, HAVE A CUP OF TEA OR COFFEE AND BISCUITS OR BOTH, WHAT EVER FLOATS YOUR BOATS. THERE ARE TOILETS SITUATED NEAR THE TEA AND GIFT SHOP. IT'S JUST PAST ELEVEN O'CLOCK; IF YOU MAKE YOUR WAY BACK FOR MIDDAY WE SHALL GO ON TO THE SECOND PART OF THE MYSTERY TOUR. PLEASE BE CAREFUL OF THE HIGH STEP DOWN AS YOU EXIT THE COACH, THANK YOU!"

Milston Gardens is a beautiful place, landscape design yet again by Incapability Saunders. The main theme of this 4-acre garden is rhododendron-lined footpaths; these can only really be enjoyed in May but there are many beautiful flowers and shrubs to catch the eye, indeed some of the tree branches need a little lopping as they can catch your eye with a terrible smarting if you don't watch where you are going.

There is a great variety of fauna to be seen here and Milston Gardens is a noted conservation area. The most prolific of all creatures here are gnats, these little gems are as psychotically vampirical as the midges in the Highlands of Scotland, as Mr Robson is just about to inform us, "Crivvens and Jings, these wee beasties are as vicious as the midges that I encountered in one o' my Scottish past lives when I was walking with J.M. Barrie at Dykehead. This lovely place was not far from his home village in Kirriemuir, a quaint village that noo has one o' the biggest heroin problems in Scotland!" Thanks for that, Rabbie, although he has never been to Scotland and wouldn't know, the last part of that statement is sadly true. And Mr Robson has more to say, "It was there that the inspiration for

J.M. Barrie's character Tinkabell was found. We were sitting at the brow of a hill enjoying a picnic o' bridies and Glenfunnel when this dandelion seed parachute drifted towards us and just hung floating in the air in front o' us!" For once Mr Robson has an interested audience that are waiting for him to tell them more of this encounter; unfortunately that is all there is, and Mr Robson drifts off dreamily and aimlessly like a ghost on roller skates.

"Anybody fancy a bag of crisps?" says Bettie the sweetshop lady. "Yes please!" says Greedy Griff and takes them gratefully from Bettie's generous hand, no time for time-wasting bag opening, Griff pops the whole lot in his mouth, and with a bang of popped crisp bag he chomps and swallows it in one fell swoop – still, at least he didn't leave any litter behind! I'd keep your tartan shopping bag moving, Bettie, or Griff will have that too!

From behind there is a commotion in the trees above, they are swaying as though the very spirit of King Kong is up there shaking them; it's actually poor Eddie Jedson having trouble with his head catching up in the branches. No one offers to help the poor lad and his forehead is very grazed and painful, no one that is except for the lovely Wendy Wilson who rushes to Eddie's aid. Wendy, with gentle coaxing, manages to free Eddie's bonce by pulling him downwards onto his knees. Out of Wendy's pocket a tube of antiseptic ointment called 'STINGALL' and a packet of self-adhesive plasters are produced. Wendy kindly smears 'STINGALL' on Eddie's grazes, and after a bit of "Ooh, Ouch, Ah!" from Eddie, she places some plasters on his wounds.

Watching this act of kindness is PC Sweetman who is seething with jealousy inside; it's more than his aching heart can bear! "Alright, alright, what's all this here? It looks like trouble to me! I'll let you off this time, but if I catch you two felons together again I shall have no alternative but to give you both what for!" says PC Sweetman with fake professionalism. Wendy looks at PC Sweetman and moves her face closely to his, whispering the name 'freak!' to him. This is possibly the most hurtful thing anybody has ever said to Fred, and a tear wells up in the moat of his eye.

After a walk around the splendid Milston Gardens, the coach party stops off at the tea and gift shop for refreshment. Greedy Griff is first in and buys just about every fruit scone in the shop. There's plenty of room for everyone to sit in the tea shop, everyone that is except for Eddie Jedson due to the low ceiling, who has opted to sit at one of the bird-dropping splashed alfresco wooden tables and benches. Again, Wendy offers her kindness by ordering a cup of tea and packet of digestive biscuits for Eddie and sits outside with him. PC Sweetman is keeping his Shaw Taylor eyes peeled just in case Wendy gets too attached to Eddie. Wendy notices that one of Eddie's plasters is peeling off of his forehead and removes it to replace with a new one. So far Eddie hasn't noticed Wendy's halitosis, but even if he does I've got a feeling that Eddie won't be bothered by it; apart from his lovely mum, he's never been treated with tenderness by a woman before – this could be love!

PC Sweetman's heart is pounding, his mouth and throat are dry and his stomach is tumbling with butterflies. He feels a tugging on his left greatcoat sleeve, it's Bettie, "Everything alright, Fred? You haven't had your Walnut Whip and Strawberry Bonbons yet, love!"

"Er, I won't have them just yet as I'm on duty, can you keep them cool for me please, Bettie?" Fred replies in a distracted manner. "Right that's it everybody, it's ten minutes to twelve and we should be making our way back to the coach, don't forget to use the toilets before we go!" says PC Fred, although it's only a quarter to twelve really, he just doesn't want Wendy and Eddie to spend too long with each other.

Wendy has a sudden terrible thought, "Where's Daddy?" She'd been enjoying herself so much that she had forgotten about her poor old blind father, where could he be? Everyone who feels in a helpful mood agrees to trace their footsteps back around the footpath in hopes of finding Blind Mr Wilson. There's no need to worry however; Mr Wilson decided to stay on the coach on account of the uneven footpaths around the gardens, and so they'll find him eventually. It's extremely careless of Wendy not to notice her dad staying behind, but I suppose when you consider that she doesn't get out very often, apart from driving on her sales rep job, the excitement overcame her and she thought about her own enjoyment for one rare selfish moment, a one-off forgivable mistake!

The gravel in the coach park is crunching under the feet of the Vernham coach party making their way back well in time to get on the coach. Everyone's onboard except for "Wait for me?" Mrs Bunkerton, who decided to go to the loo rather than search for Mr Wilson. As anyone who has been on a coach excursion knows, there is always one that will be late to arrive back at the coach, and on every annual Vernham excursion it's always Mrs Bunkerton!

"RIGHT, LADIES AND GENTLEMEN, I TRUST YOU'RE ALL FED AND WATERED AND SITTING COMFORTABLY. IF YOU WOULD BE SO KIND TO REPLACE YOUR BLINDFOLDS, WE SHALL MAKE OUR WAY TO OUR SECOND PORT OF CALL WHERE WE SHALL STOP FOR LUNCH IN ABOUT ONE HOUR'S TIME. WE WILL STOP FOR AN HOUR AND A HALF AND I'M CERTAIN YOU WILL ENJOY THE SURROUNDINGS!" announces Willy with a hint of feedback over the public address.

The duration of each journey might lead one to believing that the Vernbury Vale is a vast expanse, it's not really, it's just that Willy drives very slowly and gets a bit on the lost side now and then. There is a certain amount of skill involved in estimating the journey's duration and allowing for wrong turnings though, Willy gets the timing virtually smack on every time!

At the back of the coach there is a certain amount of gaseous grunting going on – it's Graham Bird and Mickey

Farshott having a belching competition. Finding this dyspeptic sport rather vulgar and quite irritating, Nelly Birdham who's kept herself to herself up until now shouts out, "Stop that filthy noise, you vile slobs, don't you know there are ladies onboard?" And before mouthy Mickey Farshott gets a chance to say, "Yah shaddup, ya silly old bag!" Nelly throws one of her gin bottles at him making a marksman's hit on his nose with a wonderful 'DONK!' – not bad with a blindfold eh! Prone to nosebleeds anyway, Mickey's proboscis canal floodgates open and a large pack of pre-empted man-size tissues are pressed into use – that'll keep him quiet for a while!

Eddie Jedson is lying down in the aisle of the coach and Wendy is stroking the top of his huge head with the affection of a dog owner. Witnessing this disgusting display of affection, PC Fred Sweetman decides to brave the blindfold so that he cannot witness anymore.

As yet we haven't heard a peep out of any of the two small children, normally they would have let a creepy crawly or rat loose on the coach to create havoc by now. This time they've been asleep like little cherubs most of the journey, after being up all night, house burgling. There's still time though, and if last year's excursion is anything to go by, it should be an absolute wheeze! Both of the children took extra long drinking straws made from aquarium aerator pump tubing, when they reached the final destination where Roger and Susan Spur's outside bar and extra sideshow entertainments were; they spent most of the time taking big thirsty sucks on their straws from other people's beer glasses while their backs were turned. Apart from everyone thinking they were drinking more than they had, some accusing Roger of watering the beer down, the children were at their very worst – tying people's shoelaces together was one of the lighter moments. They also got the blame for setting the palmistry tent in the laid-on entertainments alight. Luckily disgraced Fire Chief Mr Jedson was conveniently at hand with his fire extinguisher that he just happened to bring along with him – I think we can all guess what really went on! The Chiromancer in the palmistry tent looked incredibly like Miss Somerton-Jove, right down to the burgundy bouclé jacket! The sideshow entertainments at the final destination are promised to be even more spectacular this year, we shall see!

There's a sudden loud cough at the front of the coach – it's Tommy Perkins, the village strange one. He's just overheard a couple behind him talking about the Vernham Bog Stomper, and one of them seems to be rather sceptical about the whole affair. "Well, all I'm saying is that nobody calls it the Velstrum Bog Stomper, and Velstrum is over the other side of Sweetwater Marsh and they must be able to hear it as well!" says one.

"That's probably because it doesn't stomp on that side, it's a lot boggier on that side apparently!" says the other.

Tommy turns around to them and interrupts, "Excuse me," (cough, cough, wheeze) "but I happen to work in Velstrum at the bakery and people there refer to it as the Vernham Bog Stomper because they don't believe that anything so horrible could belong to them!" This is true, the people of Velstrum don't even recognise Sweetwater Marsh as having any connection with their village, much like the next-door neighbour's offensively untidy garden complete with a dismantled and rust-riddled motorbike – it's over the other side of the fence and really nothing to do with you. This Velstrum snobbery is not just directed at Vernham and its natives; this superiority complex has a wide angle of dislike and includes all of the other villages in the Vernbury Vale. And yet, anybody from Velstrum that knows Tommy has welcomed him with open arms, indeed most of his friends live there!

The couple behind look at Tommy momentarily after listening to his 'in the know' advice, then turn to each other and continue with their debate. "Well anyway, the Bog Stomper does seem to have attracted a large amount of Spruggles in a search for the beast, this could become quite commercial and very profitable for the village!" says one to the other of the couple.

"Pah! What a load of old rubbish, I refuse to dwell on the subject any longer. Is it alright if I have one of those glacier mints in your bag please?" says the other to the one.

Meanwhile Cecil Twill, the proprietor of the village toy shop, has bean listening to this debate with great interest – this could be the answer to put his shop 'Vernham Playtime' on the map. He'll be lucky, because the name Vernham is absent from most road atlases, and Silver Hill is only mentioned because it happens to be the highest point of the Vernbury Vale!

'Vernham Playtime' the village toy shop, as mentioned a little while ago, doesn't do very good business on the account that there aren't many children in the village, apart from the two little horrors onboard this coach. He has many toys that could be considered as collectors' items, still boxed without any fading to the print. He has quite a few original 'GI Joe' dolls that he scooped up when he was holidaying in America in the very early 1960s, these became known as 'Action Man' over here. He has Beatle wigs and George Harrison plastic guitars; he also has little flat boxes with pictures of John, Paul, George and Ringo's bald heads – the box is filled with iron filings and you can change their hairstyles by dragging the filings with a little red magnetic pencil. These little Beatle haircut boxes were great stocking fillers at Christmas for a while, but by the time the album 'Let It Be' came out there weren't enough iron filings to cope with the beards let alone the hair!

But Cecil's interest in this Bog Stomper subject is making his entrepreneurial cogs tick over and over; this could be the way forward in selling the massive stock of battery-powered walking robots that he purchased in 1965. No one has ever seen the Vernham Bog Stomper properly, even Monica Millstone's video tape recording with an infrared camera isn't that clear, but it did sell an awful lot of copies of *The Vernbury Trumpet*. The interest generated by the press has led to regular Spruggle invasions – all of them lining the edge of Sweetwater Marsh at night in their bivouacs, like specimen hunter anglers waiting for the big one to bite. With this lack of visual idea, and working on people's accounts and descriptions of this mythical beast, Cecil could convert the robots into Bog Stompers and give it a cute name like Bobby! He is bound to get the image wrong though; he won't know that the Vernham Bog Stomper wears a duffel coat and barrel lids for Bog Shoes! What Cecil also doesn't realise is that the toys themselves are worth a fortune to collectors and he'd probably net more cash if he sold them in their original boxes, silly old fool!

"RIGHT, LADIES AND GENTLEMEN, WE ARE JUST ARRIVING AT OUR SECOND PORT OF CALL. THIS PLACE IS CALLED 'THE PODDUM PASTRY PARLOUR', AND IF YOU HAVEN'T BOUGHT A PICNIC WITH YOU, MAY I RECOMMEND THE RABBIT AND CARROT PIE IN GOLDEN SHORTCRUST PASTRY. THE PIES HERE ARE OUTSTANDING AND PROBABLY THE BEST IN THE DISTRICT!" says Willy gleefully over the public address, only to be interrupted by Master Butcher Dick Sperling, "They're nowhere near the quality of my excellent Golden Shortcrust pastry pies!"

"OH YES, THANKFULLY NOT! FROM WHAT I'VE HEARD YOU PROBABLY GET YOUR MEAT FILLINGS FROM OLD 'SWEENEY TODD' OVER THERE!" retorts Willy, implying that alcoholic hairdresser Harry Helmson is the provider of the pie fillings.

"I certainly do not!" objects Harry who is now eight paracetamol, 2 litres of Irn Bru and four packets of cheese and onion crisps better of a hangover. "Anyway, you'll never have to come to my shop for a haircut, all you need to do is take that rug of yours to a dry cleaners!" spits Harry Helmson attackingly.

The whole coach are roaring with laughter, even wig wearer Nelly Birdham who hasn't been listening has a chortle.

“OKAY, OKAY, LADIES AND GENTLEMEN, FUNTIME OVER! IT’S ONE O’ CLOCK NOW, WE SHALL STOP HERE TWO HOURS FOR LUNCH, MAY I RECOMMEND THE RIVERSIDE WALK TO WORK OFF THOSE CALORIES AFTER EATING THE EXCELLENT PASTRIES, AND DO BE VERY CAREFUL OF THE SLIPPERY RIVERBANK, MR HELMSON, IT WOULD BE A SHAME IF YOU FELL IN! DON’T FORGET TO REMOVE YOUR BLINDFOLDS, AND I SHALL SEE YOU HERE BACK AT THE COACH THREE O’ CLOCK SHARP!” says Willy, hoping that the ridicule will stop – it doesn’t, everyone is still cackling as they get off the coach.

The Poddum Pastry Parlour is a renowned eatery, established in 1953 by one time owner Francis Winkleton. Francis was a cook in the Royal Fusiliers and his pastries were loved by the whole battalion. Convinced of his ability to please gastronomes, Francis set his business up in a disused woollen mill and made it pretty much how it looks today, although a mezzanine floor was put in during a refurbishment in the 1970s due to general demand of more table sittings. There is still plenty of headroom though, so Eddie Jedson can eat his lunch in comfort.

All of the pastry is made here with the flour that is milled from the converted watermill wheel that is used not only to grind the wheat but also to power some of the electricity in the eatery. The relentless flow of the River Poddum keeps the wheel turning indefinitely, though the wheel does need to have regular maintenance to ensure it keeps working. The Poddum Pastry Parlour is now owned by a huge chain of eateries called SPERLING’S – no relation to Dick, I can assure you, although he will attempt to make people think otherwise! “Oh yes you know, my butcher’s shop is just a small part of my successful global business empire – don’t take any notice of these old clothes, all of my money is tied up in business you see, well if you’d excuse me please? I’m just going to check on my kitchen and staff!” says Dick with bogus boastings to Mrs Bunkerton.

"Ooh, a real gastronomic mogul!" thinks Mrs Bunkerton.

Dick's mock magnate magnetism could get him into very deep and hot water. 'CRASH!' it already has – Dick's just been thrown out of the kitchen for being nosey and a silver service tray has just followed him! Dick picks himself up and dusts flour off of his trousers, "You don't seem to be able to get the staff these days!" he says with cringed and pink tingling cheeks of embarrassment. It's okay, nobody has noticed anyway, so Dick can relive his fast food fantasy again.

Greedy Griff Johnson is walking to a table with a heavily laden tray of four family-size chicken-and-ham lattice pies with mash and peas – I admire his patience, I would have put bets on for him eating them before he sat down. Blind Mr Wilson is waiting patiently for his daughter Wendy to bring his steak and kidney pie and chips to the table; she is chatting to Eddie Jedson about the merits of vegetarianism and how The Poddum Pastry Parlour only seems to cater for carnivores, they both opt for the cheese and onion pasties. Wendy and Eddie aren't vegetarians, they are just delving deep into the bottom of the barrel to the remains of their teenage rebellion, the archive of unspent youth about to be spent!

Mrs Bunkerton and Nelly Birdham are sitting outside on the riverside benches with their pre-packed picnics. Always in a fluster, Mrs Bunkerton didn't have time to make her egg sandwiches properly; if she has time, she would normally mash or slice the boiled eggs to fill the bread. This time she has put them in whole and pressed the bread around the egg, giving a sort of egg ravioli appearance to the sandwich.

Nelly Birdham's picnic is a little more delicate, Cornish wafers and Edam cheese slices with the red wax left on, it doesn't matter because her teeth are always stained with red lipstick, so no one will be any the wiser! They seem to have attracted some begging Muscovy ducks and one of them is pecking a ladder into Nelly's tights. With a swipe of an empty gin bottle on the duck's head, she manages to stop the duck from making the ladder any bigger. This act of animal cruelty enrages a nearby lady animal lover who feels the need to reprimand Nelly, “You cruel, horrid, wicked old woman! How dare you attack a poor little creature like that, you should be ashamed of yourself!” Nelly glowers at the protester and unscrews the cap of a new gin bottle, she takes a swig from the bottle and sticks up two fingers of ‘Who cares?’ in accompaniment. “Well? I’ve never been so insulted in my life, you horrid beastly women!” protests the protester, stick around a bit longer, sweetie, and I’m sure Nelly will top that!

Meanwhile back in the eatery, Mickey Farshott has managed to stem his epistaxis but is taking no risks; he has a tissue rammed up each nostril just in case. He’s having trouble with the gravy from his dinner plate soaking into the tissues and his pal Graham Bird watching this palaver, is reminded of the chromatography experiments that he used to do in his chemistry lessons at school.

Tommy Perkins hasn’t got much money, and so he’s bought three jumbo cheese straws, and at 50p each Tommy is almost bankrupt, well today anyway! PC Sweetman takes pity on Tommy and offers him some of his chips. Wendy Wilson tries not to notice, desperately trying not to think the words… WHAT… A… LOVELY… KIND… MAN! in the same way as George Sanders did in *Village Of The Damned*, trying not to think of the bomb he’d planted, so that the weird psychic children with ridiculous hairstyles don’t know of their impending doom, “Must… think… of… a… brick wall!”

And on the theme of silly blonde nylon wigs, Willy Tynebull the coach driver has pulled up a chair to sit with Eddie, Wendy and her dad. “Allo, darlin’, what’s a lovely bit of crumpet like you doing sitting with these silly old twerps?” says Willy with the only chat-up line he knows. Wendy isn’t listening, she’s still trying to unravel the knotted muddle inside her head, ‘“Eddie? Freddie? Eddie? Freddie? Oh, who should I love?” Mr Wilson, knowing that Willy isn’t talking to him, nudges Wendy, “Willy’s talking to you, my dear!”

“Oh really, I’m sorry what did you say?” says Wendy.

"Oh nothing very much, love, 'ere what's that nasty niff?" says Willy trying to work out whose pie smells odd. "It's my extreme halitosis!" Wendy huffs into Willy's face, making his wig shrivel like a cellophane crisp packet thrown onto a fire. The red in Willy's face changes to green, he needs to get some fresh air, that's got rid of the blighter!

Harry Helmson looks at his watch and thinks, "I would probably have had a right skinful by now if I was in The Grummet and Nut!" This is probably the longest Harry has been without his beloved ale for a long time; he's impatient for Roger and Susan's outside bar at the final mystery destination.

Over at PC Sweetman and Tommy Perkins' table, a beautiful Japanese woman asks if a chair is taken. Fred points to the seat as if to say, "Please be seated?" The Japanese woman grabs the back of the chair and takes it to the table where her friends are sitting. In the brief moment that the Japanese woman was at their table, Wendy was worrying to herself, "I hope Fred doesn't like sushi!" It's obviously not that as simple as, 'If he likes The Archers, then there can be no future for Freddie and Me!' for Wendy, she has secretly become obsessed with Fred Sweetman, a secret even to herself until today! What is she to do? True, she has found a new friend to care for, but the length of Eddie Jedson's head could cause quite a few problems. Take bedtime for instance, normally one could turn to their partner to kiss them goodnight and make contact with their lips. With the top of Eddie's head touching the headboard, his lips would be about four feet away. This would mean that Wendy would need to have a booster attached to the headboard so that she could be on the same kiss level as Eddie. And do they make beds long enough so that Eddie can keep his feet warm in winter? All this and more will have to be considered before Wendy makes her choice. And all this has been thought about without any consideration of how Eddie would feel about the situation, or even if Eddie has thought about it at all!

Outdoors there's a bit of a do – Mrs Bunkerton and Nelly Birdham decided to go for a riverside walk after their picnic and Nelly has just lost her footing on the riverbank. There's a tremendous splashing and gurgling going on and Mrs Bunkerton has just thrown a ring buoy to Nelly making a direct contact with her head, knocking her wire wool wig off. Nelly grabs the floatation aid and manages to get it over her head and under her arms. She is soon hauled to safety with the help from PC Sweetman who has dashed out after hearing of the dilemma. With Nelly safe on the bank and Mrs Bunkerton taking her off to the 'Ladies' to dry off and give her a change of dry underwear, which she always carries around with her in case of emergency, all that is left of the commotion is a grey wig and half empty gin bottles bobbing downstream in the River Poddum.

It's nearly 3:00pm and everyone now replete is making their way back to the coach, everyone except Mrs Bunkerton who will use Nelly's wet knickers as an excuse, but she would be last on the coach as she usually is, anyway. Ah, here she is with Nelly now!

With Mrs Bunkerton and Nelly onboard and the distinctive whiff of river water and silt accompanying them, Willy Tynebull speaks over the public address, "RIGHT, EVERYBODY, I TRUST YOU'RE ALL SUITABLY FED AND WATERED?" a dull "Yes!" is reply from the few that are listening. "GOOD! WELL, NOW WE ARE GOING TO OUR FINAL MYSTERY DESTINATION WHERE ROGER AND SUSAN SPUR HAVE LAID ON ENTERTAINMENT AND THEIR SPLENDIFEROUS OUTSIDE BAR!"

"WEE HEE, WOO HOO, WAH HAY!" reply the masses with great interest. At the same time as this reaction, Willy is looking in his rear view passenger monitor mirror, expecting everyone to be doing their impression of PC Fred 'Flasher' Sweetman. They're not, but PC Sweetman nearly forgot where he was and there was a slight twitch in his greatcoat.

"RIGHT, I THOUGHT YOU MIGHT LIKE THAT IDEA! IF YOU'D BE SO KIND TO PUT YOUR BLINDFOLDS BACK ON, WE SHALL ARRIVE AT OUR FINAL PORT OF CALL AT AROUND 5:00PM. THANK YOU, THIS HAS BEEN WILLY YOUR COACH DRIVER SPEAKING! BEEP, WHISTLE, SHRIEK, POP!"

Reverend Parsworthy, inspired and excited by the thought of Roger and Susan's outside bar, bursts into song, "SHALL WE GATHER AT THE RIVER? THE BEEAUTIFUL, THE BEEAUTIFUL A RIVERRRRRRR!" Nelly's not impressed!

Mr Robson, the counterfeit Scotsman, was slightly disappointed that there were no Scotch pies and Bridies at The Poddum Pastry Parlour, but Reverend Parsworthy is quite content that the chicken and leek pie was up to his standard but, 'could have done with a little more leek Boyo!' Greedy Griff Johnson is still hungry!

The two small children of the village are starting to be naughty; there's a sudden disgusting noise as one of them sits on his pre-inflated whoopee cushion while the other little horror cracks a stink bomb on the floor to add realism. "Ho Ho!" laughs one of the dads, as if to say 'That's my boy!' As the sulphurous niff permeates the coach, all of those who have tried to ignore it are overcome with nausea – it's bad enough being blindfolded let alone asphyxiated. Windows are getting smashed to increase ventilation, those little sliding ones aren't of much help. Willy will have to make a claim on his insurance, that's if he's remembered to renew his cover.

"RIGHT, LADIES AND GENTLEMEN, WE SHALL BE ARRIVING AT OUR FINAL DESTINATION IN APPROXIMATELY FIVE MINUTES, HALF AN HOUR EARLIER THAN PLANNED, DUE TO THE FACT THAT I DIDN'T GET LOST! ROGER AND SUSAN SPUR WILL BE THERE TO WELCOME YOU WITH A DRINK, AND THIS YEAR A BARBECUE HAS BEEN LAID ON. IT'S ALL IN THE PRICE OF YOUR TICKETS SO NO NEED TO PAY. THE USUAL SIDESHOW AND FUN TENTS WILL BE

THERE FOR YOUR ENTERTAINMENT!" announces Willy Tynebull with a crackle, fizz and pop of electronic amplification.

This year, there is a special appearance by Corrie Nation the page 9 model from Busted's raunchy tabloid *The Stun*; she'll be giving signed photos away. Corrie Nation, her real name, came into the modelling business as Corrie Nation-Street. She added the last bit to add a touch of the exotic, but her manager said it made her sound too much like a soap opera and told her to drop it from her name. She will be appearing fully clothed, thankfully!

Willy pipes up over the public address, "OKAY, LADIES AND GENTLEMEN, WE ARE JUST ENTERING THE COACH PARK, YOU MAY NOW TAKE OFF YOUR BLINDFOLDS! WE WILL SPEND THE NEXT FOUR AND A HALF HOURS HERE AT FRIMTON PARK. MAY I REMIND YOU THAT ANYBODY WHO IS UNREASONABLY INTOXICATED ON THE WAY HOME WILL BE TOLD TO GET OFF THE COACH FOR DRUNKENNESS?" Mr Robson's ears prick up with that last word, "Drunkenness? I wonder where in Scotland a place is called Drunkenness?" he thinks to himself; little does he know that he is sitting next to the fabled Drunken mess monster!

Crunching through the pea shingle of the Frimton Park car and coach park, Willy applies his brakes and switches off his ignition. "RIGHT, LADIES AND GENTLEMEN, HERE WE ARE AT FRIMTON PARK. MAY I REMIND YOU TO DRINK WISELY AS MY COMPANY RUNS A STRICT 'NO DRUNKEN SLOBS' POLICY AND IT'S A LONG WALK HOME FROM HERE! I TRUST YOU'VE ENJOYED THE MYSTERY TOUR SO FAR AND HOPE YOU ENJOY THIS, THE FINAL DESTINATION OF YOUR TOUR. WE SHALL BE LEAVING AT 9:00PM SO THAT WE CAN ENJOY THE MARVELLOUS VERNBURY VALE SUNSETS. I'D BE MOST GRATEFUL IF YOU'D ALL BE PROMPT FOR OUR DEPARTURE, AS MY WIFE IS EXPECTING ME HOME

FOR 10:30PM. THANK YOU, THIS HAS BEEN YOUR COACH DRIVER WILLY TYNEBULL SPEAKING, ENJOY YOUR EVENING!"

Frimton Park is no more than a 20 minutes walk away from Vernham, so if you are a little bit elephant's trunk and get thrown off the coach, you'll probably still be home earlier than the coach. Willy has been doing this particular excursion for over 16 years now, and it appears he still gets lost in the Vale of Vernbury. Map books and atlases mean absolutely nothing to Willy Tynebull, and getting lost is all part of the fun, apparently!

Now you'll have to pay particular attention to this bit of info: Frimton Park is in the village of Frimton, Frimton House is in Frimton Park, Frimton House is the only house in Frimton village and Frimton Park is a village surrounded by a wall. All of this nonsense came about in 1763 when the then Earl of Beastly, selfishly built a wall around his estate (well, he didn't build it exactly, men from neighbouring villages were employed for no pay to build it, lazy swine!) and called it Frimton Park. The Earl of Beastly also designed a functional folly and had it built at the edge of the estate lake. This folly is a fully working lighthouse and still has a lighthouse keeper employed to keep it going. In the 1700s of course there was no electricity and so a huge oil lamp was used. The Earl of Beastly named the lake 'Pharos Pond' after the lighthouse of Alexandria built around 280 BC. The reason for this lighthouse being built was because the Earl used to like rowing his boat around the lake late at night, and the lighthouse gave him the general direction where the jetty was when he he'd had enough – I'm sure a small oil lamp would have sufficed. The beam from this Beastly beast can be seen for miles and it's very likely that this beam illuminated areas of the Vernbury Vale during the Second World War sufficiently for old Jerry to drop a few accurate bombs on certain buildings. The Earl of Beastly during Second World War didn't give a fig about blackout regulations and it's purely a miracle that Frimton House wasn't bombed – unfortunately Grummet Hall was! Gladly, the current Earl of Beastly is a lovely rotund old chap, often to be seen cycling around on his Penny Farthing to visit summer fetes and such like. He always wears tweed plus fours, but even then he doesn't take any risks and wears bicycle clips to keep them away from the huge front wheel. He also looks forward to Roger and Susan's outside bar and sideshow entertainments, and this year he has donated space for it in Frimton Park, he definitely won't have far to go home.

In this year's sideshow entertainments there are some new features; a pain endurance test (comprising of thumbscrews and red-hot ball bearings to name but a few of the discomfort threshold tests); guess the total of maggots wriggling in Susan's tights (the gentles donated by Master Butcher Dick Sperling – a perk of being a butcher is that you can breed your own maggots on rotten old joints of meat and get a regular supply of bait to go fishing with); magnetic fishing pools for the children and, reintroduced after a three-year absence, a boiled egg eating competition (three years ago Greedy Griff Johnson was disqualified for eating the eggs shell and all).

There is also a surprise live band performing tonight at 7:30pm, it promises to be exciting! Last year Mr Selsman bored the knickers off of everyone with his phonofiddle concerto of the works of William Bainbridge. Bainbridge was a much maligned experimental music pioneer from the Vernbury Vale in the early 1920s. His music, or musick as he called it, was generally based on an arpeggio of three or sometimes four notes played over and over, but gradually changing the order of these notes as the opus progressed until finally returning home to its original order at its finale. This approach to composition was later perfected by composers such as Philip Glass and Instrucarp. Mr Selsman is not able to attend the mystery excursion this year since his Wellington Boots were stolen from his doorstep last week. He won't be venturing out until his new pair that he mail-ordered from *Country Gent* magazine arrives in the post. It goes without saying that the two small children of the village have been blamed for this Welly theft, but they are totally innocent (this time) as torturing woodlice with the pinpoint of sunlight through a magnifying glass at the time is their alibi.

Mickey Farshott is running about all over the place after being chased by an ‘early for the time of year’ wasp; his mother has booked him in with a hypnotherapist in an attempt to cure his apiphobia. He should be alright by the time the sun goes down as the wasps have to fly home by then.

The barbecue is proving to be successful, and Nelly Birdham is using its heat to finish off drying her Poddum-soaked polyester floral dress she bought from ‘Dickens’s Ladies Wear’ in 1969, they don’t make garments like they used to!

Greedy Griff’s already into his second string of sausages – I hope he waits for his next one to be cooked!

Wendy and Eddie are tucking into some gammon and pineapple kebabs and PC Sweetman is watching them with a glint of jealousy in his eye. Because of Eddie’s problem with words and sentences, he’s been afraid to speak too much and Wendy’s getting a bit tired of ‘yes’ and ‘no’. She never had a problem getting a conversation out of Fred Sweetman and can’t understand why Eddie isn’t more willing to talk; it doesn’t matter if the words come out wrong, as she would still be able to work out what he means.

Mr Robson and Reverend Parsworthy have hired the rowing boat from the Earl of Beastly for an hour. Reverend Parsworthy is rowing Mr Robson about and his oars keep popping out of his rowlocks. No matter, Mr Robson is happy singing ‘Speed bonny boat all over the Glen, over the sea to Skye’ with one of his hands trailing in Pharos Pond’s still and murky water – a hungry jack pike is following, ready to assassinate Rabbie’s ‘gnarled old bunch of bangers’ fingers.

Meanwhile, back at the barbecue, Roger Spur has scalded his hand on a very hot turkey drumstick and has plunged his fist into a fast melting bucket of ice, Susan despairs of him! “You know, Roger, this is exactly why I prefer to cook instead of you – you're so accident prone, really!" This is true, Roger has broken both of his legs, his nose and his wrist since they've been together, and he has also cut his head open three times on the same cupboard door in a week while doing the wiping up. And yet for Susan, there can be no other man, Roger is the light of her life – isn't love strange?

Ruefully this year, the palmistry tent is still in evidence, and typically there is a woman in there who will ask you to look into her goldfish bowl of dry ice and water with children's action figures that may hopefully look like that tall dark stranger that you're likely to meet. She's calling herself 'Madame Mystère' and it's definitely not Miss Somerton-Jove, not unless she has drastically lost about five stones in weight – now that would be 'The Five Stones of Impossibility', especially with her diet! No, it's someone I'm certain I've never seen before acting as the Chiromancer, she must be a Spruggle surely?

Eddie Jedson is the first to go in and cross her palm with silver. Outside the tent, Eddie's big bonce is bulging the canopy, looking like a penguin trapped under a carpet, searching for freedom. "Cross my palm with shiny metal, my precious, and I shall read yours!" croaks the Chiromancer. Eddie places a 5 pence coin in her ungrateful palm, and she decides to give him the economical version of reading. Madame Mystère was expecting at least 50p, what is she, Parsworthy's sister or something? Noticing that she still has a miniature soldier action figure in her goldfish bowl, she asks Eddie to close his eyes; this will give her enough time to change the figure to a girl's doll.

"You may now open your eyes, let me see your palm, oh, oh, oh, oh, yes!" she groans, "I can see a beautiful woman in your marriage line, a beautiful women with golden hair, look into my gold – er, crystal ball, there she is now!" Madame Mystère says with a curly, wavy finger pointing at her goldfish bowl.

Eddie knows that she is talking about Wendy Wilson and is very excited, "W-W-W-Will it be soon?" stammers Eddie.

"Let me look at your other palm, young man, and I shall tell – but cross mine with silver again first?" says Madame Mystère. Eddie plonks a 20 pence piece in her hand… you'd better be good this time, Madame Mystère, this is a serious stake! "Close your eyes, young man, and hold out your palm, my dear?" says Madame Mystère as she places an action figure of Enid Blyton's Big Ears from her Noddy stories next to the blonde dolly in the goldfish bowl. "Open your eyes, sweet boy – oh, oh, oh dear me! If you don't move promptly, you will lose her to a handsome man in uniform. Look, there he is next to her in the mists of the future, run boy, RUN!" Madame Mystère urges Eddie, mainly because she's run out of 25 pence worth of ideas.

"F-F-F-F-F-F-Flippin' 'eck, it's Flasher Fred in the-the-the-the goldfish bowl!" shouts Eddie fighting his way out of the tent. "It's a crystal ball, you ignoramus!" rebukes Madame Mystère. Eddie can't see Fred or Wendy in the crowd and hopes it's not too late. Eddie has never felt like this before about anybody and he's not sure how to cope with this emotion. There's nothing to worry about though because Wendy has taken her dear old dad to the portaloo and PC Fred is examining Willy's coach tyres for bald patches and anything else he can find to throw the book at him with.

Back on Pharos Pond, Mr Robson and Reverend Parsworthy have nodded off in the boat and are gently drifting aimlessly with the light wind that is blowing across the pond. The Earl of Beastly is standing on the north bank of Pharos Pond with a megaphone, "ER, COME IN NUMBER ER… ONE PLEASE? ER, YOUR TIME IS UP!" There is only one boat of course, bless his little plus fours. Reverend Parsworthy and Mr Robson both wake up with a start, and both believing they are shipwrecked, are shouting "HELP, HELP, MEN OVERBOARD!" Yes well, overboard would be a good way of describing them! They can't row to shore as silly old Parsworthy let go of the oars when he nodded off. Seeing that the two men are in a spot of bother, the Earl of Beastly rushes to his gardener's shed to get his chest waders – that'll ruffle his plus fours, they don't make waders with room for plus fours, but flared waders would be interesting though! In next to no time the kind Earl of Beastly is wading out to rescue the silly old twits and dragging them ashore. Reverend Parsworthy and Mr Robson thank the Earl for saving their lives and rush off to Roger and Susan's outside bar for a couple of stiff ones.

Harry Helmson, well on his way with his sixth pint of ale is boring everybody with his hairdressing stories, it's uncertain how many of these tales are true though as very few people trust Harry and his scissors!

Mickey Farshott is still being bothered by the same wasp; obviously Vespula vulgaris has got the hots for Mickey!

Wendy Wilson has made her mind up over Freddie and Eddie, she is going to propose a ménage à trios – but not tonight, tonight she will make a fuss of Eddie and play hard to get with Freddie.

It's 7:28pm and there seems to be a bit of a stir over by the concert stage and roadies are doing a bit of a sound check with lots of P's T's F's and various fricatives and raspberries being blown into the microphones bellowing out over the 5000 watts of amplification. The Earl of Beastly, with his chest waders still on, gets up on the stage to make an important announcement; he puts his megaphone to his mouth and speaks, "NOW LISTEN HERE, ALL OF YOU, EVERY YEAR AT THE END OF THE VERNBURY VALE MYSTERY TOUR, THERE IS ALWAYS A CONCERT—"

The Earl is interrupted by one of the roadies offering him a microphone so that he can be heard better. The Earl thanks him and puts the microphone inside the megaphone and carries on speaking, "AS I WAS SAYING, AT THE END OF EVERY VERNBURY VALE MYSTERY TOUR, THERE IS A CONCERT LAID ON FOR YOU TO ENJOY. UNFORTUNATELY FROM THE COMPLAINTS RECEIVED

AFTER THE LAST FEW YEARS, IT'S QUITE APPARENT THAT MOST OF YOU HAVEN'T ENJOYED IT. THIS YEAR IS DIFFERENT, WE HAVE ALL GONE TO THE GREAT TROUBLE OF ARRANGING A SHOW THAT WE'RE CERTAIN YOU WILL ENJOY. MAY I ASK YOU ALL TO PUT YOUR HANDS TOGETHER AND WELCOME... TRICKY TURNSPIKE AND THE TRANSINCIDENTALVESTITES, ER, AH, ROCK AND ROLL CHAPS!"

Suddenly the air erupts with the instantly recognisable (to those that have heard it before) opening thrash chords of 'While You Were Snoring' crashing through the PA speakers like a railroad truck. Tricky isn't on stage yet as he's busy swatting up on his lyrics so that he doesn't forget them. Then suddenly, Tricky bursts to the front of the stage and throttles the microphone stand just in time to belt out the first line 'While you were snoring, I blew maaa mind!'

Tricky looks different, his giant quiff has had an upgrade, it's now six feet tall and is encrusted with miniature battery-powered halogen lamps that flash on and off in time with the pounding beat; it's a shame it's still broad daylight as I'm sure it would be most effective in the dark! Minus his famous Braeburn sunglasses, Tricky's face is painted with horizontal black-and-white stripes; it's difficult to make his features out, he looks rather like an Everton Mint wearing a dandruff-speckled Busby!

Mrs Bunkerton grabs hold of Nelly Birdham's hand to drag her to the front of the stage. Mrs Bunkerton has been a number one fan of Tricky ever since he saved her from drowning in the great Vernham flood. Tricky and his Trannies breeze through the first number effortlessly and as Tricky brings the song to an end with the last line 'While you were snoring, you blew maaaaaaaaaaaaa MIND!' Mrs Bunkerton turns to Nellie and says, "See, I told you, it's the snoring, it'll make or break you!" Nelly can't hear but just nods to be polite.

No sooner has the first song finished and Tricky and the Trannies are into their second number 'I Believe In Santa Claus And I'm Seeing The Shrink Next Tuesday!' Mrs Bunkerton, who's completely 'booglarized' as Don van Vliet would say, is throwing off her mac and cardigan like a born again Rock and Roll hedonist. She throws off her hat and takes the pins from her hair shaking it loose as the final touch. On Sunday with her head bowed in prayer at All Faiths church, it'll be hard to believe that Mrs Bunkerton is the same woman. Nellie Birdham is still in Mrs Bunkerton's emergency underwear – it's unlikely she'll be wearing her floral dress again as it caught alight from being too close to the barbecue, plus a helpful and accidental splash of barbecue fuel from one of the two small children of the village.

Tommy Perkins is thoroughly enjoying himself pogo-ing about all over the place, giving way to the odd cough and wheeze, while Eddie Jedson is proudly leaning on the outside bar counter with an 'I don't need to be at the front, because I know the star!' look on his face. Wendy wants to go to the front of the stage though, but feels she can't leave Eddie behind, but she sees PC Sweetman boogying on down with his greatcoat flapping wildly and she feels like crying.

Roger Spur has just broken wind and is being rebuked by Susan for being so disgusting when he's serving food – poor old Roger, he's been holding on to that one all afternoon and as the music was so loud thought he might be able to get away with it – it's not his fault that it smells!

As all good gigs do, the hour performance of Tricky and his Trannies seems to be over as quick as it began and they are back on for an encore of 'While My Plank Gently Whinges'. Nowadays they do a 10-minute version and it's taken on a progressive punk rock flavour – it always goes down well for an encore! All of this spectacular has been missed by Mickey Farshott who is still being chased by that rampant wasp. By 9:00pm the sun will be so low that old Waspy will have no choice but to give up and go home – wasps use the sun for navigation. The trouble is that all of the coach party will be buzzing off too at 9:00am and poor Mickey hasn't even had a drink – I must say his beer belly seems to be a bit slimmer though, and I do admire his stamina!

Right, that's it! The day is nearly over and everyone is making their way back to the coach, and by Vernham standards everyone has adhered to the 'No Drunken Slobs' policy of Willy Tynebull's coach company, no one too tipsy, everyone that is except for Willy Tynebull, who's been quietly scooping back the cognacs all evening and is completely faeces faced. It's only about a twenty-minute walk back to Vernham, so the happy Vernhamite throng decide to enjoy the Vernbury Vale sunsets on foot.

Willy's wife isn't half going to give him a smack if he gets home after 10:30pm, if he ever gets his lumbering brontosaurian bulk home at all!

# Chapter 8

## VERNHAM GOSSIP UPDATE

Tommy Perkins has been made redundant from his bakery job in Velstrum; to celebrate, all of the remaining employees in the bakery have had a wage rise. Tommy is now scaring cats from leaving their mess on Mrs Bunkerton's beautiful garden during the night, the only trouble being that Tommy scares the mess out of them so much, they're still doing it to some degree! Mrs Bunkerton is paying Tommy £10 a night, which doesn't seem very much, but it is tax free and the DSS won't know about it when they send him his Giro. During the daytime, Mrs Bunkerton keeps faith in those enigmatic silver discs that the newspapers give away regularly; when the wind is blowing they can scare both birds and cats. These discs however are not a mystery to Mrs Bunkerton anymore; Tricky Turnspike gave her a signed Transincidentalvestites CD/radio player in the shape of Braeburn sunglasses to play his albums on.

Tricky Turnspike and the Transincidentalvestites have taken a bit of a blow from the media of recent; it seems that Tricky's new image is not going down too well, and neither is the new music. One headline in the music rag *Noise* jibes: 'CAPTAIN BOUFFANT AND HIS TRAGIC BAND!' in reference to Tricky's hyper hairstyle and change in direction of music. While it's normal for members in bands to have musical differences and indeed some members may leave because of those differences, the Transincidentalvestites use those differences to an advantage – it just sounds like they are all playing their own thing all at the same time, regardless of the song. Wilfred Sprat, a critic from music rag *Rock Shock* a competitor of *Noise*, finished his slag-off review with: 'personally I wish they'd go and run off a quiff!' It's a typical

Rock and Roll story, that the media help you up the ladder when you're en vogue, and when you get to the top they'll push you off!

Despite Tommy Perkins' job misfortune, the legend of the Bog Stomper survives and toy shop owner Cecil Twill is near to perfecting his 'Bobby the Bog Stomper' souvenir models. These models are battery-powered robot toys from Japan that he bought a massive stock of during the 1960s. Cecil has had some furry suits made up by a dress and suit maker's shop in Busted called 'Taylor's The Tailors' – the robots dressed in the suits, with the final touch of glued-on plastic bulging eyes and plastic fangs couldn't look further away from the real thing, but then no one has seen the Bog Stomper properly, so it doesn't matter.

Mr Selsman's new Wellington boots still haven't arrived, apparently the parcel was last tracked in Rajasthan – I suppose they do need Wellington boots in India sometimes? In the meantime, kindly Mr Robson has offered to do all of the shopping for Mr Selsman, and hopefully Mr Selsman's 'neaps and tatties' endurance will hold out until his new boots arrive.

Mr Robson, the counterfeit Scotsman, has been banned from the Wednesday afternoon Vernham Parish Hall Pensioners' Picture Show for crunching his sweets too loudly. That's a shame because they are going to show *The 39 Steps* and *Trainspotting* next week, although a word of advice about the latter should be given to the organiser of these picture shows – it may not be suitable for some of the regulars' viewing. Mr Robson is trying to come to terms with the softer kind of sweet; those American Hard Gums are a dickens of a beast to his dentures.

Miss Somerton-Jove was seen riding bareback on one of the mysterious daily Friesian cow visitors. Dressed only in her burgundy bouclé jacket and shouting "I'm Lady Godiva, I'm Lady Godiva!" she was arrested by PC Fred Sweetman on the grounds of indecent exposure – the words pot, kettle and black spring to mind.

Wendy Wilson has made her proposal to PC Sweetman and Eddie Jedson regarding the ménage à trois she had in mind; the boys are okay about it but both agree 'not at the same time!'…the little minx!

Milly and Molly Goldsworth the twin spinsters, have been considering a long overdue holiday and are considering closing Comfytums for a fortnight while they holiday in Newport Pagnell after seeing a postcard of Tickford Iron Bridge sent to them by a Spruggle customer who lives in Buckinghamshire. Milly and Molly have been interested in bridges since their schooldays when they borrowed a book from Velstrum library in 1929 about Isambard Kingdom Brunel, they still haven't returned it yet! This will be the first holiday they have ever had outside the Vernbury Vale, and now in their early nineties the time is ripe for adventure. Whatever Mrs Bunkerton will do about her 10:02am visits is anyone's guess.

Disgraced Fire Chief / Pyromaniac Mr Jedson is alleged to have been spotted in Busted selling matches to people on the street – if this is true, it's a sure sign of addict turning pedlar to feed his habit.

Mr Barnford the veteran ARP warden is still standing sentry in the corridors of Blagworth Junior School after being kidnapped while he catnapped in the Comfytums tearoom raid – he smells worse than ever and looks decidedly green.

Mr Swale the retired bassoonist of The Busted Philharmonic Orchestra has finally sold his cottage after being victimised by Vic and Maureen Grinham for making music at a sociable time of day. It promises to be a bit of an ugly awakening for Vic and Maureen; the new owners of the cottage are a two-man West Indian steel drum band called 'Ganjabangbong' – members Winston Reefer and Leeroy Roach are not known to be friendly and don't go to bed too early.

Mickey Farshott, apiphobic extraordinaire, has been undergoing treatment for his fear of wasps, bees and other stinging and biting things. Rather than going down the hypnotherapy route, Mrs Farshott decided on taking Mickey to phobia specialist Doctor Philip Vernham; there's no relation to the village with that name, the doctor is a Spruggle of Dumfries origin, but there may be a spiritual connection with Mr Robson. The treatment is a graduated desensitising programme – after a brief consultation the first part is to look at pictures of various bombi and vespa, gently moving through to watching a video of the same whilst slowly increasing the volume of the buzzing soundtrack in 5:1 surround sound. The next part of the programme is a tactile one; the patient is encouraged to touch dead bees and wasps mounted on boards with pins, after that a visit to a bee farm, with full beekeeper's protective clothing. The final part of the treatment is to wear a spaceman-like helmet called a 'Hive Helmet' which has a double wall. This helmet is based on Sir James Dewar's clever invention the 'vacuum flask' and is made of clear acrylic. The patient has the Hive Helmet placed on his or her head and then a miniature swarm of bees is gradually fed into the space between the two walls. To the observer, the patient's head looks as though it is completely engulfed in a ball of bees; others have likened it to looking at a strange planet from some other universe. Sadly, very few patients get to the final part of the programme, and although this method is somewhat controversial, Dr Vernham has stated in an interview for *Shrink Monthly* that the method has a 100% success rate and that he has never had a patient return for more treatment. Vernham greengrocer Jim Phillips is considering an appointment with Dr Vernham to cure his phobia of swans, but they may not have helmets big enough – it's just as well Eddie Jedson doesn't have any phobias then!

The stray bulldog has been spotted in Low Street after a long absence since the flood; he has only been seen by a few locals and only late at night. They say that he looks different somehow, almost phosphorescent and transparent and seems to be floating rather than walking.

After the virtual success of the Vernbury Vale mystery coach excursion this year, The Grummet and Nut Landlord and Landlady, Roger and Susan Spur, are weighing up the pros and cons of doing a Christmas Special Excursion. This little trip out, if it goes ahead, will include visits to local garden centres and gift shops in the itinerary. They won't be employing Willy Tynebull's services again – he still hasn't found his way home after the last excursion!

Dick Sperling, Master Butcher of the universe in his own book, is entering a sausage competition. The 'Busted Banger Bonanza' will take in competitors from all over the United Kingdom, and a strict 'Brits Only' rule will be employed this year as last year there was a bit of cheating going on. Velstrum butcher François Biscay entered into the competition under the pseudonym of Frank Biscuit and was disqualified for having too much of a French accent to his sausage recipe. A few words with François in the first place would have made it quite apparent that he wasn't all that British and saved an awful lot of time and money. One thing is for sure, if Dick Sperling is accepted as a contender he had better make sure he uses the finest cuts of quality meat for his sausages, not the usual nostrils and earlobes he normally slaps in.

Barry the butcher's delivery boy's job hangs in the balance after losing a complete delivery of Dick Sperling's pies. Barry was having a bit of a chat to Mrs Bunkerton and had his back turned to his bike. Greedy Griff Johnson couldn't resist the pies and chomped the lot while Barry wasn't looking. Barry was only aware of the situation when he heard an explosion as Griff started to bite on his bike tyre.

The two small children of the village, whose names we shan't mention, have been a bit poorly recently with runny tummies. The cause of this is thought to be the apples that they ate after scrumping them from Mr Burnheart's orchard. The apples from Mr Burnheart's orchard are one of the sweetest eating winter apples called 'Black Oxford' and are most unlikely to cause stomach upsets. Someone overheard a conversation in The Grummet and Nut, that Mr Burnheart had impregnated some of the apples on the lower branches with senna pods. It's a mystery how these apples came to the

Vernbury Vale as they are apparently of American origin – possibly Paris in Oxford County, but an interesting mystery nonetheless. As regards the two small children and their poorly tummies, who cares?

And finally, two devastating blows for Ken and Bettie Griggs of Ye Olde Sweetie Shoppe: firstly the terrible news that Killjoy's the confectioners will be churning out their last humbug at Christmas – very appropriate if you're Ebenezer Scrooge but not if you own a sweet shop. Apparently Killjoy's current manager Wesley Killjoy, the last in a long line of Killjoys with no desire to marry and keep the family name going, is an incurable gambler and does enjoy his horses – most of the company profits have sailed down the racetrack at Aintree. With only enough money left to pay off his loyal employees with a few ex gratia pats on the back, Killjoys will cease to trade after 101 very successful years of confection.

The second blow for Ken and Bettie is that they have been told that they are not to sell backdated newspapers anymore as it was confusing some of the old folk into turning up at the post office on the wrong day for their pensions. They have been allowed to keep the CDs and DVDs that are given away free with the Sunday papers. They can distribute these little discs to anyone who is interested – as mentioned before, the concept of these products of the digital age is beyond most of Vernham's natives. Mr Selsman thought that the 'Simply Red' compilation sounded like a scraping scratchy noise when he played it on his Decca Salon 10 Phonograph, and it's not one of those old-fashioned ones with the ridiculous funnel sticking out – no, it's one of those compact design ones with the sound being generated at the tone arm. Another annoying thing for Mr Selsman was that the disc didn't have a playing speed on it, and didn't know whether it should be slow, 78rpm or fast. All that angst was dispelled after Mr Selsman relaxed with his favourite 78, 'Mildred's Velvet Dress' by 'The Spinning Top Orchestra' and a full pipe of Angel's Kiss in his armchair.

# Chapter 9

## A PLAGUE OF BOG STOMPER DOLLS AND THE GREAT TOY SHOP SWINDLE (THE NASTINESS BEGINS)

It's 10.00am and another business day dawns in Vernham as Cecil Twill dusts off his toy shop window displays, flicking the dead flies into a corner where they can still be seen. Cecil has received the first batch of 100 off battery-operated robot / Bog Stomper conversions. This could be a very exciting turn in Cecil's career as a toy shop owner – today a troop of Bog Stomper hunters are to arrive in Vernham to camp on the perimeter of Sweetwater Marsh.

With luck, some of these Spruggles may take a visit to the Low Street shops and have a bit of a nosey, and maybe some will visit the toy shop when they see Cecil's proud posters advertising Bog Stomper souvenirs. The posters aren't the ones he had printed 'professionally' at a lithographic printers in Busted called 'Fudget and Scarper Litho Ltd', they were very disappointing as they weren't proofread properly and as Cecil trusted their judgement, he didn't bother with the old proof approval bit. What should have been ***BUY YOUR BOBBY THE BOG STOMPER DOLL SOUVENIRS AT VERNHAM PLAYTIME NOW!*** turned out to be ***BUY YOUR BOGGY THE BOB STOMPER DOG SOUVENIRS AT VERNHAM PLAYTIME NOW!*** Possibly a poor telephone line or a deaf switchboard operator that took the details may have been the root cause of this reject; whatever the reason, when Cecil telephoned Fudget and Scarper to explain the dilemma, nobody would pick up the phone. And when Cecil took numerous bus rides out to Busted to see if he could talk to someone of authority about the print error, the premises were empty as though no one had ever been there. So with Cecil £100 poorer, he had no choice but to make his own posters with fluorescent pink poster sheets that he purchased from an art shop and a bold marker pen – they still do the job!

The shops of Low Street are busier than ever today; over 50 enthusiastic phenomenon and legend hunters have arrived by car, making parking very difficult for the locals. This group of Spruggle anoraks are members of a club from Aylesbury called the 'Grendel Slayers'; they've never slain Grendel, but the idea of being the Beowulf that beats him in an arm wrestle inspires them. There are a number of Grendel Slayers in Comfytums the tearoom and they're enjoying Milly and Molly's pastries and tasty treats – the Cajun four-cheese omelette is proving as popular as ever. Again the specials board is being ignored, Milly and Molly might as well write 'Botulism Burger' on the board, although you can guarantee that some pillock would try to order it if they did, just to be awkward!

Milly and Molly have been kind enough to hang one of Cecil Twill's gaudy day-glow posters on their back wall, and it's just been noticed by two of the Grendel Slayers, Pete and Sharon Svelte. That surname would conjure up thoughts of a slim couple wouldn't it? Yes, well unfortunately you'd be wrong in your conjecture; they are a couple of chubby-chopped, tubby-tummied food hoovers that will probably devour the very soul of Vernham – watch out Greedy Griff, you've got competition! Pete and Sharon Svelte are antique collectors, and their ruthless opportunism has netted them a fair stash of money in the past, so much so that they no longer need to work. They aren't averse to conning the odd noddy that may turn to them for advice on how much to insure their prize possessions for, "Um, yes, what you have there is a vase from the Ming dynasty from around 1400 AD, not very sought after, you could probably have picked 'em up from Woolworth's not so long ago for about two a penny! As regards insurance, I don't think you need to worry too much as Ming vases aren't really sought after, even if I may be so bold to say? they are in as excellent" (saliva, drool and try to hide the smirk!) "condition as this. I'll tell you what, just to take the worry off your hands, I'll give you… let's see… um, £40?" Pete and Sharon discuss a visit to the toy shop over some loud slurps of tea.

Meanwhile, Cecil Twill is still sprucing up his displays. He gently dusts with a brush, a 00 scale Flying Scotsman train that Mr Robson, the counterfeit Scotsman, has had his sticky conjunctival eye on for a long time now, never quite saving enough pension money for its tag of £10. Cecil has plenty more of these beautiful smoke-billowing trains at the back of his shop; the boxes alone must be worth £10. Cecil doesn't really know how to value these toys. He has a lot of Hot Wheels cars, in particular a Green Cadillac Eldorado that he has priced at £1; this was one of the first toy cars that the young Richard Turnpike bought with his birthday money, and the influence of that image has stayed with him, except Tricky Turnspike's Cadillac is pink. Is £1 too much for these little cars? I don't know, but Cecil was selling them for 35p in 1971, so maybe they're a bargain!

Cecil looks around at the toys in his shop and notices that The Beatles one time toy's packaging, now memorabilia, have faded very badly; there was a distinctive red and white theme to a lot of these items – they are now more like yellow and cream. Tins of 'Canned Beatle Breath' sold pretty well, by Vernham standards anyway – Cecil wonders how they managed to breathe into all of them, they must have been working flat out. "I hope they brushed their teeth properly before!" he thinks. The naked little Trolls in various sizes with big fluffy fluorescent hairstyles are there, ugly and glassy-eyed, yet appealing to youngsters in the 1960s, no one seemed to dress them up very much. PC Sweetman was allowed to play with Trolls, but his Auntie Winifred knitted a one-piece woolly suit for his, which was then glued on the Troll so that little Freddie couldn't take a sneaky peek at the Troll's cheeky plastic botty.

‘Clackers’, the cause of many a playground injury, were a very popular toy in the early 1970s. These toys were just two solid plastic balls mounted on a piece of very strong cord which looked very much like the South American weapon called a ‘Bolas’. With a ring in the middle of the string, the object of the game was to hold the ring and briskly move it up and down, the resulting effect was that the two balls would start swinging apart and meet each other at the end of the swing making its distinctive clacking noise – hence the name. This was by no means an original concept of toys in Vernham as there had been something similar for hundreds of years called ‘Conkers For One’. If one didn’t have any friends and one wanted a quick game of Conkers, one would thread two Horse Chestnuts on a bootlace with an ingenious knot tied at either end to prevent the chestnuts from flying off. With the same action as Clackers you could bash away at this Bolas of Conkers until one of them smashed. You could give the chestnuts names and place a bet on the winner, but you’d never lose! This game was originally played with snail shells, sometimes with the snail still in them to give a bit of extra weight, as the Horse Chestnut isn’t native to the United Kingdom and wasn’t introduced to this country until possibly the 16th century. The first recorded game of Conkers played with Horse Chestnuts was in 1848 on the Isle of Wight, but the people of Vernham know otherwise!

Cecil looks at his loudly ticking Smith’s clock and adjusts the time as it gains 3 minutes a day. He uses his Timex ‘Snoopy’ watch as a guide for timing accuracy – this watch loses 3 minutes a day. There is a red pedal car from the 1950s on the shop floor and Cecil bends down to buff up the chrome hubcaps. He sees his reflection in the mirror-finished cap and notices that he is looking more like Albert Einstein every day, with mad white hair and moustache. The pedal car is extremely valuable in the world of antiquity; it was manufactured in 1953 by sheet metal worker Earnest Beauthorpe, father of Rodney Beauthorpe the inventor of the Beauthorpe Dentmobile. This little pedal car was originally made as a one-off by Earnest for his little boy Rodney; soon all the children in the neighbourhood wanted one and their parents were willing to pay Earnest to make them for their children's birthday presents. Often times Earnest was given a one-week deadline to produce these little marvels, including the immaculate coach paint. The price for these works of wonder was a princely £35, a lot of money in those days. Earnest built a total of 20 pedal cars to the same design but there was only meant to be 19 including his son Rodney's. Car number 20 was made when a little brat burst into tears because he 'wanted a blue car, not a red car BOO HOO HOO!' In my day I would have had a smack on the back of the legs for being so unreasonable; however, this spoilt little urchin got his own way and Earnest made a blue one. So the red car in Cecil's toy shop is that very same car. Enthusiasts and antique buyers have been looking for the missing red car for years, not knowing that it is in Vernham Playtime, still unsold. Cecil bought it from Earnest in 1959 for £20 to take it off his hands; he doesn't really know how to value this pedal car but realises it will be worth far more than the £20 he bought it for – he is open to suggestions. The car's antique value is currently £2500 and rising.

One may wonder how Cecil can continue to run his shop if nobody buys his toys – all of this is of no importance to Cecil as he inherited a sum of £5,500,000 from a distant uncle he never knew of in the 1950s and has lived well on the interest made on his investments. The toy shop is more of a pastime than a job for Cecil, but the odd sale makes his entrepreneurial pecker pucker up and so, for Cecil, success with Bobby the Bog Stomper will pucker up his pecker more than ever.

Ding-dong, Cecil's toyshop door chime signals a customer, but it's not a customer, it's Mr Robson, his eyelashes encrusted with crystalline mucopurulent discharge after a particularly bad night with conjunctivitis. "Helloo, Cecil ma auld pal, hoo are ye todee?" asks Mr Robson with feigned interest as he glides on virtual roller skates towards the counter.

"Who am I? Well I'm Cecil Twill of course; at least I was the last time I wrote my name!" replies Cecil with mild dismay.

"No, not who are ye, HOO are ye! Och ne'er mind, I've just come for a wee fondle of yer Flying Scotsman, Cecil!" explains Mr Robson pointing a crooked finger in the general direction of the model train he so desires.

"Well, you can't. I'm sorry, Rabbie, I've just dusted it and I want it to remain without paw prints!" Cecil replies in a stern voice and arms folded, mimicking the scolding that he used to receive from his long passed father.

"Och, goo on, just a wee sniff of its cardboard box then?" begs Mr Robson.

"NO, NO, NO, THRICE NO!" says Cecil, three times no less.

"Och right, pal, and may Cailleach Bheur visit ye at Christmas when you've no troosers on, ye miserable auld git!" snarls Mr Robson with the anger of a spoilt child. Cailleach Bheur is the bringer of cold winter in Scotland, also known as the Blue Winter Hag; Mr Robson often has nightmares about this ice queen and even shivers when he mentions her name. How he is so educated in the knowledge of everything Scottish is a mystery, he's probably gleaned most of it from the books in Velstrum library, another place he's been banned from for crunching his Winter Mixtures too loudly. He also likes to watch television documentaries, so he may get some of his info from those too. So with a flick of his mock kilt and a whiff of yesterday's haggis, Mr Robson stomps off in shiny brogue shoes and grubby spats, away to annoy someone else in the village.

Shortly after Mr Robson exits, Pete and Sharon Svelte both try to enter the shop at the same time. Causing a jam in the doorway momentarily, Pete wins with a powerful thrust and bursts into the shop. "Ah, hello, my name is Cecil Twill!" says Cecil with a friendly customer welcoming voice. Cecil notices the Grendel Slayer tee shirts that hardly fit the pair. "Are you beast hunters looking for some Bog Stomper souvenirs perchance?" asks Cecil hopingly.

"Err, yes sort of!" replies Pete. "We are here to spend an all-night vigil in pursuit of the Bog Stomper and have seen your poster in the tearoom over the road," says Sharon. Pete looks around with eyes agog at the antique toys in Vernham Playtime, it's as though he's died and gone to antique toy heaven.

"Yes, I have had a new consignment of Bobby the Bog Stomper Dolls in this week – can I interest you in buying one for a young child you may know?" asks Cecil.

"Um, maybe, but we'd like to have a browse first if that's okay?" says Pete.

"Ah yes, feel free? I'll be over by the counter if you need me!" assures Cecil pointing at the shop counter not that far away.

Pete wanders around the shop singing an irritating song with the hum-hum-dee-d-dee-dee that a bathroom fitter sings when he's just about to rip you off with a quote. The annoying ritual that tradesmen use of sitting down on your toilet seat, marking and measuring this and that, and finally giving you a quote of £3500.43p when they had already decided what they were going to con you for before they started, needs no musical accompaniment!

Pete picks up a Corgi 'Chitty Chitty Bang Bang' and remembers when he had one of them for his sixth birthday, shortly after it was snatched from his grasp in the school playground by a bully – ginger-haired and freckly Robin Ransom. Pete never did get over the heartbreak of losing his beloved Chitty Chitty Bang Bang, that's why he turned to comfort-food binging – it filled an empty hole that appeared when Chitty disappeared.

Sharon strokes the mane of a hair-growing dolly, much like one she used to own, and remembers how her brother Shaun cut most of her dolly's hair off so that he could dress it up in his Action Man clothes as a German Stormtrooper for his

British Infantry soldier to fight. The toy manufacturers 'Barton Toys' also made a male doll equivalent with a growing beard; these became very popular later on with ZZ Top fans. This hair-growing dolly mutilation didn't affect Sharon in the same way as Pete with comfort food; she's always hungry and has always been plump!

Cecil asks if Pete and Sharon need any assistance, which is a bit like telling the executioner exactly where to hit the back of your neck with his axe when it comes to dealing with this miscreant duo! Pete says that he's still browsing and will ask if he needs any help. Sharon looks around the shop and notices the red pedal car on the floor – how they both missed it when they first entered the shop is odd, it's quite big and very red. "Hey Pete, look over there!" whispers Sharon at the same time giving Pete a painful nudge with her elbow in his kidney. Pete turns around to see the car and nearly falls over with shock; he puts a hand in his trouser pocket and pulls out his angina spray as he can feel an attack coming on. Instinctively Pete realises that they have found the Holy Grail of pedal cars and that he must have it.

"Mr Twill, I've just noticed that you have a lovely red pedal car, is it for sale?" asks Pete trying not to show his excitement too much.

"Well yes it is, how much are you willing to pay for it?" replies Cecil with a business-like tone to his voice.

"Um, well, um… what you have here is a Beaufort pedal car made in the mid to late 1950s, not very sought after. Although made to a very limited edition of only 20, because of the lack of manufacturer status these cars never did make much appreciation in value. This particular car you have in your shop is known as the Red Reject, discarded by a child for its distinct lack of blueness. I would put the value of this run-of-the-mill toy in the region of say… £150 and um… 25p?" advises Pete with bogus sincerity.

Cecil shakes his head in disagreement and says, "No, no, I'm sorry, I am looking for something more like £1500, I can't accept anything less!" Cecil thinks that he's reeling Pete in as he sees a flicker of temptation in his eyes.

"£1500? that's more than ten times what it's really worth, I was just being kind when I said £150!" snarls Pete with vehement anger.

"No, sorry, £1500, nothing less!" insists Cecil.

"Alright I'll think about it," says Pete.

"Can I still interest you in purchasing a Bobby the Bog Stomper doll at all?" pleads Cecil. Pete and Sharon leave the shop without answering and go to The Grummet and Nut for a CON-ference meeting and a couple of pints of local brew.

Cecil looks at his Bobby the Bog Stomper army and remembers he hasn't loaded them with D-size EVERLAST batteries; there's a huge box of them at the back of the shop he bought specifically for his bunch of Bobbies. Cecil lifts the heavy box from the back of the shop and brings them to his counter. Now for the job of loading all of his 100 Bog Stomper conversions with batteries. As Cecil loads the first set of batteries through a zipper opening in the back of a Bog Stomper, the on/off switch is already set to 'on' and the Bog Stomper bursts into life. The Bog Stomper turns around as though to look at Cecil, the illuminated eyes of the robot underneath its furry suit glow through the bulbous white plastic eyes with a slow pulsation. Cecil is excited, these have turned out better than expected and he certainly didn't expect the red LEDs to shine through the stick-on eyes of the Bog Stomper suit. Cecil talks to the Bog Stomper in way that a dog owner speaks to his dog, "You're a beautiful boy aren't you?" The Bog Stomper raises its right arm and Cecil shakes its hand, "Pleased to meet you, Bobby!" chuckles Cecil. Accepting that this incident was just a pleasant side effect of malfunction, Cecil turns the Bog Stomper off and proceeds to load the other 99 of them with batteries.

Ding-dong – it's PC Sweetman, he's here to have a quick WAY HAY HAY flash at the Troll dolls. Cecil gets annoyed, "Do you have to do that, PC Sweetman?" he growls.

"What?" asks PC Fred with puzzlement.

"Expose yourself to my toys – this is a place of innocence, where children can visit and be miles away from depravity!" preaches Cecil.

"Oh, I'm sorry, I didn't realise that I was doing it!" apologises PC Sweetman.

"Did you listen to The Archers yesterday, Fred?" Cecil enquires.

"Yes I did, I hope Shula is going to be alright after that herd of cattle nudged her into a ditch!" says PC Sweetman with a tinge of worry to his voice.

"Yes, who'd have thought it, her car breaking down in that country lane and being rammed off the road by a herd of cattle?" says Cecil with equal concern.

"Oh well, I suppose I'd better be off to see Ken and Bettie to pick up my Walnut Whip and Strawberry Bonbons, bye!" says PC Fred with a cheeky flick of his greatcoat.

The daily visit of Friesian cattle are outside the shop and PC Sweetman seems to be having trouble with them – they won't let him pass. Remembering Shula and the trouble she had with cattle on The Archers, Fred tries to shoo them in the only way he knows how. It has to be said here that indecent exposure to cattle is probably always going to be ineffective, no matter how much you WAY HAY, WOO HOO, WEE HEE! give them what for! So, crestfallen and having a feeling of abject failure, PC Sweetman waits for the cattle to go on their way and then follows them up to Ye Olde Sweetie Shoppe for his daily treats of confection.

Meanwhile in The Grummet and Nut Pete and Sharon Svelte, who are now a couple or so pints of local brew blearier, are getting quite irate about not being able to rip Cecil Twill off with his red pedal car. The local brew they have been imbibing is called 'Landford's Lobotomy' which is 9.5% proof and only sold by the bottle in limited supply, and is normally known to pacify the angriest of drinkers – not so with Pete and Sharon, they seem to become more vicious with every sip. "Right,

Sharon, the way I see it is that if the old fool won't let us have the Red Reject for £150, then we're going to have to steal it!" snarls Pete.

"How are we going to do that – break in during the night?" asks Sharon.

Pete ponders on the situation and the practicality of breaking into Cecil's shop. "No, I'll hold him down and you pinch it!" says Pete, smacking and rubbing his palms together.

Roger Spur, the landlord, who is drying up a badly washed beer glass overhears part of Pete and Sharon's conversation and is quite concerned that Cecil may come to harm. Cecil Twill is mildly eccentric but likeable; there is not a single Vernhamite that has a bad word to say for him.

In the days when there were more than two small children in the village, Cecil used to have an old beer barrel filled with sawdust in his shop. Buried in the sawdust-filled barrel were toys; it was a bit unisex and often a disappointed small boy would get a dolly or skipping rope instead of a plastic soldier. So Cecil acquired another barrel and made a pink one for girls and a blue one for boys. The toys weren't for sale but could be won as a prize in exchange of a correctly answered question. Cecil would ask the child a question, which could be about general knowledge, stories from the Holy Bible, sports, maths, geography or junior science, and if the question was answered correctly then the child would get a chance to put his or her hand in the sawdust and feel for a prize.

Cecil, being a kind man, would often help the child to answer the posed question and at Christmas time he would give away prizes for the silliest answer. Poor little Richard Turnpike could never get a single question right, even his Christmas silly answers weren't silly enough! One day it all got too much for Richard and he burst into tears, "It's not fair, I never win a toy, BOO HOO!" Cecil could feel the disappointment in Richard and told him that he could have a toy because he tried harder than any of the other children and he admired his never-give-up spirit. Being so small then, Richard couldn't reach inside the barrel and so Cecil helped Richard by lifting him up so that he could reach for a toy. Unfortunately at the time of this event, the then Vernham village Bobby PC Hardly was walking past the shop and misconstrued the incident, believing that Cecil was trying to stuff Richard into the sawdust-filled barrel. After a lot of explaining, PC Hardly let Cecil off with a caution and was told to get rid of his lucky dip barrels as they were a safety issue. The educational quizzes continued, but without the surprise of the sawdust-filled lucky dip, the children got to choose a toy from the quiz prize shelf.

So not withstanding, there is not a Vernhamite who would allow Cecil to come to any harm – well if they were about at the time anyway. Roger decides to telephone the toy shop and tip Cecil off that he may get a bit of trouble from Pete and Sharon. 'BRRRING BRRRING, BRRRING BRRRING!' Cecil picks up the phone to answer, "Vernham two two two! …Yes that's me Cecil Twill… Oh yes hello, Roger… Fat couple getting drunk in The Grummet and Nut… Going to steal my pedal car… Yes, thank you, Roger, goodbye!"

Back at The Grummet and Nut, Pete and Sharon are giving Roger a bit of bother after he refused to serve them with any more bottles of Landford's Lobotomy. Pete is getting very irate and is throwing peanuts everywhere. Greedy Griff Johnson is dashing around in attempt to catch every peanut in his mouth, waste not, want not! Outside is PC Sweetman on patrol – he senses that there is trouble afoot and charges in, "WHAT'S ALL THIS THEN?" he bellows. "IT LOOKS LIKE A BIT OF NAUGHTY AND NASTY GOING ON HERE, I'M GOING TO GIVE YOU WHAT FOR!" he bellows again. And with a swish of a greatcoat opening like morning curtains with the new day sun hurting hungover eyes, PC Sweetman proceeds to give 'em what for with a "WOO HOO, WEE HEE, WAH HAY, OOH YAH, OOH YAH!" chasing Pete and Sharon out of the pub – they've never seen anything so horrid! That's sorted them out for the time being, but they've run in the direction of the toy shop.

Inside the toy shop, Cecil is trying to put the threat of Pete and Sharon attempting to steal his pedal car to the back of his mind and singing a song to himself: "I go driving in my car, Beep beep tiddle diddle beep beep, it's not quite a Jag-yoo-ah! Beep beep, tiddle diddle clang clang!" It's not working and Cecil is beginning to tremble with fear. Cecil sees the rotund rogues loitering outside his shop out of the corner of his eye and starts to panic.

Ding-dong, Pete bursts into the shop, "RIGHT £150, OR ELSE!" shouts Pete like a Sergeant Major.

"Well I'm sorry, but as I've said before, £1500 and nothing less!" says Cecil.

"Oh dear, oh dear, oh dear oh dear, oh dear oh dear oh dear, tut tut tut, Mr Twill, you have disappointed me, I was hoping that we could settle this amicably, but it seems you're bent on hurting my feelings and I don't like it when my feelings get hurt, it makes me very, very sad, and when I get sad, I get melancholy, and when I get melancholy I get murderous thoughts running through my head, and when I get murderous thoughts running through my head, people start to get hurt! Do you get my meaning, Mr Twill?" explains Pete in epic dialogue.

"I'm sorry, I didn't quite catch that! Could you be so kind to run that past me again please?" replies Cecil, wishing that he hadn't.

"RIGHT THAT DOES IT, YOU'RE TAKING THE WIDDLE OUT OF ME NOW, NO ONE TAKES THE WIDDLE OUT OF PETE SVELTE!" shrieks Pete as he lunges for Cecil and grabs hold of his throat. "RIGHT, SHARON, PINCH THE CAR NOW!"

Cecil is choking with Pete's pincer-like grip around his throat and is looking for something hard and heavy to hit Pete with. Sharon is trying to drag the red pedal car through the shop doorway but it's become stuck fast between the doorposts. Cecil gropes around and grabs a growling teddy bear to hit Pete with, and with each smite the teddy bear growls, 'BANG, OOF, GROWL, BANG OOF, GROWL, BANG, BANG, OOF, GR-R-ROWL!'

And then something strange happens – the 100-off consignment of Bobby the Bog Stomper conversions switch themselves on as though they have a will of their own. The Bog Stompers march from the back of the shop in a military marching troop, their fur suits tear open at the chest, revealing laser guns. At first, Pete doesn't know what is going on and maintains his tight grip around suffocating Cecil's throat. The Bog Stompers open fire from behind Pete and needle-sharp burning beams of laser light are stinging his legs and popliteal fossa. The pain gets too much and Pete releases his grip on Cecil and turns to kick the Bog Stompers out of the way, but as quickly as they fall over they right themselves again and continue their attack on Pete. Now the Bog Stompers are shooting higher up at Pete's body and Pete is in extreme agony; one laser beam hits Pete in the eye and blinds him momentarily. As though this assault isn't enough, a squadron of radio-controlled helicopters switch themselves on and start dive-bombing Pete.

Sharon has run away in fright leaving Pete to contend with this horror. Not being a very good runner himself, Pete lumbers towards the shop doorway and is followed by the Bog Stompers who are concentrating on Pete's legs again. A hundred intense beams of laser light ignite Pete's trousers – now that's what I call flared trousers! Pete jumps over the red pedal car with an agility that would normally be impossible from a man of 30 stones in weight, and wobbles off up Low Street to safety, trousers aflame. He disappears into the distance like a shooting star, getting smaller and smaller, finally burning itself out, never to be seen again.

Cecil, still dazed and in shock from the attack, steps over the pedal car and staggers out of the shop to get some fresh air. Cecil wonders exactly what could have happened – were these Japanese toy robots a secret military weapon, or do toys have a strange affinity with the humble toy shop man who is known as Cecil Twill? I prefer the latter!

## Chapter 10

## MRS BUNKERTON'S SPECIAL VISITOR

It's a Tuesday morning someday in October and Mrs Emily Bunkerton is excited, for today an old acquaintance is coming to visit. It's been nearly 43 years since Mrs Bunkerton last spoke to her friend Patricia Wells, shortly before Patricia and her husband Robert emigrated to Australia. Mrs Bunkerton and Patricia haven't lost contact though; regular letters and occasion cards being exchanged like Microsoft file downloads from each side of the world. Patricia, also a widow of seven years, lost her husband Robert through a terminal illness, ironically on the same date as Mrs Bunkerton lost her husband Gerald, not simultaneously though, that would be too spooky.

Gerald, Emily, Robert and Patricia were long-time friends since they met at St Spielberg's Polytechnic in Busted. The girls weren't students there, but Gerald and Robert were and they used to smuggle Emily and Patricia into the campus to play pontoon and snap. They were innocent days, both men were gentlemen and the thought of anything carnal didn't cross their minds, much! Emily and Patricia never spent the night on the campus and always went home, often nearly missing the last bus out of Busted to make the connection with other buses to arrive eventually in Vernham. Once or twice though, the girls were late enough to miss the last bus from Velstrum to Vernham, and a long cowpat-riddled walk in the dark would only be comforted by a shared cigarette or two. In the pitch black, all that could be seen was the little orange dot of the burning cigarette end, like a firefly in slow motion. They were just silly girls then and the smoking was just a brief flirtation with film star glamour. Both Robert and Gerald didn't smoke and did their level best to discourage the girls by screwing their faces up after kissing them goodnight.

Oddly enough, Mrs Bunkerton's boyfriend was originally Robert and Patricia's boyfriend, Gerald. That was until the girls decided that they'd made a mistake and preferred each other's boyfriends; gladly the boys felt the same. But somewhere deep in the secret heart of Mrs Bunkerton, a torch still flickers in a special corner for Robert – no one will ever know! The realisation of this inner feeling didn't dawn in the young Emily until the day of her wedding at All Faiths Church, Robert was Gerald's best man and Emily couldn't keep her eyes off him. Later at the reception, Robert asked Gerald for a gentleman's excuse me, and after a brief bit of dancing Robert explained to Gerald that he actually wanted to dance with Emily; Gerald yielded. While Robert and Emily danced together, Robert told her that he'd never seen her looking as beautiful as she did that day and half joked about eloping together; the other half of the joke was a true feeling, but it was too late. Emily relived that moment inside her mind for a long time; she still thinks about it now, but the pain has dulled slightly. Truth to tell, Mrs Bunkerton is thinking about that secret right now, but that's silly girl's thoughts and she must tidy up before Patricia gets here.

Mrs Bunkerton dusts the mantelpiece, 'Oh dear look at that dust!' she hasn't dusted for a week. Ooh! Steady on, more haste less speed and more precious ornaments smashed if you carry on whipping up a domestic storm like that! Mrs Bunkerton looks at the clock, it's 9:00am and hopefully just enough time to vacuum the carpet before removing some embarrassing weeds in her beautiful flower borders. She looks out into the front garden and remembers that she hasn't paid Tommy Perkins for his night of cat scaring – look, he's still running around now bless him! Mrs Bunkerton relieves Tommy of his duty and has a look at her pretty garden. The Virginia Stock went a bit mad this summer and there's still plenty of the little pink to violet flowers thriving. The Alyssum still looks like an untrodden snowscape – well, everywhere that Tommy hasn't accidentally trampled anyway! During the summer evenings, Mrs Bunkerton's Nicotiana Tabacum plants emit the most delicious perfume – so hard to understand how anything so beautiful could be connected to a deadly habit. The Papever Somniferum still standing proud and tall, even if flowerless – someone has been slitting the poppy heads with razor blades, but why and who would do such a thing? No finger-pointing here, but this poppy head slitting has only started since Winston Reefer and Leeroy Roach moved into Mr Swale's old cottage. A quick scout around the garden borders to pluck out a few dandelions and Mrs Bunkerton thinks back to time gone by, when she banned husband Gerald from gardening – he used to pull the flowers and leave the weeds, happy days!

It's nearly 9:55am and Mrs Bunkerton is whizzing off for her 10:02am visit to Comfytums, not to stop by – she can't because Milly and Molly Goldsworth are on holiday in Newport Pagnell and have closed the tearoom for a fortnight. But Mrs Bunkerton still has to go; it's one of her obsessive compulsive disorders.

After a quick run to Comfytums and a quick stroke of the door handle, Mrs Bunkerton zooms back to her cottage to prepare for Patricia Wells' visit at 11:06am. The plan is to take morning coffee and malted milk biscuits, and have a chat about old times – good and bad. Setting the table with a plate of malted milk biscuits, coffee cups and her finest silver cutlery, Mrs Bunkerton's mind goes back to when she and Patricia first shared a packet of malted milk biscuits on one of the many bus rides to Busted – maybe Patricia would like to take a trip into Busted to visit their old haunts?

The telephone rings, Mrs Bunkerton picks up the receiver, "Hello, Vernham 567!"

A women with an Australian accent speaks, "Emily? Is that you, darling?"

“Yes it is, to whom am I speaking?” enquires Mrs Bunkerton.

“Why it’s me, you silly old Pom! …Patricia!” says Patricia.

“Why Patricia, how Australian you sound, I didn’t recognise your voice!” chuckles Mrs Bunkerton.

“Listen, darling, I’m running a bit late, I’ve just missed the blasted bus from Busted to Binkley, and I’ve just been told that there isn’t another bus for another twenty minutes!” rages Patricia. The bus rides to and from Busted to Vernham and vice versa are a bit of a swine to be quite frank. For just a 15 mile ride you get on a bus from Busted to Binkley, then a bus from Binkley to Rumpstead which is only half a mile away, then a bus from Rumpstead to Renton, then Renton to Velstrum and finally Velstrum to Vernham. This journey takes just over an hour and a half and drains the patience of any saint. Mrs Bunkerton tells Patricia to hang the expense and board a taxi; she will pay the fare when Patricia arrives at her cottage. Patricia thinks that is a great idea, especially as she doesn’t have to pay.

It’s exactly 11:05:58am. Earlier than expected a taxi arrives from Busted, delivering Patricia Wells to Mrs Bunkerton’s cottage. After waiting at her window, Mrs Bunkerton gallops down her garden path to greet Patricia and pay the taxi driver. The fare is £22.50p, which is actually cheaper than the bus. It’s a misconception of most travellers that buses are cheaper than taxis – not so in the Vernbury Vale! Mrs Bunkerton pays the driver (with only two £1 notes in the bundle of money, thankfully!) and gives him two buttered fruit scones in a Tupperware box as a tip, the taxi driver of course is extremely grateful, YUM YUM!

Walking arm in arm down the garden path towards Mrs Bunkerton’s cottage with the popular ‘You’re looking well’ and ‘You haven’t aged a tad!’ lies, Patricia steps on a garden snail with a painted shell. “Struth! What the dingo’s kidneys is that?” asks Patricia.

“Oh! That’s one of Tommy Perkins’ racing snails. I employ him to scare cats from my garden during the night and he likes to bring his pets along for company. Oh dear! It’s a Humbrol Flyer, one of Tommy’s favourites, he will be upset, it’ll probably bring one of his asthma attacks on!” explains Mrs Bunkerton gaspingly.

The girls go inside for coffee and malted milk biscuits and a good old chat. First, they talk about when they first met in ‘The Old Trumphonians Infant School’ in Low Street; this eventually closed due to lack of local children and merged with ‘Velstrum School for Little Ones’. The infant school is now Vernham Parish Hall and is popular with pensioners, particularly on Wednesdays as they have a miniature cinema that shows a lot of the good old films.

The girls both agree that they had happy days at the infant school, even if the Headmistress Mrs Henty was a bit of an old bag. They recall a time when the Mayor of Busted, John Throstle-Pippet, visited the school and was presented with the children singing a new hymn that they had learnt called ‘Morning Has Broken’, and how he described the performance after hearing it as “A complete cacophonic nightmare!” Mrs Bunkerton and Patricia can still feel the cringing fear that they experienced in the classroom when they heard Mrs Henty screaming with rage in the corridor and the occasional window being smashed. And how all the children were made to feel guilty for such a poor performance, even though they had tried their best. The truth was that Mrs Henty was having an affair with the Mayor and had been dumped by the Mayor previously before his school visit. Mrs Henty hated the feeling of failure, she had failed in the affair and her school had failed to impress the Mayor, so naturally it had to be the children’s fault, rotten cow!

But there were nice teachers there – Miss Wiston, the one with the glass eye, was a lovely lady. And Mr Surly, who had very short legs, used to come to school on a strange tricycle that had the pedals on a steering column because his legs were too short to reach the pedals on a conventional tricycle. How sweet Mr Surly looked on sports day running about with those little legs that seemed to have no bend at the knees; luckily having a torso of four feet long he was a good six-footer. Then there was Miss Shapely, a pretty young teacher that taught the babies class; she wasn't there for very long as she had her own baby to teach at home after she became Mrs Smith. "Oh, they were lovely days!" both of the girls agree in unison.

Patricia asks Mrs Bunkerton how she's coped with becoming a widow, and she replies with her usual answers of "It's his snoring that I miss the most!" and "I still keep expect him to come walking in through that door, but he never does!" Patricia says that snoring is the one thing she doesn't miss and how Robert used to sound like a lion roaring when he got into top gear. A powerful surge of thrill runs up and down Mrs Bunkerton's spine and she thinks how ungrateful Patricia is, it's the one thing that tells you that your lover is still alive during the night, apart from breaking wind, although that isn't always reliable!

"Oh, Patricia dear, would you like another cup of coffee?" asks Mrs Bunkerton.

"Actually, dear, I was hoping for something stronger, darling – do you have any whisky?" enquires Patricia.

"I think so!" says Mrs Bunkerton and goes to the cupboard under the staircase for a rummage. Mrs Bunkerton gropes around in the cobwebs and finds an old bottle of medicinal Glenfunnel 12-year-old single malt. She dusts the bottle off and sees that the angels have had more than their fair share, 'Why, it's half empty!' If Mrs Bunkerton had had a bit more of a grope around, she would have found Gerald's secret stash that he used to dip into when she used to go up to bed early with one of her bad heads, and in the morning it would be Gerald that would wake up with one of his bad heads, and yet she never knew why!

Mrs Bunkerton asks Patricia if she would like to retire to the lounge with her Scotch, and Patricia thinks that's a very good idea after the hours she's spent sitting in the uncomfortable seats of various forms of transport. The girls chat about their teenage years when they first met Gerald and Robert, and how that horrible boy Pinky Watson used to hang around like a scavenger, just in case one of the girls were available after being dumped by one of the boys. Pinky did appear to be an unpleasant fellow; his main topic of conversation would be rude things – he would lure someone into a false sense of security by talking about wholesome things, and then find an opportunity to turn the thread into obscenity. The most obvious twist in conversation would be something like, "What have you got in your lunch box today then? Ooh, you've got a nice pear, ho ho!" He got the nickname Pinky because he was born with only one forefinger which was on his left hand. Considering that Pinky (or William, his real name) was right-handed, Pinky had all sorts of problems in dealing with everyday things. And yet, if people knew the real William, they would find that he was the sweetest, loving soul you could ever meet. The rude talk was just a mask to paper over the cracks of his sensitive personality; he disappeared shortly after Emily and Patricia became engaged to be married to both Gerald and Robert respectively, and has never been seen again.

Mrs Bunkerton did see the sweet side of Pinky Watson – one day when she tripped on a proud paving stone and laddered her stockings, he ran to her aid making sure she was alright and handed (or should that be fingered?) a handkerchief to dry her tears. Okay, the handkerchief was a little on the snotty side, but the sentiment was true. Emily in her youthful suspicion thought that there was probably an ulterior motive; of course there was, but not as ulterior as she believed, he just loved and cared for her. It's strange how we never appreciate the hurt that someone feels when their offers of romance are rejected by us, and how we still don't appreciate the pain that they experienced when the same thing happens to us!

Mrs Bunkerton looks out of her lounge window and sees Miss Somerton-Jove stomping down the garden path. "Quick!

Duck! Down here behind the sofa, it's that blessed woman Miss Somerton-Jove!"

Miss Somerton-Jove has been visiting Mrs Bunkerton every day since Milly and Molly went on holiday; she too has a daily habit of visiting Comfytums to fulfil and visiting Mrs Bunkerton is the best way she knows. After a quick scramble behind Mrs Bunkerton's paisley-patterned settee, the girls cower in hiding.

Miss Somerton-Jove approaches Mrs Bunkerton's front door and knocks loudly. After a few seconds of nobody answering the door, Miss Somerton-Jove knocks the door loudly again, but this time follows up with shouting through the letterbox "YOO HOO, YOO HOO, IT'S ME, MRS B, YOUR FRIEND MISS S-J!" With Mrs Bunkerton's senses being heightened by fear, she can smell and taste the sickly odour of Miss Somerton-Jove's mothballs in her burgundy bouclé jacket pocket whiffing through the letterbox. Patricia is mulling over that name Somerton-Jove – that name rings a bell and she's certain that she met a women in Busted many years ago with that name, and after all, a ridiculous surname like that would be unforgettable.

"Miss Somerton-Jove, Somerton-Jove? Crikey! It's that women I borrowed 10 shillings and sixpence from and never paid it back!" recalls Patricia, if there's something more she hates than owing money, it's paying it back! It's been said that if you put sand in the palm of Patricia Wells and she closes her fist, by the time she opens it again there will be a glass marble!

Then all goes quiet for a brief moment. Mrs Bunkerton begins to crawl out from behind the settee and she catches sight of the silhouette of Miss Somerton-Jove's bulk in the intense light of the low autumn sun blazing through her window. Miss Somerton-Jove presses one eye tight to the windowpane and calls, "Mrs B, Mrs B, are you there? It's your friend Miss Somerton-Jove!"

"What shall we do?" Patricia asks tremblingly.

"Stay put until that terrible woman goes, she's not been taking her medication of recent and she can become quite unreasonable. She's been coming here every day since Milly and Molly went on holiday – oh how impatient I am for their return!" says Mrs Bunkerton.

"Milly and Molly, are they still about?" Patricia asks with another frightening thought of IOUs. "Struth! I owe Milly 2 shillings and thrupence for a blasted toasted teacake and a wretched cup of tea!" thinks Patricia. Yes, indeed she does, but she's also forgotten the tab of £5 1/- 8d she had built up over the five years before she emigrated to Australia. "When are they coming back?" Patricia asks with great personal interest.

"Next Tuesday I think they said!" replies Mrs Bunkerton.

What a relief, that means Patricia won't have to experience the embarrassment of being confronted by Milly. Milly's memory is extremely accurate, and she would remember as soon as she saw Patricia. Miss Somerton-Jove is still pressing her mad face against the window shouting, "COOEE, COOEE, YOO HOO, YOO HOO, ARE YOU THERE, MRS B? IT'S ME MISS S J, YOUR FRIEND!" And then Miss Somerton-Jove pulls her face away from the windowpane leaving the dust of her face powder behind, as though a giant doughnut had been thrown at the window and bounced off, leaving its sugar there.

All goes quiet; Mrs Bunkerton and Patricia remain behind the settee for a while until they're certain the coast is clear. Suddenly, 'SMASH -TINKLE!' Mrs Bunkerton's pet tortoise 'Harry' comes crashing through the lounge window, wrapped in a sheet of paper. The tortoise holds its passive defence poise on the fleur-de-lis carpet for a short while and then struggles to right itself from its upside-down misfortune. The sheet of paper unfolds with the tortoise's frantic leg movements. Mrs Bunkerton, still not sure whether Miss Somerton-Jove has gone, crawls out from behind the settee to rescue her tortoise. On the unwrapped sheet of paper is a note: *Called today, sorry you weren't in, will see you tomorrow, finest regards, Miss S J.*

"It's alright, Patricia, she's gone!" Mrs Bunkerton assures Patricia.

Mrs Bunkerton telephones 'Pane's Emergency Window Repairs' in Velstrum to help her out. Pane's Emergency Window Repairs make a lot of money repairing windows in Vernham, at least once a day they have to come out to repair somebody's window. The Managing Director of Pane's recently gave each of the two small boys of the village a Black Widow catapult and a promise of £5 paid to them for every window they smash; it's honest pay, they never deny that they are breaking any windows. A recorded message with charming saxophone music from Pane's switchboard greets Mrs Bunkerton's ear, "You are in a queue, please hold the line until one of our operators can help you with your enquiry? Your call is important to us, we go to great pains (Pane's, ho, ho, very good!) to help you, please hold the line?" Mrs Bunkerton finally gets through to Pane's switchboard and in next to no time at all she has booked a window repair and the glaziers arrive promptly to repair the broken pane, almost as though they had been waiting outside! The truth is that because of the regularity of window breakages in Vernham, Pane's keep a van stationed in the village so that they can spring to action immediately, it saves on diesel too!

With the window repair done and everything shipshape, Mrs Bunkerton suggests that she and Patricia go for a stroll around the village. Patricia accepts the challenge, even though she's worried about whom else she owes money to. "Perhaps you'd like to visit The Grummet and Nut and have lunch there?" asks Mrs Bunkerton.

"Er, well… is it expensive in there?" answers Patricia with a question.

"No, no, not really, but anyway it'll be my treat!" Mrs Bunkerton assures Patricia.

"Oh well, fair dinkum then!" says Patricia, resigning herself to not having to pay, yet again.

On the way to The Grummet and Nut Mrs Bunkerton and Patricia Wells bump into Mr Robson, the counterfeit Scotsman, “Morning, gentlemen, hoo are ye todee?” says Mr Robson in his best Scottish brogue, and in his best Scottish brogues, they’re so shiny you can see right up his kilt, YUGH!

“Good day, Mr Robson, and we’re ladies not gentlemen!” replies Mrs Bunkerton with a reprimanding tone.

“Och, sorry! It’s Mrs Bunkerton isn’t it? Ma eyes are soo stucky I canna see a thing todee!” says Mr Robson apologetically.

Patricia is amused with Mr Robson and asks Mrs Bunkerton what his ridiculous accent is. Mr Robson hears this and reacts aggressively, “It’s SCOTTISH, my dear lady, SCOTTISH, ma native tongue and raison d’être!”

Patricia says that it doesn’t sound very Scottish to her and that she remembers a Mr Robert Robson from years ago that spoke with a Vernhamese dialect. “Och aye, that would’ve been me before I had ma post monition, but I’m Scottish noo, and with that I’ll bid ye ladies good dee, bye bye, noo bye bye!” bids Mr Robson with fond adieu and a swish of his mock kilt.

Patricia says to Mrs Bunkerton that she’s glad to see that Vernham still has its oddballs and Mrs Bunkerton says that she couldn’t really see them that well in the reflection of Mr Robson’s brogues. Puzzled by Mrs Bunkerton’s remark, Patricia changes the subject and asks her if she has had any romantic encounters since her Gerald passed away seven years ago. “Well, not really, although I was saved from drowning by a very handsome rock star called Tricky Turnspike in the great Vernham flood during the early summer!” replies Mrs Bunkerton with pink tingly cheeks of bashfulness.

“Tricky Turnspike? I know of him, he’s a bit of a spunk isn’t he?” says Patricia.

Stumped by Patricia’s terminology, Mrs Bunkerton says “Yes!” but has vague memories of that ‘S’ word being anathema at the tea table.

Off the girls toddle, arm in arm with giggly girlishness, excited about lunch at The Grummet and Nut. Landlady Susan Spur is an excellent cook and the few that have dined there have complimented her on her culinary delights. Sadly, most of the punters that frequent The Grummet and Nut think that eating only fills you up and inhibits the intake of ale, while others are afraid to eat there after having a bad experience with Greedy Griff Johnson scrounging at their table – he often won't go until you've given him most of your chips. And of course, a stroll down to the pub wouldn't be complete without being accosted by Reverend Parsworthy and his blessed Church door fund collection box.

Reverend Parsworthy catches bleary sight of the girls and pops a handful of cashew nuts in his mouth in attempt to mask his breath. "Ah, good day, ladies! May I be so bold as to beg you for a donation for the door of our beloved All Faiths Church?" begs Reverend Parsworthy with bogus sincerity.

"You can beg if you like, but you'll not get anything from us! You've been pestering us for ages now with that darn money box and by rights we've probably bought a new church by now! Where *is* that blasted door?" protests Mrs Bunkerton with a vehemence from deep inside she never thought she had.

Reverend Parsworthy tries not to be upset by this womanly tirade, but tears are welling up in his eyes and he can't speak for fear of his voice breaking. Reverend Parsworthy, trying not to think of his mother, tightens his lips and staggers off to pester someone else for donations. He would normally have made a killing in Comfytums, but he shall have to wait for Milly and Molly's return from Newport Pagnell and make do with street sponging instead.

The girls go into The Grummet and Nut and order some delicious food. Patricia has the Venison Roast, the most expensive on the menu and Mrs Bunkerton has a look into her purse for her bank balance and orders the Welsh Rarebit, the cheapest on the menu, but she likes that, so no hardship there! As Mrs Bunkerton pays for the food order at the bar she notices the lost property box, the very same box that her husband's glasses are in. The glasses have been there for seven years since Mr Bunkerton left them by mistake in the ladies toilet, went home and had that terrible heart attack. What Gerald Bunkerton had been doing in the ladies toilet at the time is anyone's guess. Mrs Bunkerton peers into the lost property box and sees the tortoiseshell frames of the very recognisable spectacles and thinks, "Mmmm! My Gerald had a pair of glasses just like those, I wonder what happened to his?" Whew! That was a close one! If for one moment Mrs Bunkerton had an inkling that Gerald had been a regular in this pub, all of his wholesome marital image would be shattered in a trice for her. How she never detected the alcohol fumes on Gerald's breath is a mystery – I suppose one could say she was so bewitched and barmy bonkers about him, that she was blinkered to reality.

Thoroughly enjoying their luncheon, Mrs Bunkerton and Patricia discuss plans for the afternoon and whether or not a trip out to Busted would be a suitable thing to do. They could revisit some of the old haunts they used to frequent when they were mere slips of girls – the cafés, the cinema, the roller skating rink and many more places than they can cram into a single afternoon, or even remember. 'Macaroni's' coffee bar would be a good place to start, they could have one of those long tall glasses of frothy coffee with spoons still in them that either stick up one of your nostrils while you're trying to drink, or have your eye out. One of those delicious slices of Crostata would go down a treat as well if they have any room left to eat after their lunch.

So after an unusually hassle-free lunch in the Grummet and Nut, Mrs Bunkerton and Patricia embark on the one-and-a-half hour bus journey with many changes, and apart from the usual loonies, smelly people and loud coughers behind that one encounters on this less favourable form of public transport, all goes swimmingly.

The bus fare was paid for by Mrs Bunkerton though and she's beginning to think that it would be nice if Patricia dipped into her own pockets now and again. When was the last time that Patricia paid for anything or went Dutch to ease the finances of a friend? After 43 years it's difficult to remember, but Mrs Bunkerton only seems to remember Patricia saying that she had paid the last time every time she was asked if she would pay for something. Friendship of course shouldn't be about who paid for what and when; some friends insist on paying for everything such is their affection for the other friend; some feel that they had better pay for something for fear of earning a reputation of being miserly, even if they can't afford it; some friends insist on sharing and some insist on letting their friends pay for everything – the latter is the friend that Patricia Wells is.

Patricia has absolutely no reason for being a tight wad, she and her husband Robert emigrated to Australia for business reasons. Robert moved with his company, originally based in Busted, to the town of Wingabong in Western Australia near Perth and made an awful lot of money designing and selling bathroom showers. It's fortunate that Mr Robson, the counterfeit Scotsman, doesn't know that Patricia comes from Perth because he'd immediately think that Patricia was Scottish and produce his favourite postcard of The Station Hotel in Perth that he bought in a Velstrum charity shop; he's recently been telling angling greengrocer Jim Phillips about the quality roach fishing that can be had on the river Tay in Perth city, a fact that he read in a page from an old *Angler's Mail* he found blowing around Low Street some time ago.

But I digress yet again. Robert Wells never let Patricia lift a finger to help with the marital finances; she never wanted for anything and never had to buy anything, she was thoroughly spoilt. And yet even though Patricia is loaded, she tries extremely hard not to spend anything. The price of the air fare made her depressed for weeks, often telephoning help lines to help her with her despair – freephone naturally.

This deep seated frugality in Patricia Wells is the result of a traumatic childhood experience that happened one November when she was six years old. It was a popular activity around November 5th for many children to stuff some of their father's old trousers, jumpers and jackets with newspaper and make a Guy Fawkes; this effigy would have the finishing touch of a cardboard mask fastened with knicker elastic to a dummy head made from a pillowcase, again stuffed with newspaper. One day, little Patricia Homestead was scrounging money for fireworks in Velstrum with her Guy Fawkes she had made with the help of her mum, "Penny for the Guy, mister?" she would ask with childish appeal. Most people ignored her or told her not to beg on the streets, and then one very tall man with a top hat and silver walking cane stopped and said, "A penny for the Guy? Why that's an absolute bargain!" He then threw a penny into Patricia's collection box, picked up the Guy and walked off with it so quickly that sobbing little Patricia's chubby little legs couldn't catch up with him to get her Guy back. This event left a deep, unhealed mental scar in Patricia's personality, her reasons for value, possession and friendship twisted and confused. Most people would be able to come to terms with such disappointment as they matured, treating it as a learning curve on the subject of people and trust, but people from Vernham are different. Later on in life when she was married in her early 20s, she bought the Mary Wells record 'My Guy' when it was sailing high in the hit parade without knowing why – it's pure irony that she should have the same surname!

Five buses later, Mrs Bunkerton and Patricia finally arrive at Busted bus station, but they have to wait to get off because the driver is three minutes early and he won't open the doors until the correct time (hyper pedantic twit!). Everyone in the bus sits there quietly accepting the situation; this is normal behaviour in the Vernbury Vale, in other places it would be deemed as a problem. Three minutes gone, the door wheezes open with the sound of tired pneumatics, and people spill out of the bus like rats running from a burning building.

Patricia and Mrs Bunkerton are in need of that frothy coffee in Macaroni's and make a beeline for the said coffee bar. Arriving outside Macaroni's the girls are disappointed to see that it looks very different from their memory of the place; it's now known as 'Macaroni's Pizza & Pasta Ristorante', but you can still buy the frothy coffee with the eye-gouging spoons in the glass they go in. Mrs Bunkerton asks if Patricia would like to pay for the coffees, and Patricia is put on the spot as she fumbles around in her handbag and pushes her purse out of sight to the bottom. "Well, er! Ooh look at that, I must have had my purse stolen!" remarks Patricia without a single look of distress on her face. "Sorry, Emily, I'd love to but you see I haven't got any money!" lies Patricia from the heart of her bowels.

"Oh, very well then, my treat again then!" says Mrs Bunkerton in a humble yet forlorn tone. "I suppose you want a slice of Crostata as well with your coffee?" Mrs Bunkerton asks Patricia.

"Well, if it's not too much trouble, darling!" says Patricia with pseudo consideration.

"No, no trouble at all, I'm your humble servant as usual, my dear!" Mrs Bunkerton assures Patricia.

Mrs Bunkerton orders the coffee and Crostata while Patricia selects a seat for them both. The fixed double seats and tables are probably the only pieces of original fixture from the old days of Macaroni's, old and worn but comfortable nonetheless. The seats are only truly comfortable if your choice is correct though; for instance, quite a few of the seats are fixed back to back. If you choose a back-to-back seat and you get a small fidget bum child sitting behind you swinging and banging its legs against the base of the seat, it can be very annoying. Similarly, if you get a large adult sitting behind you that can't keep still, it's very difficult eating and drinking with the whole assembly rocking and shaking. Such is Patricia's generous nature, she has found a seat that isn't fixed back-to-back, for her anyway; Mrs Bunkerton's seat is the back-to-back variety if she chooses to sit opposite Patricia. Luckily there is no one sitting in the seat behind Mrs Bunkerton so all should be okay.

Mrs Bunkerton brings the tray of two coffees and Crostata to the table and places the tray on the table. Patricia thanks Mrs Bunkerton and proceeds to slurp the coffee through the froth. “It’s interesting that the Italians should name a pastry after an extremely high-pitched singer isn’t it, Emily?” wonders Patricia.

“Actually, my dear, I think you’ll find that it’s a Castrato that sings in a very high-pitched voice!” Mrs Bunkerton informs Patricia. As if a conjurer had waved his wand, a very scratchy recording of Allesandro Moreschi singing ‘Ave Maria’ whimpers out from the in-house music player. “That’s a Castrato voice!” explains Mrs Bunkerton pointing at one of the speakers.

“It sounds like the squeaking when you strangle a non-knotted neck of a balloon with your fingers and let the air out to me!” remarks Patricia. Mrs Bunkerton rolls back her eyes in annoyance. Patricia was never the best-educated girl when she was young, she doesn’t seem to know very much now, but it hasn’t held her back.

The girls’ minds go back to Macaroni’s of yesteryear and how they enjoyed those times. Old Mr Macaroni had a soft spot for Patricia, he used to go out of his way to chat to her and give her a hug every time he saw her. He was a nice man, rather rotund and always in a string vest, but extremely likeable. Emily Bunkerton was often hurt and jealous though, because Old Macaroni used to give bigger portions to Patricia. Patricia never once offered to share some of her larger portion of cake or whatever with Emily, and yet they remained friends.

“It looks like Old Mr Macaroni’s grandson runs the business now!” says Mrs Bunkerton with a tired and faint voice. Old Mr Macaroni’s grandson Marco does run the business, and very successfully too – Thursday nights will find the place heaving with customers. Thursday night is music night and ‘Dino Martino’, a Dean Martin tribute band, really pulls the punters in. ‘Antonio Benito’, the Tony Bennett tribute band are playing this week, not as popular as Dino Martino but they are still young and will grow on people.

"I wonder if Old Mr Macaroni is still alive?" wonders Patricia. If Old Mr Macaroni is still alive he will be nearly 100 years old at least; although Emily and Patricia called him Old Mr Macaroni, he was barely 60 years old, but people of that age do look old when you're young.

"I wouldn't have thought so, he'd probably be 150 years old if he was!" says Mrs Bunkerton. And then, right at the back of Macaroni's, an old figure in a string vest and a tea towel over his right arm appears. With eye-rubbing disbelief, Emily points at the old man and says, "P-P-P-Patricia, look, look! No, it can't be Old Mr Macaroni, surely?" The old man walks down the aisle of Macaroni's until he spots Patricia; he raises his left arm and points at Patricia, slowly walking towards her.

Patricia, so excited to see Old Macaroni, is just about to launch herself into 'Why Mr Macaroni, how lovely to see you after all these years!' when the old man speaks, "You, you, you are a very naughty girl, you owe me a five a pounds-a, you rip-a me off you naughty, naughty girl!" This is true, of all the debts Patricia has marked up, this debt is one she thought she would never have to pay back.

With panic and fluster, Patricia tries to assure Old Mr Macaroni that she had paid him back many years ago. Old Mr Macaroni says, "You rip-a me off, nobody rips Macaroni off, you are very naughty girl, you never pay me back!" Patricia has two choices, pay the old man back or run – she chooses the latter option. In her haste, Patricia drops her handbag and reams of paper money that were stuffed in the lining of her gargantuan handbag explode over the floor. Patricia stops and tries to scoop all of her cash back into her handbag, but the old man is frightening her so much she flees from the ogre leaving more than she owed for him to collect, and leaves her old friend Emily behind as well. Mrs Bunkerton, severely embarrassed, gathers up the remaining money and hands it to

Old Macaroni, "Here take it all; Patricia's debt will have gained interest by now!"

"You are very nice-a lady, I never did know your-a name!" smiles Old Macaroni.

"My name is Emily!" says Mrs Bunkerton and sadly walks out of Macaroni's for the very last time.

At the Busted bus station, Mrs Bunkerton looks in her purse for money to buy a ticket for the journey home, only £5 is there. If only she had bought a return ticket for herself, but then again she wouldn't have had enough money left to buy coffees and Crostata. What is she to do, 15 miles from home and not enough money to get her any further than Rumpstead? Mrs Bunkerton, with heavy heart, slumps down on a bus station seat and sobs quietly to herself. She had seen Patricia as she really is for the first time and it could be the last time she will ever see Patricia.

As Mrs Bunkerton looks in her pockets for a tissue, handkerchief or anything to mop up the tears, someone offers her a clean handkerchief. Mrs Bunkerton looks up and sees a familiar face – it's Pinky Watson! "Pinky, I haven't seen you for ages and ages! Where have you been?" asks Mrs Bunkerton still choking on her tears.

"Oh I've been around, Emily, here and there, there and here!" Pinky answers with a friendly smile.

"Look, Pinky, I know it's been a long time since we've seen each other, and you'll probably think I'm an absolute stinker for being so presumptuous, but I've been left in the lurch and I've no money to get home!" snivels Mrs Bunkerton. "Could you help me please, I will pay you back!"

Pinky smiles and says, "I can do better than that, I'll drive you home in my new mobility car!" Mrs Bunkerton thanks Pinky very much and they drive off and chat about old times, with Pinky telling Mrs Bunkerton that he isn't surprised that Patricia ripped her off; she still owes him ten bob.

Pinky's car arrives with a squeak of brakes outside Mrs Bunkerton's cottage and she invites him in for a cup of tea and a bit of a chat. Pinky declines the offer as he has to go and pick his wife up from her amateur dramatics group in Renton. Mrs Bunkerton says goodbye and sadly walks up her garden path, opens her cottage door, enters and closes the door and feels a hopeless sense of loss. Pinky Watson, it would seem, was an alright chap after all!

# Chapter 11

## THE NIGHT OF THE PYROSPRUGG

Every first Saturday in November, Vernham village closes to all visitors for an annual bonfire event called ‘The Night of the Pyrosprugg’. Although this event was originally a ‘Vernhamites only’ ceremony, now people from other villages in the Vernbury Vale are allowed to attend for a reasonable ticket price of £1.50p. At 03:03pm precisely, barriers of blackthorn and barbed wire are placed at every entry to Vernham village to prevent intruders from enjoying the revelry.

Pyrosprugg night is much like many bonfire bonanzas of any village with deep-seated pagan roots. Although most villages eventually became Christianised during the Roman occupation of Britain, the pagan ceremonies were often continued, but only for social gatherings rather than religious ritual. One must remember here that bonfire ceremonies nowadays are carried out in November to coincide with Guy Fawkes Night, not because of religious ritual, firework and pyrotechnic availability being the key factor. Vernham’s bonfire celebration however has always been in November, and always the first Saturday. The event was originally named ‘Burnem’, which was also adopted as the village name, this of course was changed after the dawning of Norman Wisdom and the village name eventually became Vernham.

The Burnem event was a religious ceremony which entailed an offering to the Winter God by means of burning some of the vegetable harvest on the peak of Silver Hill. The reason behind this act was to appease the Winter God by offering him some of their vegetables as sacrifice so he didn’t take their food away from them during the Spring Struggle. Of course, occasionally the odd hedgehog was thrown in for good measure, but there were often more of the poor little blighters cremated than known after they'd snuggled under the pile of wood, twigs and other combustibles for winter hibernation, only to be burned alive while they slumbered. Unfortunately the Winter God wasn't appeased very often and he rotted their winter vegetable stash regardless of the generous offerings. Then one day, one of the head Vernhamites, or Burnemites as they would have been known then, thought that an offering of human sacrifice would do the trick. Outsiders were often intruding in the village of Burnem and the Burnemite warriors were instructed to lie in wait for an outsider (they would never kill their own brethren, they weren't that heartless) prior to the Burnem ceremony, capture the victim and imprison them until the ceremony. This victim would then be bound, gagged and thrown on the fire to act as a bonus offering to the Winter God. As the outsider was being mercilessly burned the gathering would chant, 'BURNEM, BURNEM, BURNEM!' Fortunately for the outsiders, this barbaric attitude faded due to the fact that they had learned to keep away from Burnem anytime close to early November.

So back to the modern day Vernham ceremony then. The barbed wire and blackthorn barriers are symbolic as a warning to all Spruggles to 'KEEP OUT OR ELSE!' There is normally a lot of merrymaking and silliness involved in The Night of the Pyrosprugg, normally fuelled by Roger and Susan Spur of The Grummet and Nut's under-the-counter 10% proof cider called 'Mindmush'. Anyone who partakes of this potion called Mindmush is said to take on the possession of souls from the ancient Vernhamites, but the truth is that it makes you very drunk in next to no time at all and is guaranteed to turn the most humble and normal Vernhamite into a slobbering, gibbering mess before bedtime.

After the first few downs of Mindmush the participants of Pyrosprugg feast on delicious food such as baked potatoes with baked beans and molten mature chin-blistering cheddar, Master

Butcher Dick Sperling's gorgeous venison and chilli chive sausages and his finest golden shortcrust pastry pies. No one is left out; there are even tofu kebabs on skewers for the herbivorous few of the village. All of this food is served outside in Low Street and is probably the warmest friendliest social gathering ever held in Vernham, the Winter darkness alive with sparklers that take on the appearance of swarms of fireflies weaving in and out of the little dark figures in the street. The use of fireworks is not always responsible here, and it's not the two small children of the village that you need to worry about, they're normally taking advantage of so many people being out of their homes and busily getting on with some good old-fashioned burgling. This irresponsible use of pyrotechnics can be quite frightening – one year poor old Mr Robson was chased down Low Street by a Jumping Jack until it finally jumped up his kilt. PC Sweetman was so excited and inspired by this happening that he felt the urge to expose himself as Mr Robson raced by… (A 'Jumping Jack Flash' then, apologies to Mick and Keith!)

After the self-imposed greedy piggy gorging, the Pyrosprugg ceremony begins to take some sort of shape; I won't use the term 'semblance' here as the event can vary a little bit depending on the amount of Mindmush imbibed. This ceremony starts at 5:33pm and a torch-lit march stomps up Low Street and then up a public footpath to the peak of Silver Hill where a ready prepared bonfire waits impatiently for ignition. The torches are lit and the procession is led by a Holy man (in this case Reverend Parsworthy will have to do) who wears the torch on his head. This purpose-made torch head dress is rumoured to have been an inspiration for Arthur Brown, although it's unclear whether Arthur has ever visited Vernham and it isn't something that any self-respecting musician would admit to. The head dress is known as a 'Torch Hat' or 'Torchat' and is quite unsafe to wear. Reverend Parsworthy is encouraged to lay off of the booze until after the ceremony as he has led the procession through thicket and thorn, and in the completely wrong direction in the past.

At the rear end of the procession walks Jim Phillips the greengrocer with a wheelbarrow full of various vegetables, turnips, swede, cabbage and that kind of ilk; he also wears a Torchat as it's difficult to hold a regular torch and push a wheelbarrow at the same time. Somewhere in the centre of the procession, a huge effigy of a disliked politician, celebrity and this year Mr Jedson the disgraced Fire Chief, is carried up to Silver Hill to be burned. Remember, all of this ritual had been going on long before Guy Fawkes Night and so this effigy isn't to be confused with a regular Guy, not unless the effigy of that person is named Guy on that particular year. It could be said that the ancient Vernhamites were bonfire pioneers, or should that read 'pyre-oneers'? Poor ex-Fire Chief Mr Jedson who normally enjoys this ceremony has to miss out this year as he's gone into hiding after escaping his arrest for attempted arson, but he will be here in spirit and the thought of Pyrosprugg night won't be far from his thoughts.

All the weirdos attend – Nelly Birdham, Comfytums pianist and stalwart gin drinker likes to dress up for this occasion; normally barefoot with a long flowing translucent white gown, sans wire wool wig, she lets her beautiful white mane flow and her face is normally painted white with Edgar Alan Poe detail and an Alex DeLarge false eyelash. Milly and Molly Goldsworth always dress up as 'Harvestians', Angel Princesses of the Harvest. Pyrosprugg night isn't just about burning dummy Spruggles, it's also about yielding some of the autumn harvest to the Winter God as thanks for a kind season – it's a sort of late and very confused Harvest Festival.

Mrs Bunkerton always refrains from this pagan ceremony, being a Christian woman; she doesn't hold with a lot of this old Vernhamite mumbo jumbo, and considers it to be very linked to the occult. Mrs Bunkerton is not far wrong though, many Spruggles that have purchased a ticket for this event have commented on how uneasy they have felt, as though there is an undercurrent of evil there. This feeling of unease can be experienced when one is watching a film that features fire, sacrifice, painted faces and chanting – it could just be a primeval survival instinct that gives this feeling of unease, or maybe that there is something demonic digging around in one's soul.

Although Pyrosprugg night is meant to be fun, all Vernhamites that participate do seem to have a slight change in character, as though they have become possessed when the drums start pounding. Eddie Jedson is one of the drummers, a duty that he thoroughly enjoys, no complicated drum patterns necessary, with the drum supported over his shoulder with a strap – this job can be done single-handed, leaving his other hand free to hold a torch. Miss Somerton-Jove has been banned from this ceremony after she appeared dressed as Joan of Arc a few years ago. At the ceremony the year before she was banned, there was a slight warning from Miss Somerton-Jove as she approached a number of people saying, "Make the most of me, for I shall last only one year!" The year after she wore a mitre bearing the inscription 'RELAPSED, HERETIC, APOSTATE, IDOLATER'; it took six strong men to hold her back from running into the already raging bonfire.

When the procession reaches the summit of Silver Hill, the drumming and chanting stops for the Holy man to offer prayers of thanks for the year's harvest. There he will stand with arms and legs as akimbo as his old bones and muscles will allow. After prayers are over, a select chosen few will take a vegetable each from Jim Phillips' wheelbarrow and throw the vegetable item in the general direction of the Holy man in an attempt to knock the Torchat off of his head into the bonfire to ignite it. For obvious reasons there is no chin strap on the Torchat as this could lead to decapitation – poor old Reverend Parsworthy has suffered two black eyes, a broken nose, a broken jaw and nearly swallowed his dentures in the years gone past. Possibly a bit of restraint on the amount of

Mindmush drunk by the select few would help their aim, those turnips can be quite brutal when they hit you!

Once the bonfire is ignited by the fallen Torchat, the effigy of the Pyrosprugg, or 'Burning Spruggle' roughly translated, is tossed onto the bonfire followed by more vegetables thrown into flames, and the drumming and chanting of 'BURNEM, BURNEM, BURNEM, BURNEM,' strikes up again. As mentioned earlier, the effigy this year is of Mr Jedson the disgraced Fire Chief; although a born Vernhamite, he lost his identity as a native of Vernham after being arrested for arson. There may seem to be a perpetual state of anarchy in Vernham, but there are rules not to be broken as a Vernhamite; the burning of a property in Vernham such as the Fire Station is breaking one of those rules. Thus Mr Jedson became disowned by the village as an outcast, and therefore denounced as a Spruggle.

Once the effigy has completely burned, the irresponsible use of fireworks resumes, and the Rumpstead Ambulance Station, always on red alert, is often pressed into use for attending superficial burns and Reverend Parsworthy's wounds.

The survivors of this annual event always like to finish off the evening with more food and Mindmush back at The Grummet and Nut. Harry Helmson, the drunken barber, is normally the first back; it's all a downhill run from Silver Hill so it doesn't take him long. If Holy man Parsworthy isn't too injured, there is a huge chalice of Glenfunnel 12-year-old single malt waiting for him; there he will down it in one scoop to rapturous applause, and finally pass out. From there, Reverend Parsworthy's limp body is taken to a place of rest, in his bed at the vicarage, where he will wake up the following morning with very little recollection of the night before, and a very dry mouth.

And there's absolutely no reason why this year's Night of the Pyrosprugg should be any different!

# Chapter 12

## VERNHAM YULETIDE

Christmas time in Vernham is not really that different to Christmas held in any other village. It's true that Vernham has its oddballs, and probably more than its fair share, and this can make Christmas seem strange to a Spruggle's concept of how to spend a Yuletide, but Vernhamites still share the same warmth, generosity and meanness as most human beings. It is the one time of year when the people of Vernham migrate to Busted to buy their Christmas gifts, because to be brutally honest, as lovely as the village of Vernham is, it's as good as useless for buying nice things for people.

This annual migration to Busted doesn't deter Cecil Twill from doing his fancy Christmas toy shop window dressing; he's busy there now, lining the shop window with cotton wool and glitter. Cecil always places his mains-operated Santa Claus that says 'Ho, Ho!' to passers-by in the window display; his Santa raises and lowers its arm holding a lantern installed with a little pretend candle that flickers. The flickering candle incidentally is not by design; it's an electrical fault that Cecil has never been bothered to fix. This Santa is dressed in the traditional green coat, not the common red inspired by Coca Cola adverts on the back of *National Geographic* magazines. The *National Geographic* magazine, in the past read by many a giggling schoolboy, chortling at all of those naked African women on parade with bones through their noses. That magazine served as an education to many young boys, that women were quite a different shape, and to some of those boys, a fantasy as well as an education! Although Cecil doesn't really sell any of his toys, he still enjoys this time of year; there's still chance that a Spruggle visitor may enter Vernham Playtime and buy a toy for a young boy or girl. The Bobby the Bog Stomper battery-powered robot conversions received a flutter of interest in the late summer / early autumn, but as the specimen hunters' interest waned, so did the interest in Cecil's entrepreneurial venture. Still, there's always next year; when the nights are less cold and long, there will be more people hoping to spot the Bog Stomper of Sweetwater Marsh again and maybe one or two may wish to buy a souvenir. Until then, most of Cecil's Bobby the Bog Stomper toys are relegated to the shop rear, but there are a few still on display in the shop window, just in case.

Christmas time is always a busy time of year for both Greengrocer Jim Phillips and Master Butcher Dick Sperling. Both proprietors generate a healthy business community atmosphere by working together. It's a back-scratching operation where Dick Sperling gives his customers a 10% off voucher for Brussels sprouts and parsnips at Jim Phillips' greengrocers with every turkey bought. A healthy business atmosphere indeed, although not such a healthy atmosphere after those sprouty things are consumed for dinner! In return, Jim Phillips gives vouchers for free chestnut and cranberry, or apple and hazelnut stuffing packs from Dick Sperling's butchery when £5 pounds or more is spent on greengroceries. This system works well for both Jim and Dick, although for the newcomer to this business idea it can be quite frustrating and, it would be kinder if Dick told his new customers that the stuffing packs are free if they first buy their vegetables from Jim. Equally, it would be friendlier if Jim told his new customers that they could have bought their vegetables 10% cheaper if they'd bought a turkey from Dick first. Those that have cottoned on to this stupidity are seen busily whizzing about to and fro between butcher and greengrocer so that they don't miss out on any of the offers. After all, when you've just bought the stuffing to shove inside the turkey of your dreams, there can't be many more situations as distressing as to find out you could have had your 'stuffing for nuffing' if you went and bought your veg at Jim's. Some people of course don't give a fig for this silliness and prefer to buy all of their bargain Chrimbo goodies from BREECHER'S THE SUPERMARKET – NOW OPEN 24 HOURS A DAY; it's only a bus ride away to Velstrum and a lot cheaper.

Comfytums the tearoom is always busy, but at Christmas it can prove almost impossible to get a seat. It's Milly Goldsworth's plum and fig pudding that everybody wants; you can eat it there or order a whole one to eat at home on Christmas day. Most people that buy Milly's plum and fig pudding enjoy eating it, but it's never the same as when you eat it in Comfytums; it could be an atmospheric thing, or it could be that it misses Milly's twin spinster sister Molly's clotted cream custard with vanilla pods to complete the gustatory and olfactory symphony. One thing is for sure, if Milly and Molly sold this Yuletide feast combo as suppliers to other food retailers, they would quickly become millionaires – or filthy rich at least!

For Mrs Bunkerton, however, it's a frustrating time. She may be the first in with her 10:02am visits, but soon after Comfytums is buzzing with noise and activity. Mrs Bunkerton endures this predicament, but it's very hard to tell people that you've recently been widowed seven years ago with that racket going on. Miss Somerton-Jove, who also makes a visit every day, suffers slightly; it doesn't seem to matter if she goes into one of her rolling about the floor tantrums when she can't get her own way – everyone is blissfully unaware that she's doing it and either step over her, or on her!

Milly and Molly also do a great three-course Christmas lunch too, the only snag being that you have to book up the Christmas before to guarantee a table because it's so popular. The three-course meal normally includes Yuletide soup and a buttered wholemeal roll for a starter, which is a spicy Brown Windsor similar to Mulligatawny but with chunky vegetables and is a meal in its own right; second course is the traditional Christmas meal but with three meats – turkey, beef and pork, and none of this bacon-wrapped chipolata stuff here, Milly and Molly insist on full-size Lincolnshire recipe sausages much to Dick Sperling's chagrin; and for the third course there is a choice of Milly's plum and fig pudding with special clotted cream custard or a smorgasbord of various cheeses and biscuits. A bottle of quality French red or white wine would go down well with this jumbo Christmas banquet, but Milly and Molly don't have a licence to sell alcohol, so there! Oh, also, after all of that lot, Milly and Molly give a whole tube of indigestion tablets free with every Christmas meal.

Directly in competition with Comfytums of course is The Grummet and Nut, although not as popular. Landlady Susan Spur's Christmas meal is to die for, in fact some people think that they have died and gone to Heaven when they tuck into Susan's food. So anyone who is unfortunate enough to miss out on a table at Comfytums and plumps for The Grummet and Nut, they discover a very good second best, some might say Vernham's best kept secret!

One thing that The Grummet and Nut did have in its favour this year, was the Christmas coach excursion that Roger and Susan Spur had arranged. This coach tour took in all of the magnificent garden centres in the Vernbury Vale and was quite useful for buying unique presents for people that you wouldn't normally be able to buy anywhere else. One of the most popular gifts to be bought at the garden centres are electronic cat-scaring devices called 'SCATAPULT', not to be confused with the ultrasonic frequency emitting devices which don't work all that well, although it could be that the scaring frequency is so ear-splittingly shrill that it deafens the cats and so eventually they can't hear it and just get on with their business. 'SCATAPULT' has an electronic sensor that detects movement, when anything breaks a 180 degree beam emitted from the SCATAPULT; a spring-loaded boxing glove is tripped, knocking the offending defecator to other side of the garden. Normally, cats make a bit of a meal doing their daily thing and so SCATAPULT has plenty of time to adjust to find the correct location before letting rip. Imagine sitting down in a public toilet, and suddenly a boxing glove shoots out from the side wall knocking you off the seat, it wouldn't take too many times before you chose to avoid that cubicle would it? SCATAPULT works on that theory. SCATAPULT is quite effective when camouflaged or secreted in vegetation, though it's a good idea to remember where you installed the device when you go for a stroll around the borders – bruised shins can occur! I wonder if Mrs Bunkerton will wake up to find a SCATAPULT in her stocking on Christmas morning?

The garden centres really go over the top when it comes to Christmas decorations, all competing with each other. This competition only leads to gross stupidity. The most popular garden centre 'Shrubbs & Potts Garden Co. Ltd' have got a ridiculous 18 feet tall singing and dancing reindeer this year.

This Christmas decoration competition isn't restricted to the garden centres – the shops and private residences in Vernham like to spruce up the outsides of their buildings as well. Obviously the shops compete with each other big time; Ye Olde Sweetie Shoppe takes on an authentic Dickensian appearance with fake snow from an aerosol coated liberally on its small paned widows. Inside the sweet shop however, Ken and Bettie Griggs show a distinct lack of imagination, the same old crepe streamers hanging up in the same place every year. Master Butcher Dick Sperling likes to hang natural bunting outside his shop; at this time of year it's surprising how effective dead pheasants hanging upside down can be. Jim Phillips' greengrocer shop always has plenty of mistletoe hanging from the ceiling, well there's always hope isn't there? Last year Mrs Bunkerton dressed her cottage up to look like a Christmas pudding, only it didn't look like a Christmas pudding because it was the wrong shape, it just looked like a Christmas cake with very badly applied icing – ten marks out of ten for imagination though!

Mr Robson the counterfeit Scotsman gets even more Scottish at Christmas; his accent gets stronger, even if it is terribly fake. He also likes to show that he has a sense of fun by wearing a special tinsel sporran and reindeer antlers on his Glengarry. PC Sweetman relaxes his professional side a little and hangs his Christmas baubles on his helmet and other places. Poor Blind Mr Wilson misses out a fair bit at Christmas; it's a very vibrant and visual time of year, but he does appreciate the seasonal fragrances and noises that are part of Yuletide though. Even miserable git Mr Selsman yields his serious side a little by wearing his special Christmas Wellingtons – they're red with sleigh bells sewn onto them that jangle as he walks. Mr Selsman has just become an author and is writing a very interesting book (for him at least!) called *The Anatomy of a Wellington*; it's a long read of *War and Peace* proportions – I didn't realise that there was so much to learn about Wellingtons!

Bringing you back into the Christmas present after the usual digression, it's just a week before Christmas and the Vernham folk are busily preparing things, wrapping things up and writing their greetings cards.

A clock ticks determinedly in Mr Robson the counterfeit Scotsman's cottage called 'Bannock Burn', a place name he plagiarised from an *Oor Wullie* annual, and harvestmen are hanging in a dark corner that Rabbie's conjunctivitis stricken eyes can't see. Harvestmen, the spiders that God forgot to give abdomens and cephalothoraxes – or are they just cephalothoraxes with legs like a child's drawing of a spider? Rabbie Robson pours out a wee dram of Glenfunnel and takes a sip. "Och, whit aboot a wee bit of Andy Stewart and Moira Anderson on thon record player, Rabbie?" he says to himself. "Aye not a bad idea, not a bad idea at all!" he agrees with himself. It's not to say that Moira and Andy didn't ever sing a duet, but not in the way Rabbie is just about to hear them. Mr Robson has two record players, he places a record of Andy Stewart's song 'I Love to Wear the Kilt' on one turntable, and a record of Moira Anderson's song 'Ye Banks and Braes' on the second turntable. This is where Moira and Andy perform a pseudo duet for Rabbie Robson – the noise that this act makes is beyond description, a crazy Celtic enthusiast Rabbie may be, Fat Boy Slim he ain't!

Whilst listening to this racket, Mr Robson likes to write Christmas cards to his fantasy friends, normally the same fantasy friends every year. There is a Christmas card for many of the characters from the *Oor Wullie* stories, Fat Bob, Soapy Soutar, Wee Eck, PC Murdoch and of course Wullie himself and his Ma and Pa. There is also a card for the Broons, but as there are so many of them they only get one card between them, and all of this lot is addressed to be delivered to DC Thompson and Co. in Dundee. "Noo let me see… I mustna forget Fife Robinson like I did last year!" Mr Robson Reminds himself. Mr Robson clears a space on his dining room table, moving old books and coffee mugs away that are festooned with more cobwebs and dust than Miss Havisham's wedding cake. Mr Robson licks the tip of his quill already loaded with writing ink and receives a very blue tongue; he begins writing with such calligraphic beauty that it's difficult to believe that such work has been executed by such an untidy man. *'To ma dear auld pal William Wallace, have a great Christmas and a braw Hogmanay, don't let the Sassenachs grind yer doon, kindest regards from your auld pal Rabbie Robson*' he writes and places the card in an envelope already addressed to 'Mr William Wallace, Elderslie, Renfrewshire, Scotland. Mr Robson never writes his return address on the back of the envelope, so there's no fear of unwanted mail being returned.

The postman arrives at the door of Bannock Burn and forces a huge handful of mail through Mr Robson's letterbox, tearing the polythene cover of a brochure from the Scottish Tourist Board that Rabbie had ordered just in case he felt like going on holiday next year. The mail lands with an impolite slap on the dirty doormat followed by the angry snap from the alligatorian jaw of the letterbox cover, Mr Robson goes to his front door to investigate. Apart from the ever unwelcome bills and junk mail, a *People's Friend* magazine, the Scottish Tourist Board brochure as previously mentioned, there is also a Christmas card. Mr Robson is filled with kilt-flapping excitement – this is the first Christmas card he's had for a long time, and it bears the postmark of Dundee. Rushing to his living room, Mr Robson takes a dirk from a plaque that it's mounted on to slit open the envelope. After slitting the envelope open, Mr Robson takes the card out of the envelope to read, *'To Dear Mrs Bunkerton, Wishing you a very happy Christmas and an equally happy New Year. Thank you for being a great customer, from all at People's Friend'*, but the envelope is addressed to Mr Rabbie Robson, there's obviously been a mistake. No matter, kindly Mr Robson will deliver it to Mrs Bunkerton later, and perhaps after all, he's found a soul mate!

Meanwhile at Mrs Bunkerton's cottage, the postman has just delivered some mail to her; amid the melange of different coloured envelopes, there is also a card from Dundee. Mrs Bunkerton isn't interested in the slightest at the moment as she's busy baking for the Vernham Parish Hall Pensioners Christmas bash party. Unnoticed, a mouse scurries across the kitchen floor to dine on a piece of orange peel and a few currants and sultanas that have been accidentally dropped in Mrs Bunkerton's frenetic cake-mixing haste. Mrs Bunkerton can't remember if she's put any mixed spice in the cake mix, so she puts some in just in case – it won't do any harm as there's enough Demerara sugar in the mix to counteract any bitterness from the extra spice. Mrs Bunkerton plops the cake mix in a large butter-greased and baking parchment lined cake tin. She places the cake tin on the middle shelf of her gas oven which has been pre-heated to gas Regulo 2, that'll be in there for two and a half hours at least. "Ooh 09:48am, nearly time for Comfytums at 10:02 am," Mrs Bunkerton thinks to herself, she's just enough time to pop in and say hello to Milly and Molly Goldsworth and whizz back to make some mince pies.

At the vicarage, Reverend Parsworthy is writing his sermon for the Christmas service to be held on Christmas Eve; some may call it Midnight Mass, but this auspicious occasion inevitably ends up as Midnight Mess with lapsed church goers necking the communion wine. It's customary, if not sacrosanct, in most normal churches to have been baptised to deserve the right in the partaking of communion wine; in Vernham however, falling in the River Poddum and blaspheming qualifies. But Reverend Parsworthy's sermon is honest and has the dynamics of anything Dylan Thomas has ever offered, drunk or sober. When Reverend Parsworthy delivers his sermon, the congregation is often spellbound and hanging on to his every word, it's just a shame that Reverend Parsworthy doesn't heed his own words and follows the road of his conviction; still, it's the thought that counts, especially this time of year. "We are here gathered tonight, no! We are tonight gathered here, no blast it! We are gathered here tonight… to celebrate the birth of a man who… was born… unto a virgin… her name was Mary…" writes Reverend Parsworthy. The sermon always starts off that way and often ends there before he leans on the pulpit and stares at the congregation before improvising, often expressing the true horror of 'no room in the inn' and telling stories of his tragic childhood in Tiger Bay.

It's true that David Parsworthy's mother was a virgin when she met his father, Irish merchant sailor Fergal O'Rear, but an immaculate conception it wasn't. Reverend Parsworthy's mind's image of his mother is nothing but pure, so we must allow him that thought of his own, it's all he has left in this life to cling to. Reverend Parsworthy's sermon serves as a confession, and an unburdening of sadness for him. David Parsworthy, a Welsh-born Spruggle, was accepted into the Vernham community because he was a man of God – if he wasn't he would have been given short shrift, and yet he fits into the Vernham jigsaw puzzle so well as though he is a true Vernhamite. Reverend Parsworthy stops writing and runs his filthy fingers through his equally filthy hair to pause for a big swig of something boozy. His face grimaces after reading his words and shouts, "NO, NO, NO, IT'S ALL WRONG, SO

VERY WRONG!" followed by a smashing of glass and strewn cashew nuts.

Meanwhile at Mr Selsman's home, there's a chime on the doorbell, it's the Earl of Beastly making one of his thoughtful 'Are you going to be alright on your own this Christmas?' calls. Mr Selsman opens the door and growls, "Yes, what do you want?"

"Hello, Mr Selsman, I just thought I'd pop round to see if you've any plans for this Christmas – are you spending it alone?" enquires the Earl.

Mr Selsman glowers at the Earl of Beastly and erupts, "EVERY YEAR YOU ASK ME THIS SAME QUESTION, AND EVERY YEAR I TELL YOU THAT I DON'T HOLD WITH ANY OF THIS SEASON OF GOOD WILL NONSENSE, AND I'M TELLING YOU NOW THAT THIS YEAR IS DITTO, DITTO!"

The Earl of Beastly gulps and apologises to Mr Selsman for disturbing him and wishes him a merry Christmas. Mr Selsman slams his door and the Earl mounts his Penny Farthing, with a wobbly front wheel he makes his rickety journey on the cobblestones of Low Street to Mrs Bunkerton's cottage.

Mrs Bunkerton has arrived back at her home after a bit of a chinwag with Milly and Molly Goldsworth. As she inserts the key in her door lock she hears a loud crash and clatter as the Earl of Beastly makes a bit of a pig's ear of dismounting his Penny Farthing velocipede. The Penny Farthing may look silly in comparison to the modern day bicycle, but cast your mind back to 1970 and the Raleigh Chopper – it was like a Penny Farthing in reverse. If in 1871 there was such a thing as a Farthing Penny, the owner of such a contraption would be avant-garde and coupled with a banana saddle and ape hangers, the term 'Cool Dude' would have been a Victorianism. Apart from crumpled plus fours, the Earl of Beastly is quite unharmed and as he attempts to puff his trousers up to satisfaction, which is something he would normally do after taking his bicycle clips off anyway, Mrs Bunkerton invites him in for a cup of tea.

"Oh that would be lovely, Mrs Bunkerton, very lovely indeed!" says the Earl of Beastly, his eyes watery with emotion and his cheeks pink with pride. The Earl of Beastly lives in Frimton house in Frimton Park, which is in Frimton village, a village surrounded by a very selfish wall. Frimton House, the only house in Frimton village is massive, and it rattles with loneliness regardless of the kitchen and house helpers that work there; after 09:00pm everyone's gone home and Frimton House becomes solitary confinement for the Earl, despite its size. The Earl of Beastly, the last in a very long line of Beastlys and no wish to procreate, is a very sweet and caring man, unlike his predecessors. The Earl of Beastly looks forward to visiting the villagers of Vernham; unfortunately some of those villagers give him the old Spruggle treatment which is something he finds quite hurtful.

The Earl and Mrs Bunkerton sit and have a chat in the kitchen – they talk about Christmases gone by, of times when it always seemed to snow on Christmas day and when Mr Selsman was a little friendlier at that time of year. Mrs Bunkerton agrees that Mr Selsman is a bit of a disagreeable old goat and can't work out why he has to be such a grumpy old git. "If anyone deserves the title of Beastly, it's Mr Selsman, ha, ha, he, he!" chortles Mrs Bunkerton.

The Earl looks puzzled. The Beastly that the Earl is named after of course is a place not a personality trait, but the Earl has never thought of the name Beastly and the term beastly as having any similarity. So with Mrs Bunkerton's joke plummeting like a lead balloon, she changes the subject to Christmas cake recipes. The Earl is most interested and asks Mrs Bunkerton if she could bake one for him, and if she would care to share some of it with him on Christmas day at Frimton House. Mrs Bunkerton agrees to both offers and the Earl is very happy about that, as it means that he will be able to share Christmas day with someone else.

There's a knock on Mrs Bunkerton's front door – it's Mr Robson, the counterfeit Scotsman, with Mrs Bunkerton's Christmas card from *People's Friend* magazine. Mrs Bunkerton opens the door. "Helloo, Mrs Bunkerton, it looks like there's been a wee bit of a mix-up with Christmas cards this year – this was addressed to me but the card inside is for you!" explains Mr Robson as he runs his gnarled old forefinger under Mrs Bunkerton's name to demonstrate.

Mrs Bunkerton invites Mr Robson in and asks if he would like to take tea with the Earl of Beastly and her. "Aye, aye, that would be most enjoyable, dear lady," accepts Mr Robson.

Mrs Bunkerton apologises to Mr Robson as she hasn't had a chance to open her mail and pours a cup of tea for Rabbie before gathering the mail together to see if there's been a card for him in amongst it. "Right, Mr Robson, here is my post, let's see if your card is in amongst it!" says Mrs Bunkerton shuffling the letters and cards like a professional gambler.

"In Amongst It? Aye that's a new film production company in Glasgow, I've heard of them!" chirps Mr Robson.

"No, no, I mean to see if your card is in with my mail!" smiles Mrs Bunkerton. "Ah here it is, a card from Dundee, you may open it to see if it's for you inside," says Mrs Bunkerton handing the card to Mr Robson. Mr Robson asks if Mrs Bunkerton has a dirk that he can use to open the envelope; she says she hasn't and the Earl of Beastly offers him his silver pipe knife.

Mr Robson slits open the top of the envelope and whisks the card out to read. It reads, *To Rabbie Robson, Have a braw Christmas and fill yer breeks, Love from Oor Wullie, Fat Bob, Wee Eck, Soapy Soutar and PC Murdoch at the Oor Wullie Fan Club.* Mr Robson feels complete and has a bit of a dirk dance in the kitchen while holding the Earl's pipe knife. The Earl invites Mr Robson to Christmas dinner at Frimton House and Mr Robson asks him, "Will there be anything Scottish there?"

"Well now let me see, I've got a very special 25-year-old single malt from Islay, um, a fresh salmon caught in the Spey and flown down by helicopter, um, Drambuie-soaked haggis, um, Clootie dumplings and—"

Mr Robson interrupts the Earl, "Stop it, man, stop it, yer makin' me drool, drool I tell ye!"

The Earl finishes off the bait by adding, "…and a special Dundee cake with icing and marzipan," and he winks at Mrs Bunkerton.

"Oh yes, Mr Robson, Dundee cake!" exclaims Mrs Bunkerton, knowing full well he wouldn't know the difference between her Christmas cake and one from Dundee. "That's fixed it then, ma man, I shall honour ye with ma noble Scottish presence!" says Mr Robson holding a rather camp and Celtic pose.

"Oh splendid, splendid, I'll pick you both up on Christmas day, 10.30am sharp then!" says the Earl of Beastly bidding both Mrs Bunkerton and Mr Robson good day. It looks like it's going to be a lovely Christmas for at least three people this year.

Mr Robson puts his arm around Mrs Bunkerton's shoulders and asks, "So tell me, ma good lady, hoo lang have ye been of the Scottish persuasion then?"

"I'm not sure what you mean, Mr Robson," says Mrs Bunkerton with bemused expression. Mr Robson explains saying that anyone with a tendency to buy anything from Scotland must have a link with the Celtic folk; Mrs Bunkerton explains that she only buys *Peoples Friend* for the knitting patterns. "Right that's settled then, Mrs Bunkerton, you can knit me an Arran knit sweater!" demands Mr Robson, and with that he takes his leave, gliding out on very enhanced virtual roller skates.

Wendy Wilson is preparing some food for Christmas day, mince pies and stuff, she's just about to ask her dad, Blind Mr Wilson, if it's alright if she has a few guests at the table for Christmas lunch. "Daddy, would it be okay for Freddie and

Eddie to come for Christmas lunch please?" asks Wendy expecting a stern 'NO!' from her dad.

"Yes, that would be nice, dear, we haven't had friends visit us for Christmas lunch for a long time have we, dear?!" says Mr Wilson with an unusual openness and sensitivity.

"Oh! Oh thank you, Daddy dear, thank you!" says Wendy with a silly girl jumping up and down whilst clapping hands glee. The reason for her jubilation is that ever since Mrs Wilson passed away ten years ago, Mr Wilson has been reluctant to share Christmas with anyone except Wendy. Christmases at the Wilsons' were always a jolly affair, and Mrs Wilson was the finest entertainer you could ever meet. There would be games and singing and always plenty of food and drink; people always felt sad having to go home, wishing the experience would last for ever. Mrs Wilson died on a Christmas Eve and there hasn't been any Yuletide jollity for the Wilsons since that day. It's strange that Wendy's problem with halitosis began shortly after her mother died; there's no irony or relevance there, it just started then. This benevolence on Mr Wilson's part is a revelation, particularly as he doesn't agree with men exposing themselves and has always held a dim view of PC Fred Sweetman – well that is if blind people have dim views. As regards Eddie, Mr Wilson hasn't anything against people with large heads or speech impediments, he just doesn't like him very much. However, the spirit of Christmas seems to have entered into the heart of Mr Wilson, so even if it's just for one day it's a start.

The Earl of Beastly arrives at the vicarage and rings the doorbell; the Reverend Parsworthy opens the door, shouting "JEHOVA'S WITNESSES, BE OFF WITH YOU!"

"Er, it's me actually, David, the Earl of Beastly!" explains the Earl. Reverend Parsworthy tells him he'd better come in and have a drink, if there's any left. The Earl suggests that it's a little too early to imbibe and that he'd best abstain as he is a responsible Penny Farthing rider. Offended that the Earl won't join him in his indulgence, asks him if he wants a cup of tea instead. “No thank you, Reverend, I’ve already had a cup at Mrs Bunkerton’s, I’ve purely come here to invite you to Frimton House for Christmas day lunch and however long you wish to stay after that!” offers the Earl.

“Why, that’s most kind, Boyo, yes I’d love to, that’s if I can remember to come!” agrees Reverend Parsworthy. The Earl, almost pleased but not quite certain that he’s gained another guest, leaves the vicarage to drum up some more Christmas guests from the village.

At the police station, PC Fred Sweetman is pondering on the good things he remembers when he was a small boy. Fred remembers when walnut whips used to have a walnut at the bottom inside the chocolate cone, not just on top, when bananas seemed to have little black seeds in them for every bite and when you couldn’t put a whole Wagon Wheel in your mouth at once because they were so big. And then he remembers Christmases at Uncle Toby and Auntie Winifred Sweetman’s home, and how he never saw any television programmes all the way through because there may have been something rude or swearing in them. He remembers that he did have to endure the whole of The Queen’s Speech at 3:00pm, and how one time he accidentally broke wind and was sent to his room without any Christmas tea for being so disrespectful, and yet he remembers that his Auntie Winifred used to make funny smells, but she was never sent to her room! That was all such a long time ago now, but the memory of unjustly treatment he received still seems to hurt and is likely to stay with him forever. Fred opens a box of Christmas lights and wonders whether or not to hang them on his little tree that he bought from BREECHERS THE SUPERMARKET – NOW OPEN 24 HOURS A DAY. Just then, Wendy bursts into the police station to shed her excitement, “Fred, Fred! Daddy has just agreed to have both you and Eddie round for Christmas lunch! Isn’t that fab?!”

“Oh that’s marvellous, Wendy! What has changed his spirit to make him so generous?” puzzles Fred.

"I have absolutely no idea, I just hope he doesn't change his mind before Christmas – we do have a plan B just in case though; that lovely Earl of Beastly has offered for us to go to Frimton House on Christmas day if we've got nothing better to do!" enthuses Wendy. PC Sweetman walks around with his greatcoat open shouting, "WEE HEE, WAY HAY!"

"What about Eddie, is he going as well?" enquires Fred. Wendy says that she hasn't asked Eddie yet, but if they have to put plan B in to action, the Earl doesn't seem bothered by their Ménage à trios – the more the merrier apparently!

The Earl of Beastly has just arrived at Master Butcher Dick Sperling's shop with the idea of cajoling Dick into going to Frimton House for Christmas. Dick seems reluctant at first as he had planned to go chub fishing on the River Poddum. "There are mammoth pike in Pharos Pond! I'll join you after dinner for a spot of piking while the others are socialising if you like?" says the Earl with a knowing smile. Dick doesn't have to be asked a second time and suggests that Jim Phillips may be interested too as he is a keener angler than himself. Dick also offers to supply a massive turkey for the meal with an unusual and uncharacteristic generosity.

So with Jim Phillips a dead cert for a Christmas guest and also a supplier of sprouts, spuds, parsnips and a few walnuts and satsumas chucked in for good measure, the Earl goes to Vernham Playtime to ask if Cecil Twill is interested in sharing Christmas day with him and a few friends. Cecil jumps at the chance and offers to bring some of his board games that he has in the shop, the Earl says that'll be good as long as it won't be games that cause any unpleasantness or arguments.

Milly and Molly Goldsworth are chest-deep and flustered with more customers in Comfytums than they can manage this year – they're considering limiting the tables next year as it's becoming too much for the old pair. Coupled with the problem they are having with Greedy Griff Johnson dashing in to have a sneaky bite out of Milly's famous plum and fig puddings while they're not looking, things couldn't be more stressful. As she passes by looking into the shop and noticing the turmoil, Landlady of The Grummet and Nut, Susan Spur offers to take some of the overflow from Milly and Molly as she has plenty of tables and plenty of food to go around. Milly and Molly graciously accept their defeat and are grateful for Susan's help – this could mean a lucky break for Roger and Susan Spur, and once word gets around about Susan's excellent food, serious competition for Comfytums

Mickey Farshott and his belly-battling chum Graham Bird are running down Low Street with their big bare beer bellies hanging out whilst belching loudly, for no other reason than to be disgusting. Noticing this ungentlemanly behaviour, the Earl of Beastly refrains from inviting Mickey and Graham for Christmas day.

The Earl of Beastly has just asked Miss Somerton-Jove if she would like to join the happy throng on Christmas day at Frimton House. She responds by jumping on him and forcing him to the ground, rolling around and giving the Earl a good old tonsil-tickling snog. Miss Somerton-Jove picks herself up after giving the Earl a good seeing-to and dusts herself down. She declines the Earl's offer by saying, "No thank you!" The Earl decides he's had enough of inviting people and Penny-Farthings his way home, slightly dishevelled and lipstick scarred.

We now move forward to a cold, crisp and sunny Christmas morning and the Earl of Beastly has arranged for all of his guests to be picked up about 10:30am, which is fine for Mrs Bunkerton as she will still be able to perform the 10:02am Comfytums' ritual, even though Milly and Molly are closed for Christmas day.

Mr Robson, who's not long woken up from a nightmare about waking up in bed with Cailleach Bheur the Blue Winter hag, is doing the finishing touches to his tinsel sporran and reindeer antlers on his Glengarry. He insists though, that they are red deer stag antlers from the Highlands of Scotland. Obviously the red deer in Scotland have antlers made from red plastic and glitter, unlike the red deer anywhere else – I'm no expert, so I wouldn't argue with him.

Reverend Parsworthy, staggering around in his kitchen, has forgotten his invite, and proceeds to open a bottle of beer from the fridge which is never plugged into the mains; he just uses it as a storage place for his booze and cashew nuts. And yet, he knows that there is something he should remember, all that he has is the heavy words rattling around inside his bonce from his Midnight Mass sermon he gave last night.

It's 10:30am and a PARP! PARP! can be heard outside Mrs Bunkerton's cottage – it's the Earl of Beastly here to pick Mrs Bunkerton up in his black Stretch-Model T Ford, a slow lumbering jalopy that is a bit of a swine to drive around the tight bends of the Vernham country lanes. It's quicker to walk to Frimton House, but it's Christmas, and it's the thought that counts. Mrs Bunkerton waves to the Earl from her living room window to gesture, 'I'm nearly ready, won't be long!' In no time at all she's closing her cottage door behind her and skipping down her front garden path, Christmas cake in an old Quality Street tin under her arm, to the ultra-long old banger, and the Earl asks her to sit in the front as his special guest. This is obviously a thrill to Mrs Bunkerton, and she's never been referred to as 'special' before. The Earl asks Mrs Bunkerton if she's had a lot of Christmas cards this year and it dawns on her that she hasn't received one from Patricia Wells, her old friend from Australia that visited her a couple of months ago; she thinks that maybe it's best though, Patricia did turn out to be a bit of a bad lot.

"Yes quite a few, Mr Earl," Mrs Bunkerton answers the Earl.

"Ha, ha, ha! You don't have to call me Earl, you can call me Philip!" chuckles the Earl.

"Did you get many Christmas cards then, Mr Philip?" asks Mrs Bunkerton by way of return.

"No, I never receive any, in fact, I can't remember the last one I received," says the Earl with severe melancholy. Because a person has an important title, most people assume that, that person would naturally get more cards than he or she could possibly read, but alas not the Earl of Beastly. Mrs Bunkerton takes heart and takes out an emergency Christmas card from her handbag, one of a few she carries around with her just in case, any time of year, and proceeds to address it to 'Mr Philip' – no easy task in a bumpy old car.

The Earl of Beastly's car arrives outside Bannock Burn and Mr Robson is waiting outside; not to say that he's keen, but old Rabbie has been ready and waiting since 10:00am just in case the Earl was early. Mrs Bunkerton tucks the Earl's scribbled cobblestone-enhanced Christmas card into an envelope.

"Och ye took yer time, Cailleach Bheur has been nibbling at ma kneecaps, mon!" moans Mr Robson.

"I'm sorry, old bean, but I did say around 10:30am if my memory serves me well!" the Earl apologises.

"Ach, well aye, maybe ye did, maybe ye didna!" sighs Mr Robson.

The Earl of Beastly's car pulls up outside the Reverend Parsworthy's vicarage, and miraculously he's waiting outside. Reverend Parsworthy hasn't remembered that he was being picked up by the Earl but pretends that he has. Reeking of booze, the Reverend throws his inebriated bulk into a seat next to Mr Robson, and falls asleep.

Next stop is Cecil Twill's place; he lives above his shop Vernham Playtime, and is waiting outside, his arms heavily laden with board games such as 'Go for Broke', 'Mouse Trap' and 'Scrabble'. If Mr Robson plays Scrabble, it'll be interesting to see if he comes up with any Scottish names, although if he insists on placing words such as 'NOO' and 'CRIVVENS' on the board, there could be a fight!

Jim Phillips and Dick Sperling will be making their own way to Frimton House, with their wealth of fishing tackle; they'll need to go by Jim Phillips' van. It's just as well that they're making their own way really as they've both got a huge supply of dead bait such as mackerel and herring – it would prove to be a bit of a pongy ride in the stretch Model T.

At the Wilson's house, Fred Sweetman (as he's known off duty) and Eddie Jedson (as he's know to everyone) have turned up together; Wendy Wilson greets them at the door and invites them in. Within moments of Eddie entering, he's having trouble with his long head and the low-hanging Christmas decorations. Wendy ushers the boys into the living room, Eddie leaves a trail of destruction with streamers torn down as he walks in. Fred and Eddie are greeted by Blind Mr Wilson who offers them a drink; I hope he doesn't try to pour it out for them. Wendy brings in the nuts and nibbles just in time to stop Daddy dearest from knocking the drink decanters off the trolley.

"It's okay, Daddy dear, I'll serve drinks for the gentlemen; you sit down and I'll get one for you as well!" says Wendy with wise advice.

Eddie has a Scotch and Soda, while Fred opts for a Port – this is met with immediate disapproval from Mr Wilson, "Port before dinner?" he gasps, "What's the matter with you, man? we only serve Port here after dinner as a gesture to tell our guests that it's nearly time to go home. If you're going to be like that about it, young man, you might as well go home now!"

Wendy gently reprimands her father, telling him that Port is drunk before dinner as an aperitif in Portugal, and to be kind to the guests. Mr Wilson mumbles under his breath, "If I knew the blighter was Portuguese I'd never have invited him!" Mr Wilson demands a conversation with Eddie, "You don't say very much do you, Eddie young man?"

"N-N-No!" says Eddie.

"Well, tell me about yourself – what do you do to earn a crust?"

"I'm a-a-a-a chef at Starerakes tresaurant in in in Busted!" Eddie proudly stammers. Wendy interprets, "Eddie's a chef at Raresteak's restaurant in Busted, Daddy!"

“What is he foreign as well, needs an interpreter does he?” Mr Wilson sneers. Wendy apologises on behalf of her father for his grumpiness.

At Mr Selsman’s home, things are a little less Christmassy. Busily picking dried sheep droppings from the tread of his Wellingtons on the kitchen table with his pipe knife and trying to pretend that he doesn’t care about his Yuletide loneliness, Mr Selsman sings some Christmas carols in tearful defiance. There’s a knock on the door, Mr Selsman goes to answer – it’s Cecil Twill, “Hello, Mr Selsman, Merry Christmas to you, I know you don’t hold with any of this Christmas malarkey, but I just wondered if you have had time to reconsider?”

Mr Selsman grabs hold of his dogtooth jacket with teddy bear leather patches, puts on his Christmas Wellingtons and says, “I thought you’d never ask, what took you so long?” And so, with another Christmas chum aboard the stretch Model T Ford, the happy throng trundle and chug their way to Frimton House.

At Tommy Perkins’ home, there is a certain amount of Christmas cheer going on. Mrs Perkins is wrestling with a capon, the eunuch of the chicken world; on the kitchen table, the capon is winning. It is said that it is better to be a live capon than a dead rooster, though most of the cockerel chicks identified by the brown patches in their down, are killed for bird of prey feed. In the end, if you’re a chicken, capon or rooster, as sure as eggs are eggs, you’re a goner someday. Mrs Perkins is having trouble stuffing the capon with Dick Sperling’s free hazelnut and apple stuffing that she obtained with the voucher from Jim Phillips’ greengrocer shop after buying £5 worth of parsnips, potatoes, sprouts, carrots, satsumas, mixed nuts and dates. Dick Sperling was a bit miffed that she didn’t buy one of his turkeys, but Mrs Perkins always finds turkey meat a bit dry and liable to make Tommy have one of his coughing fits at the table. There aren’t many more unpleasant things than seeing bits of Christmas dinner shooting out of somebody’s mouth while you’re trying to enjoy your meal – well there are worse things, but at the time it seems pretty bad. While Mrs Perkins is performing the Boston Crab on the capon, Tommy is painting walnut shells for racing snail prototypes; snails are a bit hard to come by in the winter, cobnuts are too small, brazil nuts are too rough, pecan nuts are too shiny to paint and so walnuts will have to do.

Christmas time at the Perkins' home is always a sedate affair; no one is too bothered about the Perkins. The Perkins, a much maligned family after a false and unfair rumour got out that Tommy was the illegitimate offspring of old Mr Williams' pet St Bernard. As mentioned before, kindly Mrs Perkins used to walk ailing Mr Williams' dog after he'd had a hip operation and found it difficult to get about let alone walk the hulking great brute. Tommy is the son of Mr Perkins, who left Mrs Perkins just before Tommy was born after having a fling with Tina the barmaid at The Queen's Ankle in Velstrum. Tommy had whooping cough when he was eighteen months old which left him a bit chesty and he does tend to bark a bit, which led people to believe he was half man / half dog. So, through people's stupidity and cruelty, the Perkins have been ignored, which is all the sadder at Christmas. We shall leave the Perkins alone to enjoy their Christmas as they usually do… peacefully.

Back at the Wilsons', things are going from bad to worse with Blind Mr Wilson laying into Fred Sweetman for being a flasher, "I think that the liberties you take as a policeman are an outrage, just because you are a policeman doesn't give you the right to jangle your giblets in public and get away with it!"

"Now come on, Daddy, this is supposed to be the season of goodwill, please be polite to our guests?" Wendy reprimands her father.

Well yes, I suppose Mr Wilson is being a bit impolite in his last statement, but the last part of it has a sort of seasonal feel to it, especially if you're making gravy! Both Freddie and Eddie are feeling extremely uncomfortable, and Wendy is close to exploding with rage.

“Anyway, what kind of thrill do you get out of displaying your wotsits to the general public?” asks Mr Wilson with a demanding tone.

Wendy butts in before Fred has a chance to open his mouth, “Actually, Daddy, we both enjoy exposing ourselves, but we don’t consider ourselves as exhibitionists, we are more like impromptu naturists!” states Wendy with a ‘get out of that one you silly old goat!’ tone to her voice.

Mr Wilson gets up out of his chair and bellows, “RIGHT THAT’S IT, THAT’S ENOUGH! GET OUT OF MY HOUSE ALL OF YOU!” and then he addresses Wendy, “And you, young lady, don’t even consider coming home until you have a decent apology for me!”

Wendy suggests that they have their Christmas dinner at Fred’s police house; the turkey, parsnips and potatoes are nearly roasted and only need another half of an hour to finish off. “And you, you, don’t even expect me to come home until you’ve a civil tongue in your head!” says Wendy after gathering the nearly cooked Christmas dinner and slamming the door as she leaves. Freddie and Eddie both feel they ought to leave as well and close the door a little more quietly.

The stretch Model T Ford arrives outside Frimton House with a crunch of pea shingle. The Earl of Beastly’s Christmas guests jump out of the car and are ushered into the great house, Jim Phillips and Dick Sperling arriving just after. The guests walk into the entrance hall and gaze in wonder at the ridiculous and unnecessarily neck-aching view of the high oak-beamed ceiling. Hanging from the ceiling is a Supermarine Spitfire, still sexy and ageless after all of these years. The Earl had the Spitfire delivered in kit form and reassembled it himself inside the house; it’s his pride and joy and once a week he gets up there to dust and polish it. Lining the walls are portraits of a long line of Beastlys going back a couple of hundred years, each one hiding their misdemeanours and cruelty behind their oil paint smirks. The marble floor in the hallway has a water feature with a replica of Le petit Julien having a tinkle in the pool, bulging with koi. The size of these common carp in drag are almost too much of a temptation for Jim Phillips and Dick Sperling; the Earl looks at their faces and smiles saying, "No, not those, they're my babies!" Anyway, Jim and Dick both agree that it wouldn't be sporting to fish for them in such small confines.

The Christmas meal at Fred Sweetman's is going well, Eddies already opened six Christmas crackers and he's wearing all six of the paper hats – he isn't quite confident enough to read the jokes though. Fred has decided to wear his paper hat on his policeman's helmet, ah such jolly japes! Wendy insists on not wearing her paper hat because it will mess her hair up – party pooper! Everyone seems to be having fun, except that Wendy can't stop thinking about her old dad; he won't have had a meal and he can't really prepare a cooked meal for himself as he has had quite a few accidents with the gas stove in the past. Wendy asks Fred if it's okay to use his telephone to call her dad as she's a bit concerned about him; Fred says that's okay. Wendy calls her dad, but there's no answer, there won't be because Nelly Birdham called round to see him and has taken him back to her house for lunch. Wendy asks the boys to excuse her while she checks to see if her daddy is okay.

Landlord and Landlady of The Grummet and Nut, Roger and Susan Spur have invited Mickey Farshott, Graham Bird and Tortoise Terry for Christmas dinner, there'll be no lack of good food and booze there. The special Christmas crackers that Roger and Susan had specially made at a factory called 'Completely Crackers' are going down a treat, each cracker personalised for each guest, very expensive at £20 each. Inside Terry's cracker is a pair of false rubber ears, a joke for some, but for Terry, a dream come true.

Christmas dinner at Frimton House is proving to be a treat for the Earl of Beastly's guests, everyone tucking into turkey with chestnut stuffing, bacon-wrapped chipolatas, roasted potatoes and parsnips, carrots, sprouts and peas – everyone that is except for Mr Robson the counterfeit Scotsman who's diving into a plate of neaps, mince and tatties, “Braw, Jings, Help ma boab and Och Aye!” he says with evident relish. Reverend Parsworthy’s enjoying himself so much that he’s forgotten to drink anything and has almost sobered up, almost. With Milly and Molly’s plum and fig pudding and oceans of clotted cream custard, they’ll have to have a good walk around the estate to work it off and make themselves more comfortable, and make things less embarrassing this afternoon.

Mr Selsman has just had a choking fit, a bit of turkey has just gone down the wrong way. The Earl rushes to Mr Selsman’s help by shouting “A-A-A-A-H-H-H-H!” into his ear, which seems to have done the trick.

Jim Phillips and Dick Sperling are rushing to finish their dinners, they keep casting glances out of the window at Pharos Pond and fantasising about a gargantuan Esox Lucius snapping at their dead baits. Jim will be using smoked mackerel and Dick will be using Arbroath Smokies for bait, the latter at the complete horror of Mr Robson who considers this action to be almost sacrilegious.

Mr Selsman, who is full of seasonal cheer and untypical benevolence, asks, “This is all very lovely, dear boy, but who’s doing the washing up?” The Earl tells him not to worry; he’ll be sorting that out and tells everyone to enjoy themselves. “I’ll help you with the washing up!” says Mrs Bunkerton with apparent affection. The Earl tells her not to worry; he’ll be doing it late at night after everyone’s gone home. “I’ll help!” insists Mrs Bunkerton with a saucy wink. The Earl blushes slightly and says, “Well, we’ll see!”

So with a possible burgeoning of romance between Mrs Bunkerton and the Earl of Beastly, we shall go back to the Wilson’s home, where Wendy has just discovered a note written by Nelly Birdham on the hallway telephone table, it reads:

*Dear Wendy,*
*No need to worry about Mr Wilson, I have taken him to my place for a nosh and booze up.*

*Best regards,*
*Nelly (already three sheets to the wind) Birdham.*

Wendy is quite worried that Nelly might get her daddy too pickled. This isn't the first time that Nelly has tried to lead Mr Wilson astray and she let him walk home on his own last time; he bumps into things when he's sober, so if she's tanked him up, well! Wendy decides to pop over to Nelly's home to see if everything's alright.

While Wendy is away, Fred's home resembles the community refuse tip in Rumpstead with beer cans strewn all over the place; she's only been away for 15 minutes. The boys are watching *The Sound of Music* and Eddie remembers when he used to think that Julie Andrews was the most beautiful woman in the world; well, none of us will ever know who the most beautiful woman in the world is or ever was, Julie was a cracker though! Fred remembers when his Uncle Toby and Auntie Winifred wouldn't allow him to watch *The Sound of Music* because they felt that as it had women dressed as Nuns that were unlikely to be Nuns in the cast, it was likely to be blasphemous. And then Fred remembers having a sneaky look around in his Auntie Winifred's boudoir, when he was trusted to be able to be left on his own at home while Uncle and Auntie went shopping, and inside her wardrobe was a Nun's Habit. Was Auntie Winifred a Nun, or did she have a strange Habit habit? Whatever, Fred is thoroughly enjoying this Christmas day – it's the first time he's ever been accepted as a chum, and Eddie and Wendy are his chums, but where is Wendy?

Wendy raps the gargoyle knocker on the door of Nelly Birdham's house; a small swaying figure comes into view through the frosted panes of the door. Nelly opens the door, and without saying anything gestures with her hand to invite Wendy in. Wendy finds Mr Selsman sitting in Nelly's lounge with a huge cigar and a big red glass of cherryade, and uncharacteristically donning a party hat. "I see you're alright then, Daddy!" says Wendy. Mr Wilson says that he's fine and is really enjoying himself, Nelly walks over and puts her arm around his shoulder, and it seems that there is more of a bond between these two than Wendy first thought. Mr Wilson tells Wendy not worry as he's fine and to go back to her friends and enjoy her Christmas, and that he may not be at home when she gets back.

Afternoon blends into evening, and the early winter dusk cold kisses the faces of Jim Phillips, Dick Sperling and the Earl of Beastly – pike anglers three. After an uneventful blank afternoon, the anglers pack up their fishing tackle and head back to Frimton House, stinking of smoked mackerel, kippers and sardines. It's going to be cold tonight, not a single cloud in the sky, and intense early starlight pierces the rods in one's retina. The grass crunches under the anglers' boots; a frost so early heralds a tooth-chattering shiver of a night. Pharos Pond will be like a sheet of glass tomorrow morning as even the busy wildfowl that stir in the night are beaten into submission by the encroaching ice.

Mrs Bunkerton, Cecil Twill, Mr Robson and the Reverend Parsworthy decided not to watch television this afternoon; instead they opted for walking the sprouty ones off over the Frimton Park estate. The flatulent four are arriving at Frimton House at the same time as the intrepid pike anglers, just in time for tea.

Mr Selsman opted out of the post-Christmas dinner trudge around the park, for fear of getting his seasonal Wellingtons dirty.

After a brief removal of deer pooh on the boot scraper at the entrance of Frimton House, the outdoor refreshed seven and Mr Selsman settle into the dining room for a spot of tea. Nothing exotic for tea here – just cold meats, cheese and pickles, crackers, crisps, jelly, trifle, mince pies and Mrs Bunkerton's Christmas cake, and quite right too!

After tea, Mr Robson decides to have, "Just one more wee slice o' that braw iced Dundee cake, and perhaps a smidgen of that there haggis on top!" Mr Selsman looks at the Christmas cake which now resembles a pie chart with the open section a measure of greed, and wonders why a plasticine made from ground almonds, icing sugar and egg albumen ended up with an effeminate name as Marzipan. Mrs Bunkerton remembers that even after the war days, Mother used to make emergency Marzipan from soya flour, powdered egg, saccharin and almond essence bound together with water, and then tries to forget.

The Reverend Parsworthy who's now disturbingly sober is having his third cup of tea; he's forgotten what it's like to feel sober and is quite enjoying it. Cecil Twill helps himself to a schooner of Crème de Menthe which is staining his Albert Einstein moustache green, but it will soothe his indigestion.

Mr Robson, now feeling more Scottish than ever, is sipping a very good and extremely expensive 25-year-old single malt from Islay called 'Barnacle Goose'. He stands in front of the crackling coal fire, kilt selfishly depriving the room of valuable heat and tries to think of an anecdote, or complete Celtic fabrication to impress people with, "Noo, this particular wee dram of Scottish nectar reminds me o' when I was attacked by the wee monster midges and savagely bitten in the Trossachs—"

Mrs Bunkerton interrupts Mr Robson mid fib with, "Ooh that sounds painful! Did you get an ointment prescribed?" followed by a Barbara Windsor like cackle. Everyone present bursts into childishly hysterical laughter, this angers Mr Robson, but he manages a faint smile as the comedy of his statement dawns on him. "Aye, aye, very good, ma lady, very good! No actually it was my forearm that was bitten, swelled up michty terrible too. All that I needed was a tattoo of an anchor on it and I could have been Olive Oyl's boyfriend!" This statement gets howls of laughter and rapturous applause from his now huge fan base. Appreciating that he'd finally cracked the iceberg of humility and friendship, Mr Robson does a little jig in front of the hearth, while an unexpected crack and spit of red hot coal shoots out from the fire like a comet and catches his polyester weave tartan skirt alight. With a frantic squirt from the Earl of Beastly's soda siphon the flaming kilt is extinguished, unfortunately the laughter isn't.

Over at PC Fred Sweetman's home, things have got a bit boozy and snoozy. Wendy Wilson comes back completely satisfied that her dad is safe and cared for to find Fred's place a complete Christmas slob's aftermath, Freddie and Eddie both fast asleep on the sofa. Infuriated by their typical man behaviour, Wendy grabs hold of a brass dinner gong that Fred uses for an ornament and beats the living doo dah out of it, waking the boys just millimetres away from a heart attack. "You could have least done the washing up, you lazy brutes, look at the place it's a mess!" Wendy moans.

Fred says, "Yes it is a mess, and it's my mess in my place!"

"Y-Y-Y-Yes," says Eddie. Now this could be nasty, true it's Fred's place, true it's his mess, but that's no way to speak to your intended.

"Look you two, if there is going to be a future for the three of us, you will have to learn to keep things neat and tidy, now clear this mess up at once!" Wendy says with a stern motherly tone. The boys sit on the sofa with their bottom lips tightening as small children do just before they 'WAH HAH' burst into tears. Wendy bangs the gong again and Freddie and Eddie both spring into domestic house-husband mode, with Eddie creating even more devastation to Fred's home with his huge bonce.

At Nelly Birdham's home, things are a little more harmonious with Nelly tinkling the ivories and the ebonies of her terribly out-of-tune honky tonk piano. Blind Mr Wilson is enjoying himself, belting out Christmas carols with gay abandon; that is if the last part of that statement is permissible in today's politically correct environment.

Vic and Maureen Grinham, the 'want everything their way' unreasonable neighbours, knock on Nelly's door to complain about the noise – they can hear it from the other end of Low Street, outrageous! Nelly tells them in no uncertain terms to jolly well copulate off and get a life, followed by her signature V sign and blows a big raspberry to top it off before slamming the door in their flabbergasted faces. What Vic and Maureen don't know is that Winston Reefer and Leeroy Roach from the West Indian steel drum band Ganjabangbong are having a party tonight, with the intention of making a racket until 06:00am Boxing day and lots of smoky strange whiffs billowing out of their windows… Do have a restful night Vic and Maureen, won't you?

Frimton House and the Earl of Beastly's Christmas guests are peaceful and giggly as they watch a few of the Earl's home movies of Vernham fetes and events from long summers past; there's a few clips of Vernham village green sports days, with old Mr Barnford participating in the egg and spoon race and Mr Selsman hopping like mad in the sack race. A clip of a very debonair Mr Robson in a trilby and pinstripes encourages Mrs Bunkerton to pass a compliment to the old Scottish fake, "Why Mr Robson, you were a bit of a catch weren't you!" Mr Robson gets a pink tingly cringe of embarrassment in his cheeks as he coyly replies, "Aye, that woulda been the Rob Roy trying to get oot o' me." Mr Selsman wonders if he was wearing his Wellingtons in the sack – it could account for the lack of agility in his jumps. Jim Phillips and Dick Sperling see a brief clip of themselves as young boys and both brush tears from their cheeks. Mrs Bunkerton laughs at a clip of Milly and Molly Goldsworth selling cakes from a trestle, they haven't changed; they still wear the same old floral dresses even now.

It's getting late, Wendy decides that she has had enough of Freddie and Eddie for one day and makes her way home to watch television on her own with her shoes off. And on her own Wendy will be, as Nelly is tucking her dad, Blind Mr Wilson into a clean aired bed for the night.

Fred Sweetman and Eddie Jedson crack open some more cans of beer and packets of crisps to watch the Christmas Ghost Story on BBC2 called 'The Creeping Finger Of Hate', and they're both extremely frightened.

Harry Helmson the hairdresser has decided to go for a lonely stagger on the cobblestones of Low Street, where the two small children wait with a sniper's patience to try their new air pistols out on a few kneecaps. Mickey Farshott and Graham Bird will be rolling out of The Grummet and Nut soon too, so there will be a fair bit of sport for the little beasts to experiment with their 1.77 pellets.

The Earl of Beastly sits at his harmonium to wheeze out a few Christmas tunes. Led by the powerful Welsh voice of Reverend Parsworthy, the Earl's Christmas guests sing along; 'Silent Night' humbles them as the faint ping, ting of icicles tinkle the lounge window of Frimton House. Mr Robson the counterfeit Scotsman fighting tiredness loses the battle and nods off as the beautiful Franz Xaver Gruber melody lullabies him. As the Christmas guests finish the lovely carol, they hear more voices singing outside. The Earl rises from his harmonium stool and walks to the lounge window to open the dense red velvet curtains.

"Who are they, Beastly?" Mr Selsman asks with reserved worry.

"They're the Necrochoir, they visit me every Christmas!"

"Necrochoir?" questions Mrs Bunkerton.

The Earl of Beastly goes on to explain, "The Necrochoir is an ensemble of the passed souls of Vernham, not yet passed over to the other side." With that, the Earl throws open the curtains to reveal a gathering of spectres with recognisable faces. There is old Mr Barnford in his ARP uniform; the Environmental Health inspector that left his shoes on Sweetwater Marsh after a bit of a chat outside The Grummet and Nut with Dick Sperling; and Mrs Henty, the miserable Headmistress from The Old Trumphonians infant school, to mention just three.

Mrs Bunkerton gasps as she sees her husband Gerald without his glasses, standing next to him is his old friend Robert Wells holding his wife Patricia's hand. Mrs Bunkerton thinks, "That explains why I didn't get a Christmas card from Patricia this year!" Well actually no, not really, Patricia had no intention of sending a card to Mrs Bunkerton after her acute embarrassment during her visit in October. Having been challenged by Old Mr Macaroni in his Busted restaurant for owing him £5, she fled for her home in Wingabong, Australia and ran into the path of a very convenient ambulance – she died from her injuries later that day in hospital.

At the far right end of the Necrochoir is the stray bulldog, howling away in total discordance with the ensemble. A bright blue light in the night sky steadily draws closer to Frimton house, getting bigger and bigger, and finally taking the shape of a beautiful woman. Dressed in a blue translucent gown she stands with her hair flowing, and yet there is little breeze outside – it's Cailleach Bheur, the Blue Winter Hag. Cailleach Bheur taps on the window and Mr Robson opens his eyes to see her, sits bolt upright in the chair, falls back and then closes his eyes again. The Necrochoir cease singing and a lone bagpipe serenade whines in the darkness. The Necrochoir, hundreds deep with Vernhamite ancestry, separate at the centre to form a long corridor, in the distance, a figure can be seen walking down the corridor towards the lounge window of Frimton House.

The apparition gets nearer and nearer until the familiar form of Mr Robson the counterfeit Scotsman materialises. Dressed smartly in a Glengarry, tunic, authentic kilt and sporran, tartan socks with spats over the shiniest brogue shoes, he plays the bagpipe properly with a haunting rendition of 'O Come O Come Emmanuel', chilling the spines of the Earl of Beastly and his Christmas guests. Reverend Parsworthy wonders how Mr Robson slipped outside without them knowing and turns around to look at the chair in which the old Scots fraud was sitting. Mr Robson the counterfeit Scotsman is still sitting in the chair, well at least what used to be Mr Robson the counterfeit Scotsman – he's very dead. It would seem that Vernhamites can't go to Heaven; Heaven is a place for Spruggles! And yet a Spruggle that passes away in Vernham dies a Vernhamite, in limbo with the rest of the unrest souls of

Vernham, hence the Environmental Health inspector's place in the Necrochoir.

In Vernham village, Harry Helmson is still meandering zigzag on the cobblestones of Low Street; he stops outside Vernham Playtime to look at Cecil Twill's green Father Christmas. The flickering candle inside of the green Santa's lantern flicks out two sparks, igniting the cotton wool snow lining the shop window display… Where's Mr Jedson the Fire Chief when you need him?